RECKLESS GRACE

DIANA MUÑOZ STEWART

Reckless Grace, copyright 2023, Diana Muñoz Stewart
Published by Diana Muñoz Stewart
Cover by Elizabeth Mackey
Interior Design by www.formatting4U.com

All rights reserved. Thank you for respecting the hard work of this author. No part of this book may be reproduced in any form or by any electronic or mechanical means, including information storage and retrieval systems—except in the case of brief quotations embodied in critical articles or reviews—without permission in writing from the author. This book is a work of fiction. The characters, events, and places portrayed in this book are products of the author's imagination and are either fictitious or are used fictitiously. Any similarity to real persons, living or dead, is purely coincidental and not intended by the author.

Books by Diana Muñoz Stewart

HIDDEN JUSTICE (Spy Makers Guild Book 1)
RECKLESS GRACE (Spy Makers Guild Book 2)
DARING HONOR (Spy Makers Guild Book 3)
FIGHTING FATE (Spy Makers Guild Prequel Novella)
BROKEN PROMISES (Bad Legacy Series)
AMOR ACTUALLY (Holiday Anthology)

Chapter 1
Gracie

I've learned three valuable things in the last two excruciating hours driving around Mexico: the fetal position is only comfortable in the womb, my deodorant isn't trapped-inside-a-hidden-compartment strength, and blood circulation can be lost in your forehead.

There has to be an easier way to break into a sex-slaver's home than being smooshed inside this malodorous secret compartment while my brother and his frenemy, Victor, drive me onto the compound as they pose as mano-a-mano live "entertainers."

Sweat salts my eyes, slicks my skin. The good news? If I die, the House of Hades will feel like a spacious oasis.

This is it. The absolutely last time I take part in my family's insane, secret-society-type schemes. Sometimes, I wish I'd never been adopted into this mess. Ugh. Okay. That's not entirely true. I mean, I'd do anything for my family—*including* risk my life. Which is why I'm here, rescuing my sister's boyfriend.

With a flick of my jaw, I click my mic. "How much longer, Justice? I'm roasting."

"Please, you've been in there for two hours. People smuggled out of Mexico stay in that compartment for days."

Days? Days pretending to be the back seat of a car with your legs tucked awkwardly, foam padding sticking to your skin, right arm going numb, right hip screaming, and tasting exhaust. God, those poor people—and it only goes downhill from there. "Yeah, well, not me. If my cyber skills weren't needed to rescue your boyfriend, nothing could get me into this Dante's Inferno. Nothing."

"Just because you're as tall as a fifth-grader doesn't mean you should whine like one. Chill. You're almost inside the compound."

My sister scores zero on the empathy meter. Ze—*ro*. "Easy for you. You're on a hilltop, stretched out, overlooking this whole scene through a scope."

"Just playing to my strength. I'm the best shot."

True. She is a good shot. *Still...* "You know, this bull-poop has been going on since childhood." Despite the fifth-grader comment, I mimic a child's high-pitched voice. "'Gracie's the smallest; she can fit in that pipe. Gracie's the smallest; let her squeeze through the vent system. Gracie's the smallest; put her in the smuggling compartment so she can break out Trojan Horse-style inside the compound.'"

"Bull-*poop*? If you cursed, you'd realize bull*shit* is way more satisfying." Despite her teasing, Justice sounds focused on whatever she's seeing through her scope. "And it's not my fault you're a shrimp."

"Being petite isn't a talent."

"You also have great red hair and hot underwear."

Oh. God. I'm never going to live that down. "Good thing. Otherwise, I'd have no excuse if they find me. Assuming they don't shoot before I explain that Tony and Victor hid me here as a surprise bonus to their sex show."

"Trust me, no red-bloodied male—or female, for that matter—would shoot you after getting a look at that thong."

Humiliating. Even as hot as I am, I can feel the blood rushing into my cheeks. The curse of being a fair-skinned redhead.

I should've kept my mouth shut in the plane hangar when we were discussing the mission ahead. Instead, I'd felt the need to prove myself when Justice had said, "Sure, Gracie, pretending to be a stowaway entertainer is better than nothing, but we don't have a costume for you."

With challenge in her eyes, Justice had looked around the desolate plane hangar, thrown up her hands, and teased, "We're shit out of eight-hundred-dollar bras, and there's no Agent Provocateur in sight."

There's something so uncontrollable about being challenge-teased by a sibling. It just seemed like a good idea at the time, but what happened next will probably go down as one of the top five most embarrassing moments of my life.

Trying to dramatically prove to Justice I wasn't suggesting something I hadn't thought out completely, I'd dropped my pants and lifted my shirt.

And then... and then... Justice had burst into laughter.

Tony had sputtered.

Victor had whistled. "Damn, Red, if I'd known you were hiding that, I would've been nicer to you."

Is it my fault that I like nice underwear?

Yeah. Top five. Definitely. And being in this car is probably in the top ten most uncomfortable places I've ever been. Well, maybe top fifteen, as my family does really ask the impossible of me.

"Our boys are pulling up to the compound gate," Justice's voice hums low in my earpiece, "so stay quiet."

Not liking when she treats me like I'm too stupid to live, I hiss back at her, "They wouldn't hear me if I screamed."

Not a pleasant thought.

The crunch of gravel vibrates under the wheels and through my bones as the car turns into the compound. "Seriously, I could die trapped in here."

"There's a release lever."

Yes, but the arm by the lever is numb and heavy.

The car jerks to a stop and my forehead *thunks* against metal. I zip it—without being told because, despite what Justice thinks, I *am* a professional.

Because I'm as quiet as a mouse, I hear the *click* in my earpiece before Justice says, "There're five men at the gate, including the head of security—a big, USA-hat-wearing dude. He's leaning down to the car to talk to Tony and Victor."

Straining to hear through the metal and padding, I catch the sound of a deep voice with an American Southern accent.

Southern?

Justice says, "He's gesturing our boys out of the car."

The car doors open then shut, and I picture Tony and Victor getting out.

Justice snorts through the headset. "Victor pirouetted to show he has nothing to hide. Hysterical. Man has balls."

And then some. A mental image of that fine Latino pirouetting in his Magic Mike costume pops into my head. Honestly, I don't envy Victor or Tony's roles. They're pretending to be men hired to feed Walid's sexual proclivities—watching men inflicting pain on each other while having sex.

"They're checking the car."

Oh God. The front car doors open with a squeak of hinges. My heart jumps so high into my throat it chokes me. I can't even swallow. Sweat rolls down my face, perches on my lips. I hold my breath.

They're going to find me. They're going to hear my hyper heartbeat, like in Poe's, "The Tell-Tale Heart." *Ba- boom, ba-boom, ba-boom.* They're going to shoot me. *Boom.*

Someone climbs into the back seat and my blood *whoosh-whoosh-whoosh*es in my ears.

My hearing tunnels and focuses in tight on the squeak of metal springs and the weight of whoever climbed in. Is his knee pressing on the padding over my left butt cheek?

Oh Lord, please. If I survive, I'll go back to running my bar in Pennsylvania and live a normal life. A regular life. Sure, I'll keep doing my cyber-warrior stuff on the side, but I'll stay far away from field operations and guns and traffickers. I'll leave that to Justice or Tony or any of my other twenty-seven adopted siblings.

Well, the older ones.

His weight shifts onto my arm. Even through the numbness, the padding and the springs press painfully. I sense—or imagine—him running his hands along the edge of the seat.

No big deal. No big deal. If they find me, I'll play it cool. I mean, I've heard Mexicans love redheads.

Is that racist?

Gracie, stop overthinking.

The pressure lifts, then slides along my body and off. The door shuts with a slam.

Thank you, God. I meant what I said about the cyber stuff, remember that.

Someone gets into the front, starts the car, backs it up, then drives away.

What's happening?

The car stops again, and the door creaks open then slams closed. Hearing the absolute silence now, I risk a low, "Justice—"

"Fuck. Parked it outside the compound. You're like twenty feet from the front gate. You're east of the guard tower."

Fudge. It would've been so much easier if I'd been inside the gates so I could sneak out and turn off the electric fence for Justice to get inside.

Okay. Stay calm, get out of here, get inside, then turn off the fence. Hoping I sound more confident than I feel, I tell Justice, "Got it."

Honestly. The very last time I do this.

Chapter 2
Dusty

At this particular moment in my career in the FBI—guarding the front gate of a ten-thousand-acre cattle-ranch-turned-bad-guy's-hideout—I can't help but wonder if I have the luck of an '80's action-adventure star. John McClane's brand of luck.

That *Die-Hard*-er could be scarfing down burgers at a Steak 'n Shake and *still* run into a shitshow. Not that I'm anywhere near that fabulous testament to my nation's culinary prowess. In fact, you could say I went looking for trouble. Being undercover in Mexico, trying to catch a family of American vigilantes isn't exactly staying out of the line of fire.

In my defense, I'd spent months cultivating my relationship with Tony Parish to try to get an *in* with his family—the suspected vigilantes. So, when he offered me a part in this operation... Well, I'd gone all-in.

Sure, Tony, I can needle my way in as a psycho sex-trafficker's head of security.

That'd raised a few eyebrows at the Bureau. Uptight shoe-polish divas. If you can't stomach a little cow patty on your boots, you shouldn't stomp around with the bulls.

Up to my knees in it now.

Problem with working as a spy for a bunch of spies is that you never know when they're going to fuck you. Would've been nice to get a heads-up from Tony that this was happening tonight.

This last-minute bullshit must've been sparked after Walid—discovering the Parish family was after him—captured Sandesh, Justice Parish's boyfriend.

Damn.

Could've, would've, should've are lining up at the pasture gate in my mind.

I motion Tony and the Latino guy with the sparkly G-string out of the car—supposedly so I can frisk them. Not that there's anywhere for either of them to hide a weapon.

Tony, clearly less comfortable in his G-string than his partner, shifts from foot to foot as I run a wand over his outstretched arms. "Dusty."

Even though it's barely a whisper, I freeze. Guy's gonna call me by name? Here?

Pretty stupid.

Or desperate.

"Take off your boots," I tell him when the steel-toes set off the metal detector.

He sits on the compact desert dust and pulls off the boots.

Kneeling beside him, I make a show of checking the shoes inside and out, though I'm really giving Tony cover to talk.

Looking down, he whispers, "Gracie's in back of car. Can you get her to Security?"

That definitely wasn't the original plan. The original plan included two men coming in and getting close enough to kill Walid with Justice Parish on a nearby hilltop with a scope, serving as backup.

I have no doubt she's out there now. Judging by Tony's security request, she's waiting for Gracie, the family's cyber expert, to take down the electric fence. Something I have not a single clue how to do. Computer geek, I am not.

Damn it all to Hell.

How am I going to get Gracie inside without my men starting to suspect me? Sure, they trust me—hard not to after months here—but they aren't total idiots. Poorly trained? Yes. Happy-go-lucky? Yes. Total idiots? No.

I stand back up. "Put your boots back on and," I give a curt nod and motion toward the golf cart waiting to take them inside, "get into the cart."

Tony slips his boots on without tying them. Exchanging a look, he and his buddy walk forward then slide into the cart.

Good. Can't afford to keep talking to them with my men looking on.

Now all I have to do is find a way to get Gracie Parish inside the compound without raising suspicion, while Tony sacrifices one sadistic sex-slaver to the cause.

This better gain me an invite into the Parish family inner circle—an invite I sorely need to keep my boss off my ass and get the evidence to catch the big fish—the Parish matriarch and global tycoon, Mukta Parish.

Casting my eyes to the sky and whatever heavenly powerbroker might happen to own stock in this shit show, I silently beg, *Please, Lord. No more surprises.*

In answer, an alarm shrieks from somewhere inside, setting off every little hair on my body. That alarm then echoes from speakers perched on posts throughout the compound.

I grind my teeth as a muscle in my jaw tics. *Thanks a lot.*

The two-way radio on my belt sparks to life and one of my men reports the alarm started in the old mine, AKA, the dungeon. Looks like Justice's boyfriend Sandesh got restless waiting on a rescue.

The men around me start to shift nervously. Which makes me nervous. Never can tell what poorly trained men will do when they feel threatened. Something I would've mitigated had I gotten word that *this* was going down tonight.

Instead, I've got the worst-of-the-worst at the gate right now.

Ordering Tony and Victor out of the golf cart and onto their knees, I try to get a handle on things by showing my men it's all under control.

"Down, Victor," Tony says, getting onto his knees a moment before his partner complies.

Mishearing him or fearing him, one of my guards, a recent hire whose name I can't even recall right now, gets in Tony's face and shouts for him to shut up. "¡Cállate!"

Obviously, he thinks something's up. That the alarm and these two guys arriving aren't a coincidence.

Not entirely true. Not entirely untrue.

"Stay calm," Tony says.

Fury and fear on his face, my guy pulls Tony to standing and shakes him hard. "¡Cállate!"

Adrenaline brushes its chemical magic across my blood, and the entire scene slows, snaps into bright, glaring focus.

Justice undoubtedly has her scope on this scene. Wouldn't be proper backup if she didn't.

"Slow your roll," I say to Newbie, speaking calmly in Spanish with my most pleasant voice.

Newbie's head swings toward me. His eyes are wide and panicked.

Tony puts up his hands, trying to appear harmless. But Newbie, head turned toward me, is caught off guard by the gesture. He pushes Tony back, reaches for his gun, then begins to raise his weapon.

I step forward and shout, "No. *Para*—"

Pop. A bullet hole in Newbie's head splatters blood across Tony and me.

Aw, hell.

Tony and his pal take off running toward Walid's villa, aided in their escape by the cover fire peppering the ground and scattering my men.

Like them, I run for cover. Unlike my men, I do so in a zigzag pattern, making for the car outside the gate because I know Justice won't shoot near her sister.

Bullets chase me.

Yep. John McClane's luck. I'm gonna die so friggin' hard today.

Chapter 3
Gracie

I'm trying desperately to work my way out of the hidden compartment under this darn seat when an alarm sounds in the compound.

My heart speeds up—way up. It's outpacing a Ducati right now.

Growling under my breath, I work my sweaty numb fingers against the metal escape lever. They're about as responsive as a fish on the deck of a ship.

The *pop, pop, pop* of Justice's gun comes through my headset before it clicks off. Why is Justice shooting? Does it have anything to do with the alarm?

Crud. How did I get in this situation? If I were still with John, I'd probably be a soccer mom, have a garden and soft moments, and not this crazy stuff.

Okay, stop, Gracie. Focus on squeezing that metal between your fingers. Not regret. Not the man you lost. Not the child you had to let go.

Easier said, thought, and repeated again and again than done. I think of John all the time and our son, Tyler. At work. At rest. At play. And now, here in this sweaty, uncomfortable, uncertain place, because I'm afraid, and my biggest regret is losing them.

My fingers cramp as I angle my wrist back, grasp the latch, and pull. The wrist muscles yelp, but the spring gives way with a dull *click*.

Breathing heavily, I push the padding. The seat cracks open a little, then stops dead. *Fudge buckets.*

Wait. Those shots are close by. Someone is firing from behind the car? Someone is using the car for cover to fire at my sister?

Someone is so dead.

With a grunt, I angle my toes, curve my shoulder, get leverage, then push against the seat. Much to my relief, it begins to open.

Let's hope whoever's firing is too interested in shooting Justice to peer through the heavily tinted windows into the car's interior.

The car door creaks open and I freeze.

"Let me help you there, Gracie."

I flinch back, bang my head. *Ouch.* Southern Accent? Southern Accent knows my name?

The car shifts as someone gets inside, someone big judging by the way the car rocks. There's a creak, then the seat is yanked open.

Air. I suck it in with relish, pull my shoulders loose, then sit up, blinking at fresh air and man.

Um. Oh.

Sunset-brown hair topped by a USA ball cap, a big, easy grin defined by the persistent crease of overused dimples, labor-tanned skin, and the manliest nose I've ever seen. A roughly carved block, his nose adds challenge and strength to a too-handsome, sun-rugged portrait.

My heartbeat skitters between dread, alarm, and horrifying and unexpected arousal. Hair already plastered to my head, my skin heats to a temperature rarely seen outside a volcano. Surely my face is lava-red.

USA Ballcap grins at me.

Of course he does. What man wouldn't when faced with a woman who's obviously taken with his rugged good looks? My curse. My body paints every emotion upon my skin in red hues. From pleased pink to rust-colored anger to chili-red lust.

Top most embarrassing moment, please take a step down.

As if my reaction has given him a right, his eyes bounce along my body, taking in the red-velvet bra, the matching thong, the ruby piercing snuggled in my bellybutton, and the tattoo along my right side. The tattoo, a woman's long, elegant hand curved with vicious scarlet nails, clutches an enchanted apple, holding it out, as if implicitly offering it to the person whose eyes now consume my body.

His eyes are deepest amber, drunk on sun, sex, sand, and Southern Comfort. The desire behind his eyes practically licks me.

Without taking his gaze from me, he reaches down blindly, gropes and finds his two-way. He lifts it to his mouth, but before he presses the button, says, "Darlin', don't be upset by this. I'm on your side. Trust me."

With that, he clicks the radio on and in Spanish gives instructions for his men to go out and hunt Justice. He clicks off.

Don't be upset? Does this idiot realize that's my sister?

Teeth clenched, I extract my gun from the hidden compartment and point it at him.

A muscle along his thumb twitches, but he keeps his Glock 19 down. He smiles.

Really? *Oh, buddy, let's see how quickly I can wipe that smile off your face.*

"No, no," he says, clearly reading my intent from my furious face. "Don't shoot. I'm working with Tony. I had to send those men so Walid wouldn't suspect what's going down."

Tony? "My brother never mentioned you, and you just sacrificed my sister so Walid, a sex-trafficking supervillain, won't suspect you?" I fight to keep my finger from tensing against the trigger.

He shakes his head, smile gone. *Smart.* "I did that so Tony still has a chance to get to Walid. Plus, your sister is good and those guys can't shoot. No fooling. One of them shot himself in the foot trying to take his gun out two months ago."

"Gracie?" Justice's strained voice comes through my headset.

I click my mic with a flick of my jaw. "Go. I've got USA."

He does smile at that. "I'm Agent Leif McAllister. FBI."

FBI? Nuts and bolts. The email. The email I sent via a secure site to the FBI. The one I'd sent when Tyler was sick and I'd been helpless to go to him and it'd all seemed Momma's fault. The stupid email that proves I'm a traitor to the family and the Spy Makers Guild.

I swallow a wave of panic. "FBI? In Mexico?"

"Yeah, well, I'm sort of off-duty right now. No need for the agent part, actually. Just thought that would make you more comfortable. My friends call me Dusty."

"Dusty?"

"Been told I could talk a stone to dust." He reaches out with his free hand. "I'm going to help you out of here. Okay?"

"You touch me and I will shoot."

His hand drops. Good. Nothing like setting the boundaries from the get-go.

Chapter 4
Dusty

Even though she's pointing at gun at me, even though we're in the middle of a shitshow, not going to lie, this woman has my number. Give me the ruby. Give me the nails. Give me the apple. Yep. I want to lick my way down the whole damn tattoo and across that too-pink skin.

But first things first. Getting her not to shoot me, which means being honest with her. Well, no. Not honest.

Telling her the FBI got an anonymous tip about Parish vigilante activities and I'm investigating her family and using her brother Tony to get in with them would probably lead to her shooting me. Would likely cost me my job and definitely let the person I want most to bust, Mukta Parish, go free.

I give her my cover. "Your brother recruited me to help take out the sex-slaver. I've been working here for months, replacing every decent shot with a lousy one, and learning this place and its quirks like the back of my hand."

She squints at me. Weighing whether to believe me, shoot me, or both? She shrugs in a way that tells me she's still not certain and says, "Give me your gun."

"That's a no-go." And a *hell no*.

She opens her mouth to argue—I'm guessing—because after only two minutes of knowing her, I already know that's Gracie Parish's strong suit.

I cut her off. "Look, we're running out of time. Right now, we're hidden in this car, but if any of my men see you with a gun on me, things are going to get real complicated. You need me, so risk trusting me."

Her brows draw together. "Fine, I'll give the gun back when I'm safely out of the car."

That's trusting me? This woman is going to get us both killed.

Nearly choking on the big helping of yes-ma'am she served me up, I place my gun on the floor and inch out of the car.

The SUV full of men I sent after Justice sits empty, high on the ridge with the doors open. There's a chase afoot. I almost feel bad for those guys.

At the other end of the compound, past the barn, main house, and entrance to the old mine shaft, another vehicle tears out the back gate. Road grit flies into the air as the car screams away.

Some of Walid's men are already abandoning ship. Good.

I take out my two-way and yell that I've got it under control and for them to stop. I never yell about anything. Sound a bit desperate, too. They go faster.

Perfect.

My Glock in one of her hands, her small-framed Beretta Tomcat in the other, red-velvet bra, colorful tattoo, and belly piercing, Gracie steps from the car as hot as bourbon whiskey.

With a stone-serious expression, she motions me back.

I take two steps, arguing the whole way. "We really don't have—"

She turns to the hilltop her sister was on, surveying the area, and flashing me with a thong-strapped ass as round and juicy as the apple tattooed across her abs.

"Tiiii…" My voice goes up like a hay bale doused with gasoline torched by a flamethrower. Liquid lava steams through my body and irons out the wrinkles in the front of my cargo pants.

She turns back, catches me looking, drooling, and admiring, but there's nothing I can do about that now, so I smile at her as goofy as a teenage boy.

A bullet *thunks* into the steel of the car as reality slaps me upside the head for the stupid fool that I am.

I drop a hair's breadth slower than her.

Crouched by the car, I raise my two-way and tell my men not to shoot, then return myself to the problem at hand—the woman crouched next to me, still somehow holding a gun on me. "You need to give me my gun. I can get them..."

She ignores me, raises her Tomcat and shoots over my head.

Someone cries out.

Damn it. "Don't shoot. Honestly, these guys..."

She jumps to her feet and runs up the dirt road and through the now-unmanned gate.

What the hell? I should let the idiot get herself killed, but that won't get me into the Parish family fold.

Aw, hell.

Anxiety putting spurs to my legs, I sprint after her. *I* must be the idiot to chase after a woman with a gun in each hand.

She's not slow, but I've got longer legs and know where I'm going. I catch up to her. "Stop. You're going the wrong damn way."

She pulls up behind the guard tower, taking cover inside the booth.

I follow her inside.

She says, "Which way is faster?"

The noise from the alarm pulsing against my eardrums, I put my hand up to the interior camera to block us. "Give me my gun. I'll convince my men I'm taking you prisoner. We can walk through here without killing anyone or getting killed."

She squints at me with doubt as heavy as an elephant. "And my gun?"

"Yeah. You'll have to give me that to convince my men you're my prisoner."

Shaking her head, she hands me my gun but keeps her own. "It's dark, and it's a very small gun. If I keep my hands low like they're cuffed in front of me, they won't see that I'm holding it."

I seriously cannot believe this lady.

Gun in hand, I drop my palm from over the camera, nod in the right direction, and tell her, "Make it look good."

She lowers her shoulders and puts her head down like she's been captured, then starts walking.

On my belt, my two-way squawks again—more trouble going on in the mine.

Damn it, Sandesh. Sit tight.

"My Spanish isn't great," Gracie says as we walk forward. "Did they say the mine?"

Aw, hell no. The last thing I need is her panicking and starting to run again.

With a flick of my fingers, I lower the volume. "No."

She twists her head and casts a look over her shoulders that hits me like a bucket of ice water in the face. She knows I'm lying. In fact, her Spanish is probably excellent.

The moment lengthens, draws out as clear as crystal, as clear as a blue sky on a bright, cloudless Easter morning. Too late to take it back, because the decision has been made, the box has been checked.

Her beautiful face is telling me, *I know you're lying, and I will never trust you.*

Chapter 5
Gracie

Dusty marches me into the octagonal, wood-framed yurt of a security center as if we're going to meet resistance. Besides a few stools, two of which are overturned, a coffee station, water cooler, and multiple screens and computers, the room is empty.

Dusty's eyes go wide. His mouth opens then closes. They must've just left. I can still smell the sour stench of body odor and fear. Apparently, his men are abandoning ship at warp speed.

He points at a central computer. "There!" he shouts over the alarm, which is somehow louder in here than outside. "Main security computer."

He says something else, but I shake my head because his words are lost to the bleating alarm. He picks up paper and pen from the desk, writes something, then hands it to me.

The security password. That's not what I'd expected, but I have to say this *man* isn't who I expected. I still don't trust him one bit.

I cross the room, place my gun close at hand, then get to work.

Sweat slicks my palms as my fingers fly over the keyboard. The alarm is so loud it seems to be vibrating throughout my body, in time with my pounding heart. When the adrenaline wears off, I'm going to be one shaky, chattering mess.

A series of commands and I get the alarm to stop. The sudden silence throbs against my eardrums. As expected, once inside the control room, the security here is simple. For me, anyway. I quickly take care of the electric fence. With that down, I make sure to change the password so no one can undo my good work. Justice should have no problem getting inside. Now, to get her boyfriend, meet up with the others, and get the heck out of here.

Dusty's two-way squawks with instructions that I can't hear through my still muffled ears.

He answers, then clicks off. "Sandesh is acting up in the mine. They're sending reinforcements."

He tips up his ball cap, then wipes sweat and strands of honey-brown hair from his forehead with the back of his hand. "We need to get down there, get him, and get out before they arrive."

Descending into a dark mine wearing next to nothing while men with guns race to our location isn't the best idea I've ever heard.

I press my slick palms against sweaty thighs then pick up my gun. "Let's go."

#

The old wheel-and-pulley elevator squeaks like a giant hamster wheel as a steel cable slowly—*achingly* slow—lowers us past rough, sooty stone walls and into the mine. I could reach out and touch them if I wanted. I don't want.

The single light at the top of the elevator cage has zero warmth. Shivering, I keep my booted feet wide to brace against the rocking cart as I repress a coaldust-laced cough.

Standing at my side, Dusty has one hand on a bar across the top of the open iron cage. "Kind of romantic way to meet," he whispers.

I ignore him and the little flutter in my belly, which I'm absolutely certain is annoyance. What man would call this situation romantic?

At the bottom, the cage creaks to a stop. Dusty slides the gate open with a resounding *clack* that echoes up and up the shaft. "Usually, it's ladies first," Dusty says, "but I'm gonna take the lead if you don't mind."

I shrug. His gun braced on the flashlight fisted in his other hand, he scans the area.

I follow, but without the flashlight. I don't have one. We're not far when we come to the bodies of two men.

"Oh, damn," Dusty says, whispering a soft prayer as his light sweeps over them.

I have no doubt this is Sandesh's work, which means he's close by and likely waiting to see who arrived with the elevator. Impressive that he nearly made it out without us.

Following Dusty, I step over the feet of one of the dead guards, avoid looking at his face, and head straight for a stairway carved into stone. It's unlit and the steps seem to disappear into darkness.

Dusty starts up. For such a big guy, he's ninja quiet.

My boots sweep against the gritty steps with a swish, swish. It's a wonder I can even hear the sound over my heartbeat, which has taken up residence in my ear canal.

At the top of the stairs, Dusty moves expertly into a dimly lit hallway. He says, "Whoa, now. I'm on your side." He lowers his gun and flashlight.

I peak around him and see the outline of a body on the ground and Sandesh curled up behind it, using the corpse as cover. He has a weapon pointed at Dusty.

I move quickly in front of Dusty. "Don't shoot," I tell Sandesh. "It's me."

"Gracie?" Sandesh says, lowering his weapon. He lifts a blond head crusty with blood. His face is bruised and his voice sounds as if his vocal cords were replaced with rocks. He blinks partially swollen blue eyes. "Are you rescuing me in your underwear?"

So relieved to see him, I'm nearly giddy, I say, "All the cool kids are doing it."

Groaning, he stands up, looking worse for wear with his battered face and tattered pants, but he isn't dead. And with the camp emptying out and Justice on her way inside, I feel like it's going to be okay. Chances are good, we're all going to make it out of here alive.

Chapter 6
Gracie

Two months later

Anonymous in my dark-visored helmet, black leather pants, and matching leather jacket, I inch my low-riding, custom-made Ducati through Philly's historic Manayunk district.

The thing about this bike is it likes to go fast, and it's not so great with going slow. I weave back and forth or place my foot down every few feet as traffic in the popular area is highest on Saturday nights.

Cars and high-end stores line the bustling block, colorful awnings stretch over crowded outdoor seating, and people jaywalk through the streets without a care.

Finally at the light, I take a right and get million-dollar-jackpot-lucky as a car pulls out of a prime parking space. This is closer than I should park, but I won't be long.

In my rearview mirror, I spot the familiar three-story brownstone where my ex, John, lives. Squeezed among a long row of houses, his home has a balcony with a few chairs and a tier of herb pots.

Swinging off my bike, I stroll back to the corner and up to the Italian ice cart. The man at the stand, shorter than me with skin the rich brown of Brazilian leather, rinses the ice cream scoop in a water-filled Bazooka gum bucket.

"Wha'd ya want?"

I flick up my visor. "Watermelon."

My favorite. I feel about watermelon-flavored anything the way most people feel about chocolate—a fact I'm careful not to share with my dozens of gun-toting sisters. Who needs that argument?

Leaning against the side of a building, suitably blocked by a utility pole and the water ice cart, I wait.

It doesn't take long.

The moment I see him, my heart leaps in my chest, a smile springs to my face, and the tension melts from my shoulders.

My son.

Tyler carries his guitar onto the balcony, and I realize he recently got his hair cut. I can see his green eyes, so like mine. They're bright against his sun-loving Mediterranean skin—so not like mine. With all those dark curls, he looks like his dad. They share the same build, too, though Tyler is thinner simply because of his age and the growth spurt that's made him shoot up too quickly.

He starts to play, and I inch closer. It's hard to hear over the street noise, people talking, and music spilling from pub speakers.

I listen closely to the ache, the longing in Tyler's music. In this, he's different from his father, who plays beautifully but never makes up his own songs. John prefers even his music to be defined for him.

Or he had when he'd been younger. Truthfully, I don't know who John is now that he has Ellen. She might've changed him. Likely has. Love tends to do that to people, especially a love like they have, with no dark family secrets and violence to tear them apart.

I have many dark secrets, including the Spy Makers Guild—an organization that does global ops all over the world, an organization I gave Tyler up in order to protect him from. An organization that might've permanently distorted my ability to know the difference between right and wrong.

Was it wrong to let him go? Could I have fought harder? Should I be spying on him now?

I toss my empty blue-and-white cup into a bin. Maybe I shouldn't be here, taking in these few glimpses of my son, but I desperately long to know him. A desperation that's grown since that operation in Mexico where we rescued Justice's boyfriend, took down the bad guys, and lost Tony.

The image of Tony's body lying on the floor of Walid's villa with Justice crying over him snaps into my brain as lethal and piercing as a gunshot.

Oh, how I miss him. Oh, how I regret all the things I'd left unsaid. I don't want that to be my legacy with Tyler. I don't want to be like my biological mother, who'd reached out to me only after she'd been diagnosed with cancer. We'd built a relationship but had had so little time together, a lot of which was marred by her illness. A teen and unexpectedly pregnant, I took care of her until the end.

I wish, like my bio mom, I could find a way back into Tyler's life. Not as his mother, because he has Ellen for that, but as someone he can rely on.

Putting aside his guitar, Tyler rests his elbows on the railing.

I smile, because my fifteen-year-old son is so very beautiful.

He brings his gaze directly to mine.

My adrenaline spikes.

He isn't looking at me. He can't be.

I'm a stranger on the street, hidden mostly behind a utility pole. I never wear the same thing here. I never uncover my hair.

But... he is. Tyler is staring at me.

He waves.

My heart balloons in my chest like it's filled with helium. It rises and rises, pops, then drops into my churning stomach.

Danger. Danger. Danger.

Turning away, I flick down my visor, walk back to my bike, get on, then drive down the street. What have I done?

What would Momma do if she knew I'd broken the terms of the custody deal I'd made with John? The deal that keeps John silent about The Guild? The deal that ensures Tyler will be kept unaware of The Guild—safe. The deal that makes sure Momma will never follow through on her threat to use her advanced technologies to alter John's memories?

What would Momma say if she knew I'd broken the deal that let everyone continue with their lives?

Everyone but me.

Chapter 7
Dusty

Standing on the crowded city street in Manayunk, I have to admit I'm not sure what just happened. Or why. Something spooked the usually unflappable Gracie Parish.

Hell, I've seen less reaction from her in the middle of a firefight in Mexico. So, I gotta ask myself: why did she tear out of here after Balcony Boy waved at her?

Using my cell, I get a close-up on the kid then expand it. A little blurry, but the kid does have green eyes like Gracie's. Could they be related? Maybe. But in what way?

After crossing the street, I match the apartment with a number and name. John, Ellen, Tyler, and Henry True.

Turning from the building, I begin to walk back to my car as I do a quick search using the company portal on the first name. Passing a pretty woman who grins up at me, I smile and nod, but barely break from my search.

John's son is Tyler True. He married Ellen when Tyler was three, so the mystery as to who Tyler's mother is continues. Henry came along five years ago and is the son of John and Ellen True. I put in a request for Tyler's birth certificate, but, judging by his age, it couldn't be Gracie, could it? She's barely old enough to have had the kid. She'd have been, what, sixteen, almost seventeen? Plus, her file says she's never given birth.

Still, the kid means something to her, and, according to these records, John's close to Gracie's age and grew up not far from her bar, the infamous Club When?

Consider my suspicions raised.

Back at my parking spot, I slide into my company vehicle and start her up. I'm not surprised when my cell rings. Unhooking it from my bat-belt—thing has near everything, a good knife, folding lock pick, mace, and an EMF jammer—I answer. "Hello."

"Tell me you have something, Dusty." The voice of my SAC—Special Agent in Charge—blares through the speakers.

I lower the volume. "Hey, Mack, just the man I wanted to speak with."

He grunts in disbelief, because he's not a stupid fellow. "Give me something, Dusty."

Wasn't going to mention it, but it's all I got. "I followed Gracie Parish today. She came to Manayunk in a roundabout way, using a pretty good surveillance detection route to see some kid. Had a hell of a time following her."

She'd changed getups in a garage and left her car for the motorcycle. If it weren't for her height and the specialized bike, I might've missed her. She's got good situational awareness, but I'm better.

"Seems like a lot of trouble for some kid. Could she be after the father in some way? Maybe he's a target for her family?"

Seeing an opening in traffic, I pull out onto the street then coast through the light. "I don't think so. I ran a quick check on the dad, John True. He's a regular guy, married a local news anchor a few years ago, and has one other son. Interestingly, he grew up down the street from Gracie's club—the one she started when her biological mother came back into her life. And he's near Gracie's age. This is all preliminary, but Tyler does have Gracie's eyes."

"You think he's her kid?"

Making a left at the light, I head back for my little rental a handful of blocks from Gracie's club. "All that effort to avoid being followed... she sure didn't come for the sweet ice. At the very least, the kid means something to her, but there's no record of her giving birth."

What are you hiding, Ms. Gracie Parish? I mean, besides the fact that your family is into some illegal vigilante activities?

"In other words, you've got nothing that'll help me reopen the case."

"I take it the Bureau isn't reopening the Parish investigation."

"No. Despite all the rumors about Mukta Parish, the power she's amassed, satellite companies, pharmaceutical and biotech companies—all useful to support deadly covert activities—officially, the woman is a dead end. She has a lot of fans and a lot of money, and it doesn't hurt that that exclusive boarding school she runs is filled with VIPs."

"Hard to believe that, even after that drone strike at the school, she'd still have people covering for her." The drones had dropped small explosive devices on the school a few months back. No one hurt, did little damage, but it had scared the bejeezus out of everyone.

Mack grunts a rich-people-live-by-their-own-rules sound. "Hard to argue against her when the team combed every inch of the campus—even scanned the place via satellite and thermal spectral analysis. I reviewed the scans myself and if there were a secret underground anything, it would've shown up. There's bupkis."

"Come on, there's something there. We know she's running her own covert ops. She *has* to have a secure facility to gather intel and do training. The school is the perfect cover." Annoyed, I drum my fingers on the steering wheel. Feels like I'm on my own out here. "In Mexico, I saw the Parish siblings in action. They are highly trained, lethal operatives."

"Don't remind me of that colossal failure. You went undercover for months, ate up a lot of company funds, and it went nowhere."

"Nowhere?"

"The principal was never implicated, your contact poisoned himself while poisoning the sex-slaver, and you backed off from bringing in the sisters."

My shoulders rise as my neck grows tight. I right-lane pass a car making a left and unclench my teeth. "Backing off isn't how I see it. They'd just lost their brother."

"You wouldn't even help me find the brother's body so we could determine cause of death and use it to put pressure on the siblings."

My stomach rolls at the thought of using Tony that way, and, honestly, I have no idea where I buried his body. Those last hours in Mexico remain a blur of pain and regret. "These people are as loyal as Labradors. I'm not going to bully them into turning on Mukta."

Besides, if the tip letter is any indication, Gracie and her siblings were adopted, trained, molded, and made into covert agents. If that's the case, they're victims.

"That's why I'm giving you this time to bring me something—anything—we can use to implicate Mukta Parish. You do that and this will go from a drawer to a full-out investigation. Just ring that bell."

The steering wheel brushes against my palms as I complete another turn. "I still believe Gracie is the key." I'm nearly certain she sent that anonymous tip. "If I can get her to give me an invite into the family operations, I can locate their headquarters. If it's not on campus, it's somewhere else. When I find it—that'll do more than ring a bell; it'll blow this thing wide open."

Mack grunts and I can't tell if it's agreement or doubt or something between the two, but he doesn't hang up, so he's got more to say.

I wait.

He clears his throat. "I have word on your dad."

My stomach does something it hasn't done since I'd been seven and terrified of the man—it drops, shrinks to the size of a pea. "Yeah."

"He's sick—something wrong with his kidneys—and is in the hospital."

"Of course he is." After all these years, my father, the faith healer who'd let so many sick people suffer and die—

because if God didn't heal you, you didn't *deserve* to be healed—is seeing a doctor.

Fuck. I jerk to a stop at a red light.

The woman crossing gives me the *pay-attention* glare I richly deserve.

With a tip of my baseball cap, I let her know I'm suitably chastised. "What of his congregation?"

"Has his whole congregation paying for his care and praying for him because he says a faith healer can't heal himself. It's hard to believe people can be that damn gullible."

I bristle at the word. "Thanks for letting me know. And if you continue to have eyes on that little part of the world, keep me updated."

"Will do."

I hang up, turning up the air until I can feel it practically spitting ice at my face. I accelerate through the green.

I'm angry at my dad and heartbroken for his followers, those people who raised me for a time. I know a lot of folks think those people get what they deserve, but I'm not one of them. I know what it's like to be brainwashed, to be dying from a simple bladder infection and to believe that God has deemed you unworthy of living.

It's why I'm doggedly investigating the Parish family. Following up on an anonymous email from someone who also knows what happens when family cuts you off from the wider world, from real facts and information, and replaces them with a narrow, dogmatic view.

It's why I'm risking everything to bust Mukta Parish, the woman who brainwashes young girls and turns them into her own personal army.

It's why I went undercover for Tony Parish to work for that scumbag sex-trafficker in Mexico.

It's why I intend to step from the shadows and reacquaint myself with one Ms. Gracie Parish.

Chapter 8
Gracie

Sunday is my day off from managing Club When?, the club where I work and live. One day off a week, so I usually spend it at my computer. Today's no exception. Below me, the club is as quiet as a mouse. Here, on the upper levels, my keyboard and the distant hum of The Guild's computer servers are the only noises.

If I can streamline this database, it should work not only for The Guild, but for law enforcement as well, to help identify creepers seeking children and vulnerable women on the dark web.

Rubbing my sore eyes, I realize I've been at this for hours. I need a pee break. Pushing away from the desk and the multiple screens starting to blur to my tired eyes, I roll my head left and right.

My cell rings.

It's Sunday, nearly dinnertime at the Mantua Home, so I don't need to see who's calling to know who it is.

Getting up, which sends my chair rolling back to the wall, I pick up my cell.

Swallowing my rising dread, I dive right in. "Hello, Momma. If this is about dinner, I'm sorry, I have plans."

"Are they unbreakable plans? I would consider it a sincere kindness if you came tonight."

Surprise flashes down my body. A "sincere kindness" is as good as a summons. Momma doesn't make demands like that without reason.

And, normally, that would be all it would take, but not this time.

I can't.

Ever since Tyler waved at me, I've been unable to chain up my need to be part of his life—something I can do only if I can convince John to amend the deal. Something he'll only consider if he knows I'm no longer a part of The Guild. Which is something I can only accomplish if I distance myself from my family. And that is awful and heartbreaking, and I'm not even sure it'll work, but I have to try.

"No. I'm sorry, I'm busy."

"But your newest sister, Cee, asked specifically for you."

"Cee asked for me to come to dinner? I'm the person who said she shouldn't be adopted into our family. I know she knows this because she confronted me about it when she came to the house. I had to explain my reasons to her. It was awkward."

"Perhaps your explanation suited her because she seems to have let it go."

Hmmm. No. "Cee doesn't strike me as the type to let things go." Attested to by the fact that during Cee's rescue from a sex-slaver, she shot and killed one of the bad guys. She said she'd done it to rescue Justice, but I'm not convinced it'd been absolutely necessary. "What aren't you telling me?"

Momma sighs and it's as tired a sound as I've ever heard from her.

I bite my lip to keep from asking her if she's been taking care of herself. She's not as young as she used to be.

"If you must know, she sees how you live in but also outside The Guild and is intrigued by it. It seems she's become restless with the restrictions we've placed on operations since…" There is a long pause, long enough that my heart hurts even before she says, "Tony's disappearance."

Red pain lances my head, and I want to shout into the phone that he's dead, not disappeared, but I know better. If there's one thing I've learned growing up as a member of The Guild, it's that you don't open your mouth, even when it feels wrong to keep it shut. "I can't, Momma—

"Is it something I've done?"

"What?"

"You have always been less active with the family, Grace, but ignoring one of your siblings' requests, someone who wants to get to know you... It's not like you. Have I done something to drive you away?"

That stings. Mostly because it hits the mark. Yes, it *is* something she's done.

Running a global and unauthorized spy ring that's always been more important than my life is something she's done. Threatening John's memory so I was forced to send him and Tyler away is something she's done. Lying about Tony, pretending to the press he's on sabbatical when he's dead, is something she's done.

And I can't say any of that because she'd want to talk about it, go to therapy, bring other family members in to talk about it. That's the *last* thing I want. I'm having a hard enough time keeping a lid on my feelings.

"It's not..." My words dry up like the moisture in my mouth. Reaching for the octopus-shaped bowl on my desk, I pluck out a Jolly Rancher, unwrap it, then pop it into my mouth. *Mmmm.* There's no stress watermelon-flavored corn syrup can't help ease.

"Well then, is it the family?"

"Of course not. I love those lunatics."

"It's The Guild then? Do you no longer want to work for the organization? Perhaps you wish to disavow our work."

Ouch. That word, *disavow*, has my neck and cheeks warming with heat. I had done that, hadn't I? When I'd sent that anonymous letter to the FBI, I'd disavowed The Guild, but I'd been out of my head with grief because Tyler had been so sick and I'd had no way to get to him, to be with him.

The truth is, I *do* believe in the good work The Guild does. Not just the secret work of helping the helpless, freeing the wrongly imprisoned, and rescuing victims, but also the educational work of our family's world-famous boarding school,

The Mantua Academy, does. And the groundbreaking research of Parish holdings—the charities and the foundations.

Crud. I can't disavow them again, not my family and not The Guild. I owe them. "I'll be there in a half hour."

After dressing for dinner, I exit my club and enter into the sunny sauna that is July in northeast Pennsylvania. This is not the weather to leave my hair down for or to pour myself into a magenta sequined shirt, black skinny jeans, and turquoise power heels. Yet, I have.

The crunch of gravel loud under my heels, I head for my car. I wish I had my bike, but it's my secret vehicle. I leave it at a garage halfway between here and Tyler's, so that I can do a vehicle switcheroo whenever I go to see him. I can't be too careful.

My cell blares a fox-whistle sound and gooseflesh rises on my arm. I haven't heard that sexy sound from my cell in over a decade. It's a text tone I saved for one number.

John's.

Heart in my throat, I read the text.

I know you've been spying on my son, stalking him. Remember our agreement? Stay away from Ty. I'm not putting up with you and your family's craziness in our lives. Don't come around again. This is your one warning.

My son? Hurt and anger land a punch to my lungs. I gasp for air. My hands shake as the screen grows dim.

Thirteen years.

I've been re-sharing my contact information with John every six months, waiting and hoping to hear from him, to get one word about Tyler. He's never sent me anything, not even when Tyler was sick in the hospital.

His first text to me in thirteen years is a threat.

Feeling my control slipping as anger, shame, and panic start to overwhelm me, I use my Guild training to find calm by focusing intently on my breath and the sounds around me. The whoosh of a single car passing, the bark of a distant dog, and the crack of a—

I drop without a thought, hitting the ground a split second before the bullet *thunks* against my car door.

There's another shot, but I'm already under my car, drawing my Glock from my purse, safety off.

The flood of adrenaline mutes everything but the sound of my heartbeat. My eyesight sharpens as I methodically scan the parking lot. There's another shot and another, and I flinch with each one. Stones pop up and hit my car, *tink*ing into steel like heavy rain, but they don't reach me.

Scooting toward the other side of the car, I roll out into a crouch. Quietly, I stalk to the end of the car and gaze out at the wooded area that lines the back of the parking lot where the shots came from.

I can't see anything moving among the trees, but I give it a moment then two before I sprint forward, gun raised.

I enter the woods and duck behind a tree, listening for any noise. Controlling my exhale, so that my ears can focus on any unusual sound in the woods, I hear nothing. Swinging away from the tree, I continue into the brush.

It's shaded here, dimmer than in the afternoon sunshine, but I still easily spot the pile of dirt and leaves where someone had created a berm, a place where they could lay down fire as well as hide behind if they had to take fire in return.

Someone had been in here, lying in wait for me.

How long had they been here? Had they known I'd be coming out at this time?

These heart-stopping questions filter through my brain as I accept that this is no random act of violence. In fact, this obviously trained person, judging by the silencer used, had been here to kill me.

Someone had sent a hitman after me?

I bend down and examine the area, picking up shell casings as the sound of running footsteps filters in from the parking lot behind the club.

Spinning, I raise my weapon, step to the tree line, and aim.

Chapter 9
Dusty

The finger-snap of a silenced gun brings the hair on my neck to attention and sends my heart into double-time. Nearly at Gracie's Club When?, I break into a run.

I'd suspected something was up when my phone alerted me that the surveillance camera I'd set up in the club's parking lot had quit working. It's well hidden, so I figured it'd malfunctioned. I'd decided to hoof it to Gracie's club from my rented apartment, enjoy a nice stroll in Doylestown, and go check out the camera.

Now, another shot—and another—have me jumping over a timepiece sculpture that looks like something right out of *Alice in Wonderland*. It's one of two hippie sculptures that mark off the drive to the parking area for the club.

Jogging down the driveway—a stretch of asphalt squeezed between a warehouse and Gracie's club—I pull up short and scan the parking lot.

No one around. Trees line the far edge of the parking lot where I'd placed the camera. Someone is moving in there.

I jog toward the trees and that someone steps out with her gun raised.

I lower my own weapon so as not to confuse the issue. "Whoa now. It's me. Dusty."

Gracie's eyebrows inch up, but she doesn't say a word. She takes a good long look at the area and then me before lowering her weapon.

I holster my own gun. "You okay?"

Readjusting her disheveled shirt, covering the strap of a crimson bra but not the raspberry scrape on her arm, she bends to retrieve what turns out to be her purse and phone from under her car. She straightens with practiced nonchalance. "Of course."

After one more sweep of the area, the weapon and phone go into her big bag. She opens the car door, puts the purse inside, slams the door shut, and turns to me. "Why are you here?"

Is she serious? Not even an excuse; she goes right to the counterattack? "I heard gunshots."

"Some nut tried to rob me."

She says this as if it's nothing to be alarmed about. Which sets off every alarm in my body. "Someone tried to *rob* you with a suppressed weapon?"

"Yes. I had a gun, and when I took it out, he ran off."

"Really?" I say, temper starting to rise. "Thought I proved I wasn't dumb as a box of rocks when we were in Mexico and I saved your ass."

She flinches, and I realize the last time she saw me was when she was leaving Mexico, so she could take an injured Victor out and I could take care of her brother's body.

Pain stabs me between the eyes at the memory. I stop myself from rubbing at it as something insistent whispers, *Leave it go, man. Leave it.*

Recovering, she smiles, the kind of knowing smile that makes men drop to their knees or lose their minds. "Stop trying to confuse the issue. Why are you in town?"

I lose my mind. "Right, Gracie. Someone tried to rob you with an expensive silenced weapon. It surely doesn't have a lick to do with your family and whatever shit y'all are into."

She studies me long and hard. "Why are you checking up on me? Showing up in the nick of time? Do you want me to believe that's a coincidence?"

"Why don't you explain to me why someone wants to kill you?"

We stare at each other, and I swear there's an electric current running between the two of us, because it's zapping my skin and my awareness, and creating a low, heavy heat in my balls.

She sent the letter, right? She was reaching out for something, wasn't she?

She steps closer to me. My heart starts its engine and revs, waiting for the green in her eyes to signal *go*.

Her eyes flash invitation and challenge. "Do you want to kiss me?"

"What?" I step back—the opposite of what I want to do. I want to wrap her in my arms, kiss her senseless, reassure my pounding heart she's safe—but not like this. Not as a test, not as a game, and not when she's trying and succeeding in controlling this interaction. Too bad a certain part of me hasn't gotten the message.

She huffs at the distance I created. "You obviously want to kiss me." Her eyes slide over the front of my jeans. "So, maybe you lied to Tony when you told him you were no longer with the FBI. Maybe you're undercover and would feel bad about kissing me while you're investigating my family."

She's not stupid.

She quirks her mouth, runs her tongue along her upper lip with exaggerated slowness. She put all her cards on the table, showed me her hand, and I'm holding nothing. But since she obviously already knows the truth and I really want to stop her mother, and denial is part of the job and something she should really expect...

"I'm not undercover. I'm here because Tony introduced me to a life I want a permanent part of."

She gives me a look as filled with doubt as any I've ever seen.

And since I really *do* want to kiss her and since the invitation is out there...

Grabbing her by the waist, I pull her flush against my hard-on.

Her eyebrows rise in surprise, but she doesn't pull away. She wiggles against me.

Damn. I drop my head and slide my lips restlessly over hers.

She opens wide for me. Soft. Wet. Sleek. Her glorious tongue strokes mine, sends my heart thumping in my chest.

She deepens the kiss, latches her fingers through the belt loops on the back of my jeans and uses them as leverage to grind against me. The rough friction has my dick straining in my pants. Okay, she wins. I need to stop, to…

Oh, good Lord.

What is she doing with her tongue?

She breaks the kiss.

Head spinning, breath hot, I kiss along her cheek and whisper-moan into her ear, "Darlin', let's end this upstairs."

She laughs softly, squeezes my ass. "Sure. I'm going to boink your brains out and then give away all the family secrets while you lay satiated beside me."

Boink?

She swats my ass, steps away. "Moron."

Wait. What?

My head clears. Slowly.

Yep. I walked right into that. I'd seen the trap, watched her lay it out in front of me, pretty as a picture, told myself to not go near it, then jumped inside. She's right; I *am* a moron.

Grunting, I put my hands in my pockets to hide a still-raging boner.

Gracie grins at me like she knows what I'm about, and I have to fight my own smile.

Which isn't right, because I'm pretty pissed off right now. "Okay, Gracie. Suppose I'll see you soon."

With her laughter following me out, I stroll off, unhooking my phone from my bat-belt to make sure the feed to the camera is back on. It is. Seems the "robber" used a jammer. I'll have to devise a way of keeping track of her that's less vulnerable to interference.

I watch her on my screen as she runs a hand through her hair, leans against her car, then, after a moment that goes on long enough to boost my confidence, turns from checking out my ass to get into her vehicle.

Chapter 10
Gracie

The club's theme for the next eight weeks is beginning to take shape. Red, white, and blue flags and fighter jets hang from the copper ceiling panels, along with strobe lights that will add to the Fourth of July fireworks show. The sound of workers using drills and hammers to remove the old decorations and put up the new ones pounds in my ears.

I feel like a kid in a candy store, and not just because I'm sucking on a Jolly Rancher. This is my happy place.

My bio mom used to warn that it'd get boring for me, that I'd regret the choice to have Club When? change themes based on a time period or specific event in history, but I never have. I even purchased the warehouse next to the club in order to store our costume changes.

Wearing workaday jeans with a button-down over my Club When? T-shirt—a giant gold question mark over a clock—I remove another tube of red, white, and blue foam padding from the storage box and fasten it to the gilt rail bordering the dance floor.

The only problem with the decoration change this time is my paranoia. A hitman and being threatened by an ex-lover woke me from the delusion that I'm safe simply because I'm not doing day-to-day field operations.

I keep watching the workers and evaluating the new ones employed by the contractor I use. I shift to standing as one of the men comes over with a framed *Independence Day* poster—

an alien ship beaming an aggressive red light onto the Empire State Building. He's a big guy with a lanky build and holds himself like someone who's had training, maybe military.

He says, "Where you want this?"

My heart does that ready-in-a-whisper acceleration. I place my hand on my hip so I can quickly get at my concealed gun.

I nod toward the picture of Prince in all his glory hanging between two art deco stained-glass windows near the bar. "Replace that one."

He smiles, a kind of goofy, kind of sweet smile. "You've got it, boss."

I exhale a full breath as he walks away. I know I'm being unreasonable, but I can't help it. I'm not used to dealing with threats without some kind of backup. I have none. But not because my family doesn't care. If they knew I'd been shot at, they'd be all over this place and me right now.

I can't reach out to them if John, even as far-fetched as it seems, might've had something to do with the hitman. Which means I have to be vigilant, paranoid, and update my security on my own.

A loud *bam* resounds through the club, and my hand snakes under my shirt to my holster while my heart springs to attention. No one else reacts, and I realize the noise was a worker dropping a metal Statue of Liberty sculpture. *Paranoid much?* My cell rings. I jump out of my skin, get control, then thumb the Accept button. "Hey, Victor."

"How's my favorite peliroja?"

His favorite redhead is a nervous, paranoid, and worried wreck. "Thanks for returning my call. I hate to ask, you know I do, but I kind of need a favor."

"Uh-oh, that sounds serious. Like you're going to ask me to put on a G-string and dance in public. You know I'll only do that if it's private. Me and you."

Normally, I don't mind Victor's harmless flirting. The man *did* risk his life for me and my family, after all, but today I'm all business. "I sent you an email through our secure site with some details. Can you check it out?"

After Mexico, we'd become friends. So much so that he stopped calling me Red, in English, and started calling me Roja, red in Spanish. It's a little thing, but it feels more personal. Friends, and because we each had something to offer the other—him contacts, me cyber skills—I set up a secure communication site for us.

"Give me a sec."

I listen to him tapping his keyboard.

He whistles as he works then says, "Got it."

I wait for him to read the email. He knows more than a lot of people about me and my family. Momma wanted to "alter" his memories after Mexico, but Sandesh, Justice, and I had thrown fits, so Victor remains one of the few people outside the family who knows about our secret business of rescuing and aiding women globally.

"Madre de Dios," Victor says. "Someone took a shot at you?"

"Keeping reading. That's not all of it."

He does, issuing a few choice curses in Spanish before saying, "John texted and threatened you right before someone shot at you?"

"Yeah." It could be coincidence. It could be. "But it gets worse."

The silence indicates he's gone back to reading. For the first time I'm actually glad that Victor knows about John. A few weeks ago, we'd gotten drunk together and started sharing secrets, and because Victor has no judgment and has also had a really mind-blowing life—more than even mine—I told him about John.

The shrill whine of a drill cuts through the club, and I press the phone closer to my ear as Victor says, "First, I want you to know that I'm in. Whatever you need, because no one messes with my peliroja. Second, you're not telling your crazy-ass family?"

"Don't call them crazy."

"Twenty-eight kids from all over the globe, all of them with some tragic backstory, adopted by a mega-wealthy woman and trained to do covert ops for her. Yeah, I'm sticking with the crazy part."

Well, I can't really argue with his reasoning, and, honestly, it feels good to be able to talk to someone outside The Guild about The Guild. "Did you read the whole thing? I can't tell them."

"I read it. John might be involved, Dusty from Project Mexico is in town, and you think he might've stumbled onto the whole 'make buds with Tony' thing because of your letter to the FBI."

Another confession my drunk self hiccup-cried to Victor was about the letter I'd sent to the FBI. I'd had a powerful headache the next day, but, surprisingly, no regret. "Yeah. I do."

I hear him moving around, probably pacing with that slight limp he still has from the injury he'd suffered in Mexico.

After a moment, Victor asks, "Only five people?"

My email included a list of five people who might want me dead. John and his wife—her because I suspect she knows more than she should—top the list, then a hacktivist I'd unveiled as a corporate shill, another, an uber-wealthy sexual predator I'd drugged in my wilder days, getting him to admit the truth, and a macho pilot-turned-arms-dealer I'd dated long enough to bring him to justice. Is that all? Could I be missing someone? "Yeah. Five. Just them."

My heart jumps as Dusty walks in through the front door of my club. What the heck? The sign on the door reads *Closed*.

Dusty nods and greets workers, stops to help someone with a ladder before making his way around tables and chairs toward me. It's as if his easy gait connects paddles to my chest and unleashes current into my heart which *ba-boom, ba-boom*s in time to his long-legged stride.

"He's here," I whisper, though Dusty is too far away to hear me. "FBI."

"Careful, chica. I might've been out of it after being shot, but I remember the hot chemistry between you two."

He doesn't even know about the kiss that had immolated my soul and burnt all previous records for sexual heat to ash.

"You there? Or did you melt into a puddle?"

Focus, Gracie. "Um, can you handle the first two people on the list?" John and Ellen. "I don't have the objectivity."

"Sí." He makes a sound like regret or worry, then says, "There might be more people to add to your list."

"What? Who? How would you—"

"Take care of FBI and handle your side of the list. We'll talk."

He hangs up and I stand there filled with a sense of foreboding.

A sense that heightens when Dusty stops feet in front of me.

He stares down at me. His seductive honey eyes roll over me, and, despite being dressed like a schlub, I feel like I'm wearing a negligee.

"Hey, Gracie. Came to see how you're holding up after that *robbery attempt.*"

That Southern accent makes even sarcasm sound good, and because I'm focused on how good he looks, I stupidly say, "I didn't know FBI agents could wear jeans."

He snorts and grins at me. He's really cute in a gray T-shirt stretched over his wide chest and tight against biceps large enough to make me wonder how many pushups he can do.

Probably a lot.

His gaze locks on me so intently, I can't look away.

"Is that eagerness or wariness in your eyes?"

Eagerness, because after eighteen months without sex, a mummy could light my spark, never mind someone as hot as him… "Suspicion. What are you up to?"

His breath pushes out from his mouth so fast it's as if I punched the casual right out of him.

"Honestly, I was worried about you. Not just about the other night, but about how you've been since Mexico."

He flinches on the word *Mexico* and reaches up to rub at his forehead.

The sincere concern in his eyes takes me by surprise and reminds me that he knows the truth about Tony. A truth he also seems to be keeping quiet, like my family. The family line is that Tony ran away to find himself. Anything else simply isn't talked about in public.

I mentally shake myself for getting caught in my own sorrow. I whisper-remind myself, "Must not feed the dragon of grief."

"What's that?"

I answer without thinking. "When I was a teen, after my mom died, I used to wonder if part of the Earth needs the energy from our human pain. Like there's this living thing that secretly survives off the electric impulses that shock our human hearts."

His face pales, and I feel as if I've made a mistake. The problem with me is I often say what I shouldn't. "But I don't actually believe that," I say, feeling flustered. "It's just a reminder to myself that grief has its own kind of energy."

He shakes his head. "My father used to talk about how the world was alive. A great snake that has swallowed us, a literal living hell. Claimed we're all being tested to see if we can escape and go to Heaven. Me, I think that's an excuse, a way to let pain shut you down. And to do that is to blaspheme the beauty of this world and the gifts we've been given. The grace."

Usually, I hate when people use my name as a pun. Not this time. His words are an invitation. He's reaching out, and even though I don't trust him, I want to reach back.

I finger the chain around my neck, swallow, and say, "I'm managing. Thanks for asking." Nerves still on edge and needing to see beyond him—he's so big, he blocks my line of sight—I take a step to the left.

He notices. "Don't blame you for being freaked out. Okay if we talk? Maybe we could go somewhere and have a drink?"

That makes me smile. I gesture at the club. "You do realize I own a bar, right?"

His eyebrows rise and he looks around as if in surprise. His face brightens. "Excellent suggestion, Gracie. We can catch up now. Never too early. And you can even make me one of those famous drinks."

"Famous drinks?"

"Now, don't hold back on me. I'm absolutely certain a girl who spent her teen years in a bar knows a thing or two about inventing drinks. You've probably named it, too. Something like Fuzzy Panda or Starry Night."

The laugh that burst from me is as spontaneous as breathing. I have zero control over it. Something inside of me reacts on a deeper level, too, as if stretching its back and purring.

Not good. Forget the fact that someone is after me and that I need to be on guard at all times, this guy is investigating me and my family. Still, the smile stays in place when I say, "It's called Blood and Guts, because you need both to drink it."

I'd meant that to sound like a dismissal, but he says, "I'm ready for that challenge."

My face heats when I realize my mistake, and I notice the corners of his mouth twitching. I have to bite my lower lip not to laugh. I don't dare say a word because I'm sure I will giggle.

He smiles. "That's an awful long pause, Gracie. What could you be considerin'? State of the Union? Temperature in Budapest? Last three deposits into your bank account?"

I can't help my laugh-snort, as it's obvious what I'm thinking about is him.

Okay, I'm not going to get rid of him that easily, so maybe I should turn the tables. Find out about his investigation, what he has on my family, and if his being around could have anything to do with whoever shot at me.

All solid reasons that have zero to do with how handsome he is.

The handsome thing doesn't hurt, though.

I shrug. "The club opens again to the public on Wednesday. I'm usually around."

He shivers. "Brrr. That's a climate-fixing invitation if ever I've heard one." He puts on his aviator glasses. Shields up. Game on. "But I'll take it."

Chapter 11
Dusty

I pick up my cell phone on the first ring because I happen to be looking at my screen, taking in the feed from the back of Gracie's club. "Hey, Mack."

"Dusty. Where are you?"

"My rented apartment in Doylestown."

My tone must give something of my thoughts away because Mack says, "It's that bad?"

"It's not the Four Seasons, but I spent months living my own version of hell at that sex-slaver compound, so renting from an older fellow with a penchant for drawing duck murals isn't that bad."

"Ducks? He's a hunter?"

"No siree. These aren't graceful, realistic ducks." I shift and the desk chair creaks under me like it's not sure it can hold my weight. Everything in this ancient room is three sizes too small for me, including the room. Bed squeaks if I breathe too heavily. "These are cartoon ducks like Daffy, Scrooge, and Donald."

Mack chuckles into the phone. "I do not miss the field."

I take in the glossy, open-mouth cartoon faces. "You're missing out. Walls and ceiling are filled with these shiny characters painted with every color in God's manic rainbow. Can't shake their goofy gazes. Honestly, I keep having nightmares."

Mack outright laughs. I smile into the phone. The only good thing about renting this room is that it's not that far from Club When?

His laugh settles down and Mack clears his throat in a very businesslike way. "Any new information on shots fired at Parish?"

"Some suspects, no motives," though I do wonder about her ex, John, "but I did find out Ms. Gracie Divine Parish has a son and a secret identity."

"Secret identity?"

"After looking into John True, I pulled his son Tyler's birth certificate. Mother's name is listed as Theresa Sylvia Hall." I tap the mousepad and bring up the notes on my computer as I talk. "Trying to find the woman caused me a bit of consternation, but I recognized the last name."

I open the photo of Tyler's birth certificate. "Hall is also the surname of Gracie's bio mom." The silence on the other end of my cell tells me Mack is paying careful attention—not the kind of attention where you look at your email while you talk to your college buddy. "A little research, and I discovered Gracie had been christened as Theresa Sylvia Hall before being adopted."

"How'd you find that?"

"Well, it's probably a sin to break into church records, but it surely isn't my first."

"Takes a sinner to catch a sinner. That's not a legal name, even if she was christened with it."

I grunt my agreement. "Money can't buy you love, but it can buy you a fake name on a birth certificate."

"Why lie?"

"You know, I'm not sure. But there's a bit of evidence—membership cards, cell phone, and gym membership—suggesting Gracie used that name for a while."

"So, she fights with her adopted mom, moves in with her biological mom, and uses her christened name to start fresh. Then she gets pregnant and because her family's into some dark shit, she puts a false name on the birth certificate."

"Spoken like a man who can put two and two together. I figured the same thing and that maybe she even planned on marrying the baby's father. Tax records show he lived at the club for two years before taking their son and leaving."

"Any idea why he left?"

"Nah." I've no idea how things fell apart with the guy, but I know it was bad enough that Gracie now sneaks around to catch a glimpse of her son. Which is a bit of a heartbreaker all around. "I do know that when we received that tip letter about the Parish family, Tyler was sick in the hospital."

Mack whistles low and long. I glance at the worn printout, smoothed out on the table next to my laptop. Practically know it by heart. *"When you're adopted into a family whose sole purpose is to train you to fight in their covert war, you lose all sense of yourself. You lose who you could've been and have to spend most of your life fighting who they told you you are."*

Gets me every time I read it. Reminds me of my own messed-up upbringing, sheltered from outside influences, taught to believe without question.

"I have to hand it to you, Dusty, you were right. Gracie Parish was the right call. She's the weak link."

I cringe at the word *weak* because, to my mind, she's the strong one. Strong enough to leave her family to take care of her dying mother—a woman who'd given her up for adoption. Strong enough to give up her own son which, judging by her trip to see him, had been a deep and difficult act of love. Strong enough to see past the culture of her family and reach out to the FBI.

"She's no pushover. Thought it'd be easier to get her to trust me. More like her brother, Tony." Closing my eyes, I rub my forehead. "He'd been pretty easy to befriend, but I can't get Gracie to open up."

Which sucks for a few reasons, like I'm worried about her and would like to help. It doesn't sit well with me that someone has it out for her.

"Are you telling me there's no action on the Gracie front?"

I know he means action as in actionable information or

action that moves me closer to Gracie trusting me, but that's not what comes to mind. I'm keeping that *action* to myself. Not my first sin and definitely won't be my last. "Nope. She's not budging on letting me get close to her. I need to find a way to spend more time with her."

Fuck. I stretch back, and the chair cracks like it's about to give way. The problem with being a tall, muscular guy in a world designed for average guys... even furniture doesn't fit. I stand up, give the chair a break. "Maybe I need to become a regular at Club When? Like Sam on *Cheers*."

"Sam was the owner of *Cheers*, but I'll let it go because I know you're too young to have watched that show."

"Yeah, well, out of the two of us, I'm the only one who actually worked at a bar."

"That's right. You tended bar in college."

"Memory like a steel trap, Mackster."

"Seems like you'd make a good addition to Gracie's club." He doesn't offer me anything other than that, but he doesn't need to. We've worked together for a long time and I get where he's going.

That's an idea. If I need to spend time at the club, why not get paid? "You're thinking about that sweepstakes promo we ran in Philly to get that guy in the Knowles case out of town?"

"I am. The one where we gave him a free trip so we could set you up as a temp in his job." Mack laughs and it sounds excited.

I've finally gotten his attention on helping with this case in a real way. About time.

"Better brush up on your margarita-making skills, Dusty."

"Will do." I hang up. I'd feel guilty about messing with Gracie's club except for one very important goal—a lifetime goal—sparing kids the kind of mind-fuck I'd had to go through to deprogram myself.

Now, if I can just cultivate Gracie into the helpful asset I know she can be.

Chapter 12
Dusty

As the flirty ladies in front of me move into Club When?, I hand my money over to the bouncer working the door. He's a short fellow with broad shoulders and a ready smile. I nod at the women. "Looks like ladies' night."

"You ain't kiddin'," he says, rolling shoulders big enough to qualify as boulders. "That's on top of a bridal party of fifteen that came in right after a bachelor party. Another bouncer said the two parties are inside competing to see who can better hold their liquor."

I take my change, hold it up. "I'll put a tenner on the ladies."

He laughs but accepts the bet. "You're on, but I'm not sure how well any of them will do. We had two bartenders quit today."

Now, ain't that a shame. "You backing out of the bet?"

He laughs again, then opens the red velvet rope to let me inside. "Not on your life. Don't skip out without paying me."

I grin. "Wouldn't think of leaving without collecting my winnings."

His laughter following me, I head inside. It's packed in here. Wall-to-wall with people drinking and dancing. There's a strobing Fourth of July light show that reflects off the ceiling and looks like fireworks. Pretty cool.

Got to appreciate what Gracie and her mom did with this club. I mean, the bones of Club When? are a throwback, with a real '50s' feel. Lots of shiny wood molding with gold stripes and strip lights. I imagine that's how she and her mom got it. It was a good deal, too, judging by the records.

But what to do with an outdated club that's already going to need a lot of work for the bathrooms and other floors? Well, why not use some cheap lights and decorations to update it and use that as a marketing tool? Creative, that's for sure.

Equally creative are the two stained-glass windows. One by the front door and the other to the left of the bar are vibrant and beautiful. I know those were installed after they bought the club, not by the records, but because they're of two women serving drinks, one with red hair and one with blond. Gracie and her biological mother.

It's a great bar. And popular. I like that even the music, photos, decorations, and the drink names posted over the bar—names like I Ain't Heard No Fat Lady Sing, a direct reference to the Independence Day movie—all underscore the theme.

Behind the bar, little Ms. Gracie Parish is overrun, making multiple drinks simultaneously, while she nods to acknowledge people and instruct servers.

One other guy is back there with her, a brunette with colorful tattoos on his neck. Doesn't look like a bartender. He's in a server's white shirt and black skirt, pulling beers and giving out shots, but I don't see him making any mixed drinks.

Despite Gracie's competence, it's obvious she can't keep up with this crowd. Never say I'm not a man to help a friend in distress.

I ease my way through the crowd around the bar, careful to tap shoulders and nod politely. I'm well aware of how my size can be misconstrued. Learned that lesson the hard way after one too many fights with people who, to me at the time, seemed irrationally upset.

When I make it to the bar, Gracie's head jerks up in surprise, then she smiles at me.

Hadn't expected that. Kind of warms my heart.

I lean over the bar, close enough for her to hear. "Stopped by to check on you and have that drink." I nod toward the packed bar. "Looks like you're slammed. Okay if I help? Worked as a bartender in college."

Gracie's face walks the line between *yes please* and *stay the hell away* then tips over to acceptance. "Thanks. I could use the help." She turns to the other guy behind the bar. "You can go back to your tables, Kyle."

The man's shoulders sag with relief, then his eyes flick to me and he smiles before heading out.

Gracie opens a couple beers and hands them to a guy across the bar, takes his money, then turns back to me. Her gaze runs up and down my body.

That kind of warms me, too. Warm enough to start a fire.

Face flushing pink, she pours a draft beer, hands it to a woman, then points to a fancy tablet on a stand. "Most payments are credit, but some people use cash. There are two parties that have a tab. They're easy. Write them down. We have the card, so we can enter the drinks when things get less hectic."

She begins making a mixed drink, efficient and calm and sexy as hell. "Drink prices are there." She points to a laminated document held together at a punch-holed corner with a silver hoop. She wings a slice of lemon around the drink she made, then hands it to a woman who hands Gracie a credit card. Running the card, she gives me a quick overview of it and the cash register.

Basically, I have to push three buttons and put in the amount. Old school. Think I actually had the same setup when I tended bar in college. Isn't she supposed to be good with computers?

That I don't say, though. "Got it, boss lady."

She smiles, walks away, then tosses back, "Thanks. Really."

Lady has a great ass. "Happy to help."

Music pulses under my feet as I take my first customer, a woman with lashes nearly as long as my arm. "Cash, credit, or other?"

"Other. Stevenson. We've got a tab running."

I find the name in the book Gracie showed me. Bachelorette party. "Got it. What'll you have?"

She smiles in gratitude, or maybe warning, and gives me an extensive drink order. I write as she talks, then put a tray on the bar because there's no way she can carry all that through this crowd without help.

The work goes quick. It's mostly craft beers, so not that hard to line up. Making the only mixed drink, I ask, "Who's winning? I got money on you guys."

She laughs the laugh of the cynical sober. "As the designated driver, I can tell you it's close. My friends switched to beer. They're at the point where they think that's strategic."

"It might help."

She shakes her head. "I think those guys ingested fourteen pounds of nachos, so they've got a cushion."

Sounds like I'm going to lose ten bucks.

Reaching for a half-eaten bag of pretzels from under the bar, I place them on the tray next to the beers. The woman, a dark-haired Filipina with a thousand-watt smile, lifts the tray. "You must really hate to lose."

I wink at her. "I just prefer an even playing field."

She maneuvers herself from the bar with the caution of a sober person in a sea of drunks. I don't envy her that job.

Quick to learn where everything is, I hit my stride. For the next few hours, Gracie and I learn to work with each other. Have to admit, it's kind of fun. Not just the work, but the way we buzz by each other, brushing hotly here and there as we reach for things or move to take a payment. Honestly, after a while, the charge I get from slipping past her or winking at her as we work, watching her blush, has got my engine revving.

Still, much to my disappointment, we can't stand in one place long enough to talk or explore that heat. The crowd keeps us hopping. A few people get handsy with me and with her, trying to get attention. Nothing we can't handle, but I know trouble when I see it.

A big guy maneuvers up to the bar, using his size to push through the crowd as if it were an insult. Impatient as hell, he puts two fingers in his mouth and whistles loud to get Gracie's attention since she's closer. She turns.

Diana Muñoz Stewart

The only thing keeping my hands from clenching is the drink I'm making. I'm hoping she ignores him so I can have a shot at the guy. He's big. I'm bigger.

I watch Gracie as I put ice in a glass and begin to pour gin. Aw, hell, I can tell by her eyes, by the way she's evaluating the guy and the situation, that she's not going to ignore him. A smile on her face, she goes right over and exchanges some words with him that I can't hear over the music and crowd. Tapping the bar, as if asking for his patience, she begins to turn.

I hand the woman across from me her last drink as the big guy at the bar latches onto Gracie's wrist. Keeping Gracie in my sights, I'm barely aware when the woman shoves some money in my hand and tells me to keep the change.

Gracie looks down at where the guy's holding her. She says something, then smiles like it's the only warning she'll give him, and I have no doubt that it *is* a warning.

The guy's face turns from impatient to mean. His knuckles whiten on her wrist.

It's not just me now. A few people at the bar are paying attention. Someone takes out a cell.

Gracie Parish on camera. Which means she isn't likely to pull any self-defense. She surely doesn't want that all over the internet.

As tempted as I am to move in and help, I know the lady doesn't A) need my help and B) won't appreciate me butting in. Plus, I kind of want to see what she's going to do.

Still smiling at the guy, she reaches under the bar, pulls out a nozzle for the seltzer, then blasts the guy directly up his nose.

Can't help the laugh that bursts from me.

Shock and the sting of the seltzer sends the guy reeling back as he releases her wrist. A few people lining the bar also spring away.

Gracie backs up, too, but keeps hold of the nozzle, aiming it like a weapon.

The smile on my face might be permanent.

I start to inch closer but stop when I see a bouncer move in for the kill.

He grabs the guy by the neck, forcing his head down before the guy knows what's up, then marches the soaked idiot out.

By the time the bouncer reaches the front door, Gracie is already handing bar towels to customers, apologizing for the mess and lining up free beers.

Now that that's over, a server and some others start to press in on me again, wanting my help, but I'm stuck watching Gracie.

Maybe feeling my gaze, she looks over.

I wait, expecting condemnation, like wh*y didn't you hot-foot it over here and give me a hand*, but, instead, she smiles widely at me then mouths, *That was fun.*

Lady is going to break my heart.

I get back to work. The next hour passes like a gentle wind without incident. The two big parties head off for greener pastures—me sans ten bucks. The work begins to slow. I find myself side-by-side with Gracie as we each make a drink.

I gaze down on her.

She looks up and stops dead with a bottle of rum in her hand.

What is *that* look? Am I imagining it or is there a slight change in her face, not just the red that makes her look so sweet, but a… softening?

Before I can make up my mind, she moves off.

An hour later, after last-call has come and gone, the club is officially closed. It's two a.m. and I am so keyed up I'm not even a little sleepy. Damn, that was fun.

"'Night," the last two servers call out before leaving.

"Let Phil walk you out to your cars," Gracie says. "'Night."

"'Night," I call, too. Kind of pleased I know Phil is the bouncer who took ten bucks from me. "Don't spend your tips all in one place."

In response, Kyle takes out a wad of bills from his pocket and waves them around. "It's all going into stocks," he says, laughing in a way that has me wondering if he's serious.

With them gone, things get nice and quiet. I continue wiping down the bar as Gracie replaces the empty shelves under the bar with clean glasses.

"'Cept for that one incident," I say, "I had a great time tonight."

She stops stacking glasses and graces me with a full smile. "Yeah, that kind of blustering happens from time to time. Oddly enough, it's usually around a full moon."

I laugh, but I know that to be true.

She finishes up and rests her back against the bar. "You did great tonight. I'm impressed with the way you can make drinks and conversation simultaneously. You have what my biological mother called the social virus."

I nearly bite my tongue on the sudden laugh that breaks from me. "That's funny. But just so we're clear, I'm clean as a whistle."

Her face heats, and she ducks her head and looks away.

Making her blush is becoming my favorite game. I finish wiping the bar, but, even with my back to her, I'm hyperaware of where she is.

All night, the atmosphere in the club has been buzzing in me, through me. I'd assumed it was a combination of her, the crowd, the music, and the action.

But, nope; it's all her.

Pretty obvious now as she brushes past me and begins to wipe the bar area right next to me. Heat radiates through the right side of my body as her leg presses mine. This is more than a softening. This is a probe of the electric current between us.

I'll take that bait. "Gracie, that spot's pretty clean now. Got another something that could use your attention, though."

She stops moving the bar rag around that same circle over and over and glances up at me.

A zing of current surges in my blood, hot and eager.

Her eyes widen. Her mouth parts.

I'm nearly thrown off balance when she drops the rag, fists my shirt, and uses it to pull herself onto her tiptoes.

"Don't talk," she says, putting her lips on mine.

Not talking works for me. I kiss her, long and slow and sweet, taking my time until I can feel that softening turn to a melting.

She moans into my mouth, plays her tongue against mine.

In no time, our breaths are labored and she's moaning against me, and I know where this is headed.

A sleepover.

I put my hands under her ass, press her body against my throbbing, thrumming cock.

She wiggles her pleasure, deepens the kiss.

I push her against the bar.

With a jerk, she pulls back, breathy and flushed. There's hunger in her eyes. Her gaze rolls over my lips. "Thanks for helping tonight. I can handle the close."

It takes me a moment to work out what she's saying. Stepping back, I take my grip from her ass, let her slide to the floor. I run a hand through my hair. "You know, you keep doing that."

"Doing what?"

"Kissing me into madness, then sending me away."

"That's because you are..." she waves at me as a way to finish that statement, "and I can't stop myself"—her eyes lower—"until I remember you're spying on my family."

She keeps saying that. Sure, it's true, but most people wouldn't keep bringing it up. As secretive as she is, she's honest in weird ways.

"You don't know that."

"I know you can't admit it."

She's one awkward honesty bomb after another. And damn astute.

I exhale a well of sexual frustration. Okay. That's that. For tonight anyway. "I'll be by for that drink sometime soon."

I move to pass her, and she grabs my hand. My expectations perk back up—*expectations* being a euphemism for *my dick*.

She squeezes my hand. Her face warms. "You're a really good kisser."

She's giving me a pity compliment. Naw. Lord, help me, but I'm not the only one who's not going to be able to sleep tonight.

I lower my head, lean toward her, close enough to whisper hot sighs in her ear. "It's not just the kissing I'm good at."

Her breath catches. Red creeps up her face.

My heart bucks like a bull released from a chute. As far as bulls go, I come equipped with only one horn, but it's hard and determined and rarin' to charge at her. "Good night, Gracie," I say, all casual-like. I feel anything but.

I'm starting to think tryin' to get close to Gracie Parish might've been a big mistake.

Chapter 13
Gracie

The morning after almost inviting Dusty upstairs to my apartment—thank God my good sense finally kicked in—I'm showered and dressed and in my pristine, upper-level office, going over all the data I've compiled on my would-be murderers.

Excluding John and his wife, who Victor is looking into, my list has been a dead end. I'm emotionally and physically exhausted and waiting for Victor to call with his update at eleven before I head down to get ready for the lunch crowd.

Yawning, I rub my eyes. I slept very little last night and not just because I worked the late shift. Being shot at and keeping it from my family has turned me into a sleepless wreck, so every noise in my apartment seemed like a threat. And because I'd been awake, my mind had turned to Dusty.

It's not just the kissing I'm good at.

Ugh. The man is wheedling past my defenses. *Thanks, hormones.* I can't let this get messy and out of control. I can't let it get reckless. I can't afford to go back to being the wild teen who got a tattoo, snuck out with Justice, fell in love with the first boy she kissed, and had a child as if none of that would end up causing me such intense pain.

Thinking of Tyler causes my chest to ache. I rub it, and, taking a deep breath, glance around my office—the comfortable and orderly white walls, the white desk, round white grandfather clock, and white leather chairs. This is manageable. A place for everything and everything in its place. This isn't the office of someone who's screwed up so badly that someone is trying to kill her, her ex is threatening her, her son doesn't know her, she's estranged from her family, and the FBI started an investigation thanks to an email she sent. Nope, this is the office of a woman who has it together.

I straighten my black silk button-down and run hands down my black slacks. I'm in control. Everything's been done that needs to be done. I've set up new security protocols at the club, added panic buttons behind the bar, and planned a refresher course in threat response for my employees. It's a bar, so they'll take the changes seriously but won't find them suspicious.

Picking my cell up from my desk, I check the time—even though it's plain as day on my computer. Sheesh, I'm that tired, and it's only 11:05 a.m.

What the heck? Victor said he'd call at eleven. Maybe I should call...

My cell rings in my hands and my heart rate flips into high speed. I fumble the phone then finally hit the speakerphone. I know I should say hi or be polite, but I say, "What do you have on John and Ellen?"

There must be something in my tone that cuts through Victor's usual flirtatious attitude. He says, "There's two sides to them, Roja. On one side, the Trues seem like a stable couple. They're well respected, with good jobs, and an adorable Instagram-worthy family."

"But..." I prod because I can hear the *but* coming.

"But when I dug deep into their finances, I discovered an unusual transfer of a sizeable sum—ten thousand dollars—that went into an offshore account."

Everything stops for me. It's exactly like people describe when they say someone goes blank. For a moment, I'm frozen—heart, face, muscles, breath. My visions dims and a voice inside reminds me gently to breathe. I inhale sharply. "When?"

"The transfer was made a week before you were shot at. Do you think you can use your cyber skills to dig up more?"

Probably. "Yeah. Send me what you have and I'll look into it."

"Will do."

"Thanks, Victor. I really appreciate your help. I don't know what I'd do without you right now."

He clears his throat. "How'd you do with your half of the list?"

"One dead. One in jail. One happily married and on a reality TV show. So far, you've come up with our best lead." *It can't be either John or Ellen. It can't.* "I need to go back and see who I'm missing."

"About that." There's a weighted silence, and I remember Victor's cryptic remark earlier in the week about having more people to add to my list. Before I can ask, he says, "What do you know of your biological father?"

"My father? Not a thing." The import of his question hits me in the stomach. I press my hand to my suddenly fluttering belly. "What do *you* know about him?"

A hissing breath, as if made through gritted teeth, slithers across the line. "Well, that's an interesting story. Back when Sandesh had been trying to discover who in your family had given away information that put Justice in danger, he'd asked me to look into Justice's closest siblings. You were one of the people he asked me to look into."

"I don't doubt Sandesh had a bad opinion of me back then. Although I was trying to protect Justice, I can see how I might've come off as... threatening."

"He said you almost pulled a gun on him."

True, but I'm not interested in reliving the past. Especially when the traitor was Tony. He'd been trying to protect Justice, too, but in doing so, had nearly gotten her killed. In the end, he'd paid for his mistake with his life, and I miss him every day. "So, Sandesh asked you to look into me and you found out about my biological dad?"

"Yeah."

A twinge of expectation rises unexpectedly in my chest. Growing up in a dynamic household full of adopted kids, many of whom didn't know or didn't want to remember their families, it seemed almost wrong to ask where I'd come from, so I didn't.

And when my bio mom had come back into the picture, it seemed twice as bad to ask because she'd been so sick, and I'd known if that information wasn't painful, she would've shared it. Of course I've wondered over the years, but I'd had two moms who loved me, Momma's right-hand man and closest confidant Leland, who was like a father to me, and a huge family, so if my bio father didn't want any part of me... Well, then I didn't want any part of him.

In my mind, I'd had way too many family members to go looking for more, but now that I'm a question away from the truth... "Tell me about him."

Another one of those reptilian breaths. "Let's do this in stages. First go to CNN.com. They have a live feed. Click on it."

My fingers fly over the keys and click on the live feed. It pops on the screen. The banner below the video reads, *From the Hyatt Bellevue in Philadelphia, Senator Andrew Lincoln Rush to announce his bid for president.*

A man with a lean physique, wearing a blue Armani suit, walks onto a stage as "Happy" by Pharrell Williams plays. The stage is already occupied by a group of people and Rush stops to kiss a few of the women and ruffle the hair of some kids.

I lean closer to my monitor as my stomach squeezes. There's a bit of gray, but Andrew Rush has red hair and green eyes. The same color hair as me, the same color eyes as my eyes. *Fudge.* "Is that my dad, Andrew Rush?"

"Yes."

I run a tongue over suddenly dry lips, transfixed by the scene on the stage—the clapping, cheering, clicking of cameras, and talking. Of course I've heard of him. I know Rush loves the spotlight. Well, duh. Introverts don't usually run for president.

When he finally steps up to the podium, the room goes

respectfully quiet. He commands their attention with a smile as he adjusts the microphone for his height. Unlike me, he's tall. Actually, a lot of the people in the background are tall like him.

"Are those his kids behind him?"

"Yeah. He's married to the tall blonde in the yellow dress, nipped and tucked to look at least fifteen years younger. Her name's Carrie. They have five boys, one girl, and ten grandkids."

"So many."

Victor snorts. "You can't be serious."

"They're so clean-cut. Photogenic. Dressed to perfection with amazing smiles."

"Yeah, it's like a Fashion Week photo shoot back there."

"How old are..." *My siblings?* My stomach flips at the thought. "... his kids?"

"The boys range from your age, thirty-two, to the oldest, forty-two. They all have some presidential name, either middle or first name."

"And the girl?"

"Layla Reagan Rush is twenty-seven and the youngest. Apparently, Mama Rush kept trying until she had that girl. *Parenting* magazine did a cover story on them, years ago. The article was over-the-top on hype, acting as if the mom was Sarah from the Bible and Layla was sent from heaven."

"She's beautiful. Who's the glasses guy with his arm across her shoulders?"

"Her fiancée."

Layla is beautiful and stylish, dressed in an iridescent green silk baroque-style dress. The kind of tailored dress that takes confidence, poise, and money to wear well.

I can't help but run my hand over the monitor, brushing the unfamiliar people. Would we have been friends? Would the boys have teased me, like Tony had?

Unexpected emotion tightens my throat, moistens my eyes. Shaking the gloom from my mind but not from my heart, I focus on what Rush is saying.

"There are few men in the world who are lucky enough to call their son not only a friend but a business partner. My son, Porter, has been by my side, running the show, since he was ten."

There's laughter from the family, as obviously this means something to them, an inside joke.

The camera zooms in on the tall man in the back, Porter, who looks exactly like his father. Honestly, except for Rush's gray hair, they could be twins.

Unlike his father, Porter doesn't appear to like the spotlight. Sweat runs down his face, and he wipes at it with a white cloth handkerchief. His father encourages the crowd to clap, but Porter waves off the applause. The camera is close enough that I can see his eye begin to tick.

Rush quickly moves on to each member of his family, giving a list of accomplishments that would put any one of them into the White House. Then he reaches Layla. The beautiful youngest child of Senator Rush seems to love the spotlight her brother fears.

She's all smiles as her father goes on about her accomplishments as some kind of cyber wizard and artificial intelligence creator. How odd that she and I have a shared passion. We don't look alike, though. She looks like her mother, tall and blonde. Rush veers from his praise of Layla to the fact that she was a blessing to him and Carrie after so many boys. Carrie smiles lovingly, and much to my surprise, Porter leaves the stage.

Maybe it was because he doesn't feel well. He sure looked sick a moment ago with the camera on him.

Rush continues with his speech, announcing his presidential run, as though nothing happened. Something happened, and I latch onto it like a detective would a clue at a crime scene.

How tightknit is the family? Could they be one bad news day from falling apart?

"Looks like some family strife," I say.

"You know, I was wondering about that," Victor answers.

"Porter was named as head of Rush's exploratory committee. Someone who would have to do opposition research on his own father or at least know about it."

Blood rushes into my ears as the possibility hits me. Could Porter know about me? Could my existence have come up under the kind of intense scrutiny that's done on a candidate before they announce a run for the presidency? Could that be why he left the stage when his father spoke about Rush's *only* daughter?

"Do you think an illegitimate kid, an illicit affair over thirty years old could..." I stop, doing the math in my mind. "How old is Andrew Rush?" It's hard to tell, because he looks very young.

"He's sixty-eight."

Sour saliva floods into mouth. "If my mom were still alive, she'd be fifty-one. That's seventeen years younger than Rush. She was barely nineteen when she had me. Rush would've been thirty-five."

"Claro. She was a lot younger than him, but still of age, and an affair isn't the reputation killer it used to be. You add in over three decades and the fact that you landed in a good place... it's weak motivation."

True. I was adopted into a wealthy and respected family, and a lot of people would even think I landed in a better place. "Maybe he doesn't want ties to the Parish family and our outspoken feminism."

"Could be. Your lot does have a reputation, but he's dipped a toe into the feminist waters a bit over the years, and it hasn't really stopped his career. I don't think fear over political fallout would be enough of a reason for him to hire a hitman. Not that I'm saying it wasn't him. I'm bringing it up because I think it *could* be him, but I'm not sure we've hit on a good enough motivation. Yet."

"Maybe he's worried about his wife, his family. Maybe they'd turn against him if they found out he had an illegitimate daughter."

Victor makes a noise of agreement. "That's a fair point.

That's a big family with lots of personalities, and there might be one—maybe even our runaway Porter—who'd be put off by his father's affair."

"All of this is speculation. We don't have a firm motivation or a grasp on the family dynamics."

"Let's split the list again, Roja. I'll investigate the lower half of the Rush family, the younger boys and Layla."

"I'll take the upper half, including the wife. Thanks, Victor."

He makes kissing noises into the phone and I hang up on him. I've learned in our brief friendship that you do not want to encourage Victor. He's not a flirt with no end goal in sight—another thing I found out that drunken night. I was drunk, but not drunk enough to sleep with my sister's husband's best friend.

I sigh as I watch the cheering crowd and Rush turning to the family that gathers around him.

There's still a lot of *ifs* and *buts*, but enough possibilities to send my gut churning and my paranoia soaring. The list of people who might want me dead has just grown by eight, and that means I'll have to enter all of their faces into my club's facial recognition software. The feature is on the club doors because of the servers upstairs that house a lot of my family's secrets.

Typically, I don't have any reason to care about the software, but I do now.

A crazy web is being woven around me. First, the money transferred from John's account, and, now, it turns out I could become Lincoln Rush's dirty little secret.

Chapter 14
Gracie

I feel every breezy inch of the blue-print summer dress skimming mid-thigh as I weave through the tables filled with a modest lunch crowd. Something flutters in my stomach as Dusty, with a fry halfway to his mouth, smiles wide at my approach.

This is a problem. Even in cargo shorts and a hunter-green T-shirt, the man is hot enough to disable my intellect.

Shoving aside this unacceptable thought, I sit next to him at the table. Close enough—because it's the best view of the bar—to know that he smells so darn good.

The corner of his mouth tips up, but he says nothing. Swallowing another bite of his burger, he sips the drink I put in front of him.

He coughs, pulls the drink out, and reevaluates the swirly blue-and-red mixture before taking another swig. He puts the drink down. "Blood and Guts. That's a game changer. And the burger... unexpected with the plantain on it, but it tastes great."

My heart lifts with his approval, as light and breezy as a butterfly's wings. I'm horrified. I say, "I'm glad you like the drink and the burger."

He wipes his mouth on his napkin, crumples it up, then tosses it onto his nearly empty plate. "Thought it'd be less busy during the day, less of an eatery."

"I accidentally hired a great chef, so when people started coming in for lunch, I expanded the kitchen and hired her some help. Together, they've made this place as popular during the day as it is at night."

He leans back in his chair with a satisfied groan, then—maybe noticing me scanning the club—says, "Guess that feels like a problem when you're under threat." He nods toward the front entranceway. "Noticed you got a guy working security during the day. What else is new?"

A lot, and with good reason, because a senator with a huge family might want to kill me. Not to mention John and Ellen and their offshore account taking a money transfer right before I was shot at. Not that I'll say a word of any of it. "Security is a little personal, don't you think?"

He laughs, easy and genuinely amused, and heat pushes through my body so fast and hard I'm surprised my shoes don't blow off.

"You crack me up, Gracie."

A man who appreciates my humor? That's a rarity, as I tend to have a humor based in saying inappropriate things. "I wish you weren't hot enough to melt my panties."

And there I go, making awkward into supremely awkward, which is, in fact, my superpower.

Dusty lets out a stream of laughter. "If security is personal, what's calling me panty-melting, Gracie? *Im*personal?"

His eyes gleam with amusement and more than a little lust—and that heat calls to me so intensely, my brain feels giddy and drunk on hormones. I try to command words despite the fact that every bit of this man attracts me.

I smile, lean in. "Couldn't you have some gross ear hair or a less perfect rear end or a less masculine nose or a horrible Philly accent instead of that killer Southern one?"

His smile widens. "Ah, the accent. It always gets them."

"Yeah." I say, running my eyes up and down his muscular chest and huge biceps. "The accent is what gets them."

He laughs again, quick and bright.

I really like the sound of his laughing. It's so appealing.

He pushes his plate away, leans toward me, and licks his lips. "Smart move with the security system, Gracie." His smooth

Southern accent is as alluring as hot cocoa when you come in from the cold. "And adding those cameras out back. Mmmm. Got any other prep work you can share with me?"

I know exactly what I'd like to share with him.

Fighting to keep my face impassive, I say, "Before you leave, I'm going to insist you come to my office and let me pay you for the work you did last night."

After a beat in which I'm sure he realizes I'm shutting down this flirtation, he nods and stands.

"Man should never turn down an honest day's pay for an honest day's work. Lead the way, boss."

A bit surprised by how quickly he agreed to my dismissal of him—and a little disappointed—I stand and turn for the back hall. He doesn't say a word as he follows, but I swear I can feel him watching my butt. I'm so consumed and delighted by the idea that I nearly crash into a someone coming out of the men's bathroom.

I jump back and reach for a weapon that isn't there. I reprimand myself for the lack of a gun then realize the man's a customer. My heart slowly returns to normal, but not my fear. I'm going to need to stop with the casual dresses and wear a concealed carry.

"Excuse me," I say.

The man, a fair-skinned guy with grease-darkened long hair and an unruly beard, eyes me with an intensity that sets my heart racing again. His hands flex in his pockets. His eyes stay glued on me, as if he he's contemplating his reaction.

Every intuitive nerve in my body tenses and readies to respond with a brutal combination of self-defense.

Behind me, Dusty clears his throat.

The man's gaze lifts from me to Dusty and his eyelids visibly widen. The man shifts back uncomfortably. "Sorry," he mumbles, walking away with his head down.

I watch him go.

He walks as if in pain or injured, and I can't shake the idea that, though he was surprised to see me, he knew who I was and had something against me.

Gah, I'm being paranoid.

Also watching the man, Dusty asks, "You know him?"

Okay, so maybe I'm not being paranoid. "No."

"Huh. You got any cameras in this hallway?"

I do, but I'm not about to tell him that. They're well-hidden for a reason, but his point is well-taken. I'll get the footage later and run an image search.

Turning, I swing through the *Staff Only* door, bypass the kitchen, then head to my downstairs office, the one where I conduct club business. My upstairs office is for cyber and Guild work.

Dusty is quiet enough that I glance over my shoulder to make sure he's following and catch his eyes on my backside. A warm thrill rolls through me, but I still reprimand him with a shake of my head.

He only grins wide at me, completely unapologetic, as I open the door to my office. I hold the door open for him, and he passes by me. I can't help myself—really, I can't. I take a good, long inhale. Maybe too long.

He raises his eyebrows. "How do I smell?"

Shutting the door, I duck my head to hide the red climbing into my face. I mumble, "Not awful or anything."

I try to go past him, but he steps in front of me.

"Hot in here?"

Stupid fair skin makes it kind of hard to hide my reactions, but I try. "It's an office near a kitchen, what did you expect?"

He leans toward me. "That's not the heat I was referring to."

I do not like being called out like this. It feels like a disadvantage.

I snap my shoulders back, lift my head, and meet his gaze. "Yes. Fine. I'm desperately attracted to you. You're hot—scorching—and I can feel you when I'm alone at night, naked, in my bed. And that makes me afraid because I'm pretty sure you're using me. Just like you used Tony."

He backs up. "Honest as a tsunami, Gracie."

"Not going to deny it?"

"Nothing to deny."

I can't believe he's admitting the truth to me. That he's investigating my family.

His intense, honey-gold eyes stay focused on me as he bends down, slow enough to let me know his intention. "Truth is," he whispers, "I'm just as attracted to you."

Heaven help me. It's not only the physical part of him that attracts me right now. It's the playful part of him, all that easygoing joy and teasing banter, the thought of that so close and attainable has me closing my eyes and lifting my lips.

When his soft lips brush mine, I whimper and rise onto my tiptoes, deepening the kiss and pushing myself against him.

That movement unleashes something in him. His hands snatch out and pull me against his hard-on, fisting a handful of my sundress in the process, dragging it up high enough I can feel the cold air on my butt cheeks. His tongue eases past the seam of my lips, deepening the kiss as electric tingles dance inside my mouth and spread down my entire humming body.

Such a good kisser. His sure, skilled lips drive away inhibition, drive it away and park it on the moon.

His hand slides down, cups my butt. He moans, "A thong, Gracie. God love you."

I need him closer, under me. Why isn't there a couch in here?

Desk. Right behind him.

I push against his chest, but for a heartbreaking moment, he misunderstands, thinking I'm pushing him away, and he pulls back, drops his hand from my butt, tries to take his lips away.

No!

I grasp his shirt with one hand, keep his lips to mine, and probe his mouth with my tongue.

He moans, deepens the kiss again.

Yes. That. So good.

This time when I push against him, he gets the message and

lets me steer him backward until he hits the desk and sits down, never lessening the expert sweep of his tongue against mine.

I brace my hands on his shoulders, lift myself, then straddle him. His hands slide around to grip my butt, capturing me against his hard body. *Fast learner.*

I'm frantic to touch as much of him as I can. I skate my hands under his shirt, run my hot fingers along the silk-skinned muscles of his back. So many muscles. So hard. Speaking of hard...

Lifting onto my knees, I reach between us, unbutton the top of his shorts, and stroke the tip of him.

He groans. "That feels good, Gracie. Keep going. There's more."

He's big and a talker. I'm a fan of both.

I try to delve deeper into his shorts, going for the rest of him, but it's impossible with his shorts on. Frustrated, I make a whimpering sound.

He smiles against my lips, lifts me up, holding me up with one big hand, and pulling his shorts and briefs down with the other.

Our lips never lose contact.

He sits back on the desk, and I slide against his arching body like I've missed him for a hundred years. A thousand. More. I'm so wet, the soft, saturated silk of my thong between us provides barely any interference as I rub myself along the length of him.

His lips take mine with fevered need. Our breathing picks up, creating a kind of music with sultry exhales and moans.

He whispers, "That feels amazing. Slick. Hot."

The slickness increases and I move faster, a frantic, pulsing action.

He sucks in a breath, tries to pull back. "That's a little too good, Gracie."

I'm so close, the coil of energy building, teasing with the pressure. Kissing him with all the fiery intensity I feel, I beg him not to stop with desperate moans rising in the back of my throat.

"Okay. Okay. I've got you," he says, helping me along by using his big hand to bounce me up and down in a way that increases the delicious heat and friction.

Oh. That feels so good.

The tension, like the rhythm of our bodies, builds to absolute madness, and as he whispers about how hard he is and how good I feel against him and all the ways he intends to have me, I gasp. His dirty promises and my absolute need for him, breaks me open and I throw my head back and come right there in my office, my core slick against him, the electric current throbbing through me, releasing waves of pleasure.

Chapter 15
Dusty

Sitting on Gracie's desk, her body hot and sweet and wet riding me, I barely hold on for another breath after she comes before my own orgasm hits me, so excruciatingly good I'm arching against her sleek, gliding wetness as I bounce her body along my aching cock.

It's not until the last shaking bit pumps out of me that I realize where I am and what we just did.

Damn. Haven't come from humping since I was in high school. That's what a woman hot enough to burn flesh and a six-month dry spell gets you.

Embarrassing.

And yet, a good time was had by all. Then and now.

Breathing heavily, but always a gentleman, I whisper my appreciation, telling her how sexy she is, how good she made me feel, and how I'd still very much want to see her naked and fuck her brains out.

For a moment, her head tucked into my shoulder, her breath hot against my neck, she almost purrs with her own appreciation, and I'm seriously considering another round, when she puts a hand against my chest and pulls away.

"Uh. Thank you, Dusty."

"And thank you for allowing my hands to make the acquaintance of your sweet ass." I squeeze said ass. *Incredible.* Do not want to let go.

She blushes and avoids eye contact. "So, I'll get you your money now."

Can't help the snort of laughter. She's joking, right?

"I mean, not for the…" She goes take-me-against-the-desk red, or, at least, that's where my mind goes, and blurts, "For bartending the other night."

Reluctantly, I release the globe of her ass and lower her feet to the floor. Woman knows just the temperature of water to throw on me. Cold.

Removing some tissues from an overturned box on her desk, I take a minute to clean up, pull up my briefs, cargo shorts, then zip myself into respectable.

Straightening her own dress, she watches me do all this. Her face is a soft, satisfied pink and her eyes a vibrant shade of green. The kind of green a meadow gets after a hard and unexpected storm.

"Lord, Gracie, that was fun."

Her eyes go wide and she moves around her desk. Huh. Looks like she doesn't want to talk about it. She skipped over it like you would roadkill.

Turning to face her, I put knuckles against her desk, because my legs are like rubber. Can barely stand. *Damn, that was so much fun.*

She opens a locked drawer in her desk. Is she…?

"Gracie, I'm not a proud man, but if you pull out money right now, I will lose my shit."

She closes the drawer, picks out a candy from a dish on her desk packed with watermelon-flavored Jolly Ranchers. Her hands tremble as she unwraps it and pops it into her mouth. "What do you want?"

Want? Besides another shot at her, one where she doesn't climb me like a monkey and dismantle every bit of self-control I have?

Trying for casual over some unexpectedly bruised feelings, I shrug. "You need a bartender. I need a job."

Her mouth works the candy silently for a moment before she manages, "You want to work at my club?"

"No. I want to work with your family." *Get access to your momma.*

Her fine red eyebrows crash together, weighted, no doubt, by heavy suspicion.

"Hear me out," I continue, scrambling to make this work. "I left my job to go undercover with that scumbag Walid to help with your family's vigilante activities—"

"That was Tony's ball of wax."

"For someone so honest, you sure do lie a lot."

She makes a surprised sound, as if I'd goosed her.

Huh. Looks like Gracie Parish considers herself an honest person. Have to admit, she's brutally honest in some ways, but she also hides a lot. It's the hidden stuff I'm most interested in. Aw, hell, that's not entirely true. Not anymore. "Look, I cleaned up a bunch of your family's mess in Mexico. It raised questions at the Bureau and got me disciplined, soon to be fired."

I let that sink in, wait for a reaction, but she gives me nothing.

Exhaling, I say, "And since I know your family does the kind of work I believe in—the kind that changes lives—and since I know they can afford my fees, I'm trying to find a way into your organization. But since you're not the trusting type, I figured we could start small."

She fiddles with the strap on her dress, and for a moment it seems there's something truly lonely, maybe even a little lost about her. She looks back up. "Don't mistake my lack of self-control for a lack of intelligence. You're investigating my family and looking for something that doesn't exist."

Her eyes dart down and away. Her face heats to a powerful red, a lying-through-her-teeth red.

I really did strike bone with that dishonesty comment.

Well, that makes two of us. The most honest thing about this conversation is the smell of cum and sweat in the air. How fucked up is that? I'd feel ashamed, but I know Mukta Parish is still adopting kids, still warping fragile minds. "Gracie, why would I tell you I'm ex-FBI if I'm undercover investigating you and your family?"

"I wondered."

"Got an answer?" I'm sure she has a reasonable guess. Her cyber skills and family connections are good enough to penetrate any cover I could've come up with, which is why I'm not lying. As far as most people, besides Mack, know, I'm on hiatus.

Considering my question and maybe her answer, she bites her lip. And it's so sexy, I have a hard time shutting down the instant replay of the last ten minutes. Her face as she came, the feel of her body riding me, those moans. Damn.

As if her thoughts are running in the same direction, she leans back on her heels and runs her eyes up and down me like I'm seven layers of chocolate cake and she's on a diet.

She says, "Fine. With everything going on, it's better to have you where I can see you. We can call it probation. See how you do."

Can't help the big ol' satisfied grin. "Probation sounds like one step away from where I'd like to be. I'm happy to take you up on that offer... and any other offer you might want to make me." I wink at her because subtle never got the job done. "*Boss.*"

Her face heats again, but this time with genuine interest. I can't help myself. I'm so tickled with her that I let out a full laugh.

I'm surprised when it prods a smile out of her. A beautiful smile. A we-both-know-the-truth smile and I'm-still-one-step-ahead-of-you.

Is she?

Chapter 16
Gracie

I usually like spending Sundays in my office, putting together databases for my find-a-creeper software, but this night off has turned into my find-a-killer night.

My research tonight has focused on John and Ellen. I managed to hack into the offshore account that one or both of them funneled money into. It's registered to an LLC, but the company is a shell, and, so far, impossible to trace. The LLC used the money to purchase Bitcoin and that Bitcoin disappeared into the dark web.

So, that sucks. It doesn't necessarily mean John and Ellen, together or separately, hired a hit man, but if I needed a hitman and were an average person without siblings who were assassins, I might go to the dark web.

Maybe I should close the club.

No.

Closing the club will bring Momma and Leland here faster than I can say Benedict Arnold, and they won't mess around. They'll discover the looming threat on my life, including what I have on John and Ellen, which would mean trouble for Tyler. I can't allow that. Besides, any investigation they do will definitely lead them to Dusty and my letter.

I shudder with the thought of what Momma would do if she knew about my letter. It would fall hard on me, but it would also spell trouble for Dusty, and as much as I don't trust him, I do trust his motives. That letter I sent made it seem like Momma was a criminal... and deranged. It was an unfair letter. If I could take it back, I would.

The ungodly loud *Legend of Zelda* theme blasts through my quiet office and I jump a mile. Rubbing my eyes, I pick up and glance at my cell. Cee? "Yeah."

Her voice on the other end is a whisper with a soft Spanish accent. "Can you come get me? I'm in North Philly."

"Philly!" Okay, stay calm. This is not how I get my new teen sister to open up. I'm shocked she is even calling me. We got off to a rocky start when I recommended Momma *not* adopt her. It wasn't that I'd had anything against Cee, but the kill she'd been responsible for during her rescue and all that anger seemed like the exact wrong thing to add to I Guild. "Are you okay?"

"Can you come get me or not?"

"Of course, but first tell me what's going on, so I don't have a panic attack the whole way over."

A long pause. "I had a fight with Momma and decide to leave home."

"You ran away? From campus?" *Impossible.* Sure, Justice and I did it fifteen years ago, but security has grown more sophisticated since then, and, after the drone attack, Cee now lives in one of the tightest security zones in the country. "How?"

Cee sighs.

Oh, sure, this is annoying for *her*.

"I carefully took out The Guild tracking chip and left it in my room, then I hid in the trunk of a car leaving school."

Ouch. She'd removed the GPS chip from her own wrist? That's creepy and also brilliant. Cee has learned from The Guild in months what it took others years to learn.

I shouldn't be surprised. Momma had her IQ tested and discovered this kid, rescued from a brothel, might be one of the smartest humans on the planet. Still, maybe *because* of that, she's also one of the most traumatized.

"Okay. Text me the address. Are you in a safe spot?"

A suffering sigh whistles through the phone. "I'm not a child or an idiot."

Temper. Temper. "Well, you got one of those right."

Chapter 17
Dusty

Crammed into the desk by the foot of my bed, I stare at my computer and the message Mack sent me a few minutes ago.

Makes no sense. According to Mack, a DC agent has been looking into the information I've compiled on the Parish family, specifically Gracie Parish.

Why would this guy want to know about her? She's a side player in all of this, not a principal. Up until Mexico, she'd seemed the Parish kid most distant from her family. Guess the best way to find out is to look into the agent.

I set to work, and it takes only a short time to get the basics. A picture starts to form, but I keep digging, and an hour later I've got some leads.

The agent is from a wealthy family, has tons of political ties, and judging by this old team photo, is a former lacrosse player. Three of his teammates are from political families that might have it out for Mukta Parish, but Gracie?

I expand the photo to get a better look at each of the kids and stop on Porter Rush. Sure, a lot of people have red hair and green eyes, but I can't deny the resemblance. Rush could be Gracie's brother. They look that much alike.

Wait a sec. When I looked into Gracie's biological mother, Sheila, wasn't there something about her involvement in politics? I pull up her file. Yep. Born in Australia, she'd come here interested in the American political system.

It's a coincidence, has to be. Yet...

I get back to work and, two hours later, have a firm connection between the Rush family and Gracie Parish. Specifically, her biological mother, Sheila Marie Hall and Rush. I found a photo of a young Sheila at Senator Rush's campaign headquarters, thirty-some years ago, when he'd first run for and won his seat.

Hell, does Rush's son Porter know his dad has an illegitimate daughter? Maybe. Porter is running his father's bid for the presidency; he's probably involved with vetting his own father.

So, Porter discovers this and then asks his old friend and teammate, the DC agent, to uncover what he can about Gracie.

Why? To hire a sniper to kill Gracie? Seems a stretch. The way these political boys get around an illegitimate kid doesn't seem so bad. But add in the fact that Gracie's mother had been young, Rush's conservative background, and the weird mythology that has sprung up around Rush's daughter Layla—like the good Lord himself had blessed the family with a girl after five boys—then maybe there's something there.

The agent had also asked around about Mukta. Now, that's intriguing. Mukta and Rush run in some similar circles, and *she'd* adopted *his* illegitimate kid. Chances that Mukta knows Gracie is Rush's kid? I'd bet the farm on yes, she knows. Makes for some awkward party talk, surely.

Come to think of it, Gracie's adoption is an anomaly for Mukta. Gracie was adopted as an infant, but Mukta Parish only adopts older kids, damaged kids, kids with some sad backstory.

Might be the sick way my mind works, but it seems Mukta could benefit a lot by holding the illegitimate-child information over Rush's head. Politically, a lot. Business-wise, a lot. And she's just the type of ruthless person to use her own kid to blackmail Rush. What might a man do to get that kind of monkey off his back?

A lot. Gracie's in serious danger.

Beep, beep.

Shiiit. That's the alarm I set to go off whenever Gracie leaves her the club. I check my phone. Sure enough, there she goes.

Is it too much to hope you'd sit still for one night, woman? What are you up to? I roll out of the chair, grab my bat-belt and my keys and remember I forgot to fill my gas tank.

Hope she's not going far. This woman is running me ragged.

Chapter 18
Gracie

I steer my Ford Focus down a well-lit street lined with duplexes and parked cars. No parking spots around or in front of the address, so I slow in the hopes Cee will respond to my *I'm here* text and run out.

She doesn't.

Fishing my cell from the cupholder, I try calling. No answer, but a text pops up from her: *I'm still inside.*

No kidding. I'm tempted to double-park, run up, and drag her out, but my training won't allow me to leave my car to be marked by anyone who comes along.

Instead, I circle the block, pull into the first vacant spot, and jog back to the house. A hoodie covers my hair and light-distorting sunglasses hide my face from any cameras. Because, though my hope is she's simply at a friend's house, I honestly don't know what she's up to.

I skirt the small metal gate, go up the steps, and reach the ajar front door.

Ajar?

Adrenaline spikes like the whine of a teakettle. My hearing sharpens, and my awareness seems to cross the threshold into the home itself.

Head discreetly down, I slip on gloves and a facemask. Stowing my light-reflecting glasses in my jacket, I remove my gun and step inside.

The room smells like skunk weed and ramen noodles. Three

people, two men and one woman, are in the home, blindfolded and tied up on kitchen chairs that've been dragged into the living room. All three are unresponsive with their heads drooping forward.

What is going on? The entire floor is a mess, strewn with thumb drives, laptops, and piles of DVDs. I gingerly step past them to check the pulses on the people. They're all steady. Looks like they've been drugged, and my guess is the ramen.

Where is Cee? Is she here? Or could this be a setup of some sort?

A startling crash from the basement has me accidentally biting my own tongue. Swallowing the metallic taste of blood, I pray Cee is okay and search for the basement door. I find it the kitchen. Soundlessly, I glide through and down.

The worn boards creak under my feet no matter how carefully I step. From below, wafts the stench of layered body fluids. Piss. Sweat. Vomit. Blood. Sex.

My heart raises the all-hands-on-deck-all-units-report-for-duty-SOS-and mayday-alarm all in one. Sweat runs down my neck and back as I reach to part a heavy felt curtain that hangs across the bottom of the stairs.

Quickly, quietly, I enter the room, scanning with my gun the large wood-framed basement. There's a makeshift studio with cameras, computer, and a red lightbulb hanging from the rafters over a king-sized bed.

By the back door, a heavyset man in black wrestles open a series of locks, including a rusty lock chain. Cee is nowhere to be found, and I'm worried that I should've gone upstairs first instead of following the noise down here.

I aim at his head. "Hands up."

The man freezes and raises his hands.

Inching closer, I order him to the ground, readying to shoot if he doesn't comply. "Gracie, it's me."

Oh, God. Cee is wearing a disguise. "Turn around," I tell her.

She does and I lean in close enough to see her fire-brown eyes through the black mask.

"Is anyone else here?"

She shakes her head. "No. Just those perverts upstairs."

Perverts? Oh no, no, no. The stacks of computers and thumb drives on the floor. The people tied up. Cee is on some kind of mission. "What's—"

Heavy pounding on the front door ricochets down into the basement. Cee jerks her head at the back door. "We have to hurry. It's the police. I called them."

She called the police while still in the house? She called the police knowing I was coming to the house?

Footsteps loud and heavy vibrate across the basement ceiling.

Toots on toast. Momma is going to kill me. Us.

Holstering my weapon, I use a lockpick to unlock the chain on the basement door. A quick scan of the area shows no police. Footsteps on the stairs behind us get us moving. We run.

We're halfway across the lawn when I hear a gruff voice from the back deck. "Police! Don't fucking move!"

The command echoes around us, but we run faster. I drop back so I can provide Cee some cover in case he does shoot.

At the end of the yard, she swings open the six-foot tall door and we charge into the alley.

A police cruiser's blue lights flash on one end, so we turn and run the opposite way. Police lights bounce into the alley at that end. Did they call in every cop in town?

We're trapped between two approaching cruisers in an access alley lined with tall wooden fencing. Nowhere to run. Nowhere to hide.

The cruisers inch forward, shining a spotlight on us.

I turn to tell Cee, "We're going to have to climb."

Cee is already scaling the fence, huge fake torso and belly halfway over.

Mad skills. Terrible teamwork.

Thanks to God I no longer wear my belly ring, I hoist myself over, ignoring the warnings from the police. I land inside a rectangular patch of yard and have just enough time to yank Cee back when I hear the low-warning growl.

The bull mastiff jerks against his chain. Through her face mask, Cee's eyes are as wide and surprised as someone woken from a nightmare by ice water to the face.

A light goes on in the house, and the sliding door on the deck screams open like the door to a haunted house. We're already running for the neighbor's yard when the man who opened the door two-finger whistles to alert the police. "They're over here!"

Things blur quickly as we sprint and climb, sprint and climb through a series of yards until I grab Cee from going over again and ask her breathlessly, "Is the padding on your disguise dissolvable?"

She nods. *Good.* She did that right at least. I point toward a covered boat in the yard. "Take off your clothes, ball them in the padding. We'll shove it under the tarp, let it dissolve away any evidence."

"Okay," Cee says and does what I say.

Before she hides the clothes, I break the seal on her foam padding, releasing the liquid that will destroy the evidence.

I shove it under the boat's cover.

Cee wipes her hands on the grass. "What now?"

"They're searching for two people, one short, one heavyset. You're neither of those." I push my car keys into her hand. "White Ford Focus parked between a black pickup and a rusty blue minivan." I stop for a minute and think of something. "Can you drive?"

Cee's sweat-drenched face looks offended. "Of course."

Of course? Kid is *fifteen.*

Pulling the sleeve of my jacket over one hand, I scrub her face clean, brush her hair out with my fingers, and push her toward the gate. "Wait for me at my club."

Cee shakes her head. "I can't leave you."

We duck as the flash of a cruiser's lights bounces off the fence. Crouched face-to- face, for the first time, Cee looks like the teen that she is, both scared and vulnerable. "Go," I tell her. "I'll be fine."

"How will you get back?"

Now she's going to try to be a team player? Would've helped if she'd told me what I'd be walking into. "Lyft. Now go."

She does, walking out looking nothing like a big, fat felon and everything like a wayward teen in jean shorts and army boots.

I stand and run in the opposite direction.

Chapter 19
Gracie

Flinging myself f over another fence, I drop onto the grass and stroll onto the sidewalk until the two cops nearby spot me. I run.

Not too fast. Behind me, there's the creak of leather gun belts, the clink of metal, and orders to stop. I stay far enough ahead that they can't tase me.

Through yards and across streets, I run, jumping fences and zigzagging to change directions. When the footsteps behind me grow distant, I focus ahead, knowing the police have phoned in my last known and that, at any moment, reinforcements will arrive and cut me off.

I round a corner and see no one. I climb over another fence, jog to the shed at the edge of the yard and hoist myself onto the low roof. Squatting there, sweat plastering my face mask to my skin, I search the area.

Where's the cop cavalry? Sure, the two chasing me couldn't keep up, but no reinforcements?

This is too good to be true.

Patience. Hold. Forcing myself to take slow, deep breaths, I wait. Three minutes later and still, nothing. If I wait any longer, they might stumble upon me.

Crawling across the roof, I jump and land outside of the yard in another access alley.

Muscles burning, I exit the neighborhood at a run, head down the road, and come out on Bustleton Avenue.

I stop beside a boarded-up corner store. Hidden in the dim

Diana Muñoz Stewart

area behind it, I pull off the hat and face mask, then yank off my hoodie and shove the whole thing into a packed dumpster.

Now, wearing a white tank top and black cargo pants, I shake out my long hair and start walking. I'm not ten feet down the road when my phone vibrates in my pocket.

Expecting to see Cee's number, hoping the kid is okay, I pull my secure phone from my pocket. The number on the screen is unexpected. *Dusty?*

"Yeah?"

"I'm in North Philly. Near Red Lion and Northeast Ave. Need a ride?"

He's no more than a half mile away from where I am right now. That's so not a coincidence. "Yeah. I'm on Bustleton. Head north. You'll spot me."

Jaw tense, I hang up.

In short order, he pulls up to the curb and unlocks the car door with a click.

I slide inside, strap on my seat belt, and notice the jammer settled on the seat between us.

Hmmm... I think I know why there were no reinforcements. Dusty played for my team, and that's kind of sweet... and extremely alarming.

He *is* lying about investigating my family, right?

My gaze rises from the box to search his face for answers.

He shrugs as if it's no big deal that he saved me, and I'm so not sure how I feel about that. Besides grateful, I kind of feel... Nope. I will think about that later. Right now, I'm still annoyed with him.

As he pulls away from the curb, he adjusts the middle vent so that it's pointing in my sweat-soaked direction. That's also very sweet and considerate.

Less angry than I was a moment ago, I say, "You put a tracker on me?"

"Inside your boots. Figured they're your footwear of choice most nights."

I close my eyes, hoping to disguise how much that hurts my feelings and insults my professional expertise. I'd forgotten how to deal with a spy. I've been taken in by all his incredible hotness, easy nature, and fun. Now look where it's gotten me.

Where *has* it landed me? Seated next to him in an air-conditioned car that smells pleasantly of Dusty's aftershave, something that reminds me of an ocean breeze. A riot of conflicting emotions circles in my mind, but I refocus on the jammer. "You ran interference?"

"Yeah." He isn't very chatty tonight.

"I'm going to need you to stop tracking me."

"I'm not sure I can agree—"

"Promise, me, Dusty. Right now."

He shifts in his seat. "Okay."

Why does that make me feel better? I mean, he could be lying, but I don't think he is. Somehow, I trust him. That's about the most surprising thing that's happened tonight. "I need to call my sister."

"I saw your car take off. Not sure who was behind the wheel, but she looked young."

Leaning my head against the headrest, I say, "She is. She doesn't even have a license."

His hands tense around the steering wheel as the car slides to a stop at a light. He says nothing in response. He's not being chatty at all.

Not having the bandwidth to figure out why he's quiet, I call Cee.

She picks up right away. "Gracie, are you okay?"

"Yeah. How's the driving?"

"I can't move the seat back, but it's okay. I'm"—she pauses as if checking something—"twenty minutes from your club."

"Okay. I'll be there about forty minutes after you. Drive safely, and don't talk on the phone and drive." I hang up and Dusty accelerates with the light change. He turns up the air conditioner. I didn't ask, but it feels great. "Thanks."

I close my eyes and wait for him to start questioning me, but he doesn't.

He adjusts the radio to a country station, and we ride with the twangy music playing.

After a short time of comfortable silence, he whispers, "What's it like with all those sisters?"

"You don't have any sisters?"

"No siblings whatsoever. At a certain point, I was raised by my uncle, and he was a card-carrying bachelor."

There's a story there, and it's one I find myself wanting to know as I answer his question. "I was the only one of my siblings adopted from birth. Everyone else has a history, another family, but for me... Well, having a houseful of siblings from all over the world is all I've ever known. For me, it's normal, and my normal has been both a blessing and a curse."

"What's the blessing part?"

There're so many ways I can answer that question because I have an abundance of love and people in my life, but I think the greatest blessing has been... "Because we have so many people from so many places in my family, I learned at an early age that if you get to know someone, really get to know and understand them, you can love anyone."

"That's sweet. What's the curse?"

I snort. "Nights like tonight. Because you can love someone who has issues, love someone who makes you angry, love someone who you don't always get along with, and that can cause a lot of pain."

He chews on that so loudly I can almost hear him, and I yawn, realizing how tired I am as the streetlights play across my closed eyelids.

After a moment of silence, Dusty whispers, "It's okay to sleep."

And just like that, I find myself drifting off.

Sometime later, I feel warm fingers against my cheek, and I open my eyes.

Staring into my eyes, Dusty says, "We're here."

He's close enough to kiss, and that's something I would really like to do right now.

As if hearing my thoughts or seeing them in my eyes, he leans forward and kisses me lightly on my lips.

Fire shoots through my body and, as my lips call for more, he pulls back.

I say, "You didn't ask me one question about what happened tonight. Not one."

His lips quirk, a little sadly. "I didn't want to get into it. Not again. You know?"

Strangely, I do. I don't want to play the game either. The one where I lie and he lies, and we both pretend that the lies don't matter because we each know the other is lying to us.

"Thanks." I swallow over a throat gone suddenly tight. "For helping me. For not asking. Thanks."

I move toward him, toward those lips, toward the one honest thing we have between us, but am stopped short by a knock on my window.

Dusty's eyebrows lift and look toward the knock.

I don't need to turn. I know who's there.

Cee.

Chapter 20
Gracie

Stretched out under my plush white comforter, with the air conditioning set to arctic, I realize I can't get up. My handcrafted California king, a gift from Momma when I first moved into the apartment over the bar, is hard to leave on the best of days. Today isn't the best of days. My body aches from all that running and climbing and tension.

Mmm, is that pancakes and bacon? Okay, maybe I *can* do it.

My stiff arms complaining, I drag off my blankets, exposing my white tank top and green silk boxers.

Bracing, I wrench myself out of bed and my legs, butt, and back scream their complaints. I've got to make a plan to get back to the gym.

After going to the bathroom and splashing cold water over puffy eyes, I shamble out to the family room. Cee had to sleep on my sofa because all I have in my other bedroom is a toddler bed shaped like a car. That used to be our room—mine and John's and Ty's—before John and Ty left. I moved into my mom's room after she passed.

The blanket and pillow I'd given Cee are folded on the arm of the silverleaf couch. In the kitchenette, the white cabinets are all open. Dishes, bowls, a frying pan, an egg carton, and pancake mix are scattered all over my limited counter space. Cee isn't the neatest of house guests, but she made breakfast, so I won't complain. I usually cook downstairs, but Cee did the hard work of cooking over an electric stove with only two small burners, then setting up all the food—orange juice, plates with pancakes and bacon—on the breakfast bar.

She must feel bad about last night or is worried I'm going to rat her out to Momma.

Cee sits on a swivel barstool by the breakfast bar, feet propped on the stool next to her. She's dressed in my white cotton T-shirt, staring at her phone. Her hair is jet black, so dark the recessed lights make streaks of purple in it.

I nudge her legs out of the way and sit next to her with a hiss escaping my mouth and a hot *you suck* from my thighs. "Good morning," I say.

Cee lowers her phone. "What took you so long to get home last night?"

Oh, I don't know. I was busy trying to avoid being captured. Taking a strip of bacon, I chew before answering. "I wasn't on a joy ride, so don't cop an attitude."

Cee's sharp jaw extends as she purses her lips. "I thought *cop* meant 'police.' *Cop* also means 'to have'?"

Whoops. Because she's so smart, I keep forgetting English isn't her first language. "'Cop an attitude' is a saying that means to act rudely." I take a couple of the scorched pancakes and add them to the plate in front of me. "Where's the syrup?"

Cee shrugs. "I couldn't find it."

I point to the fridge. "It's in there, and since I can't stand without muscle spasms, do you mind getting it?"

Blinking at me in surprise, she gets up and retrieves the syrup. She puts it down then flounces back into her seat. "You might need some better conditioning."

Says the kid who ran a quarter of what I did. Still, she's right. I haven't been to the gym in… well, since Tony. We used to train together most weeks.

Her eyes flick to the side, toward the second bedroom. "Do you miss him, your son?"

Grief as hot as a brand sears my chest. My other siblings know not to bring Tyler up to me, but Cee is new.

Drowning my pancakes in syrup, I force down the heat rising in my throat and decide to try for a little light family banter over breakfast instead. "Who were those people you tied up last night?"

Cee begins to fill her own plate, which means she'd been waiting for me to eat. How is the person who ties people up, runs away from home, and lies to me still also sweet and considerate enough to make breakfast and wait for me to begin eating?

"Six months ago, the two men you saw in that house, drugged and brutally raped a girl who went to their college." She talks with her mouth full. "She was lured to their home by a friend, the girl you saw. That is their way. They use the one girl to lure others. The girl who'd been raped tried to go through normal channels, but she was drunk and using that night. So that disqualifies her from humanity and justice."

My stomach turns as I swallow another bite of pancake. "How'd you find out about her?"

"Someone who went to the Mantua Academy was sisters with the college woman, and she confided to Jules about it. When I heard about it from Jules, I did some research and organized the mission."

Jules. Another sibling from Cee's unit, which is better known as Vampire Academy. Our weird family tradition names groups of kids who are around the same age and therefore lumped into one unit that trains, learns, shares a hall, and often forms an unbreakable bond. Cee's acting like it was all her idea, but I seriously doubt that. Cee is scary smart, but she doesn't have the computer skills to pull this off. The one person in her unit who does have those skills is Rome, Jule's twin brother.

Pouring coffee from the carafe into a cup, I take a sip and say, "That's against the rules."

"I followed the rules. I did research, verified the witness statements, uncovered the men had multiple recordings of these kinds of rape. They shared them online to make money but hid their trails very well online.

"That's proof that I left on the floor of that house. Proof that the college woman's situation is not, how you say, a single incident."

"Isolated. You mean an isolated incident." I stab the bacon in my hand at her like an accusatory finger. "And I meant you went against the rules of engagement because you are underage, have no approval, and could easily have left evidence that leads the police to The Guild."

"I was so careful."

"Was getting me caught part of your 'careful'? If I hadn't found you in the basement, I might've been caught while you got away."

Cee pours syrup over her pancakes, spears one with her fork, lifts it, and bites the dripping edge. "I didn't think—"

"Exactly. I need you to send me all of the information you've collected. You can't start a splinter vigilante group within our already illegal spy ring."

"Thomas Jefferson said, 'When injustice becomes law, resistance becomes duty.' I was merely doing what I came here to do."

Great quote. "You could've given this information to Momma, to anyone in Internal. They would've handled it, but, instead, you fought with Momma and ran away."

"I'm not a child. I want to go on missions. I want to do the job, unlike you."

I take another sip of coffee, coffee as dark as Cee's hair, as dark as Justice's hair. Cee reminds me of Justice in so many ways. All that anger and pain. "Cee, you have to get control of all this anger. It's leading you down a bad path. Anger is useful on occasion, but when it becomes the go-to emotion, it poisons. You deserve better, an opportunity to live a life free from all of that. Well, as much as possible anyway."

"I shouldn't have called you."

"Why *did* you call me?"

Cee takes a long swig of OJ, then wipes her mouth with the

back of her hand and says, "Because I wasn't sure you'd come."

"Meaning?"

"Meaning if the one person who didn't want me anywhere near The Guild came, then…" She shrugs.

That hurts. Hurts like a kick to the teeth. She's telling me that if the one person in The Guild, the person who'd admitted she was openly against Cee being adopted, showed up, showed she cared, then she'd give the family another chance.

"I deserve that, but does Momma? Why go through the adoption process just to run away the moment things get uncomfortable?"

Cee tosses a forkful of half-eaten pancake on her plate with a clang. "You do not understand." She curls her hands in her lap and fists the T-shirt, revealing jean shorts. "I came to the family to rescue, like Justice rescued me, and I can't do that in my bed by ten. I can't take out the bad guys if I'm studying math."

Gooseflesh wings across my skin. I understand how The Guild can make you feel—not just that you *can* do something about the injustices, but that you *should*. That's part of the Parish culture that messed me up so badly as a child. "The Guild rules are for everyone's good. This isn't about you, about one person, so if you don't want to play by the rules, tell Momma you've changed your mind." She's so young; she should know that she has a choice in all of this. "If you don't want adoption, that's fine. It'll be fine. We can set you up anywhere. I promise. We'll take care of you."

Cee's cell beeps and she texts something without looking up at me. Is her lip trembling?

"Cee, I'm not trying to hurt your feelings; I'm trying to help you. You took out your chip, you ran away, and just indicated Guild rules are too much for you."

Done texting, she looks at me with eyes as fierce as a tiger's. "No. I've decided. Unlike you, I won't leave mi familia."

Ouch. "You don't know anything about Tyler, about my relationship with him, and that statement is completely unfair."

Pulling off her T-shirt with heat and frustration, she stands there in the jean shorts and the tight blue tank she'd had on last night. She stamps her foot, "I wasn't talking about him," then marches toward the front door.

How did I mess this up? With a sigh, I follow. "You can't leave here without me putting in the code. I'm the only one authorized to allow unchipped people in or out of this level."

Cee pauses with her hand on the door. "What about the elevator? It is only password protected, sí?"

Kid couldn't find the syrup, but she found the secret elevator behind one of the inset bookcases?

"No, you can't use that either. It only leads to the basement." To the tunnel there that leads to the warehouse.

Cee frowns, frowns the way a smart person does when they come across something that makes no sense.

I wait for her to ask, but she doesn't.

Instead, she crosses her arms over her chest. "Then let me out. I'll call Momma. She'll send a car."

I'm not going to let Cee make me feel guilty. She ran away. She... Curds and whey on a big hairy spider, I do feel guilty. "You want to do the work? Let's start with training. I'm going to go through last night's mission on the way to Momma's. Step-by-step. I want you to know exactly what you did wrong."

"You're driving me?"

"Yep."

For a flash, the barest hint of a smile—the repressed hope of a hardened teen—flits across Cee's face, and I find my heart smiling back.

#

After dropping Cee off at the Mantua Academy, I check my rearview again. Still there. Someone in a light-blue Toyota Camry has been following me since I left my club.

Thankfully, Cee didn't notice. The last thing I need is for her to ask questions that might alert Momma to my situation. Besides, I can handle this on my own. What good is training if you never use it?

I continue to lure my prey up the long, winding road that leads to a hundred acres of heavily wooded and uncultivated land in Bucks County. It's owned by the Mantua Academy and is where the family practices drills, basic survival skills, and tactical maneuvers.

The man following me isn't hanging back nearly far enough, so either he isn't very good at his job or he wants me to spot him. Doesn't matter because either works for my plan. Though unskilled is much better for me because challenging him in the isolated woods is going to get tricky. Still, not as dangerous as letting this surveillance continue without intervention.

Hands sweaty against my steering wheel, I turn into the hidden drive, pulling up to the lift bar that blocks access to the property. I wave my wrist and the chip imbedded there that not only keeps track of me but allows me to access secret levels inside the Mantua Home, my club, and here, clicks open the gate. It rises then lowers once my car is safely beyond it.

I already feel better. If my tail is intent on following me, he'll have to do it on foot on a property he doesn't understand with a person who has considerable skills.

I drive down the dirt road for a half mile until I reach the barn, a rickety wooden structure worn with age and greened with moisture. A quick visit to my trunk where I fish out a camo shirt and hat from my bugout bag and grab some zip ties.

My heartbeat and my hope begin to accelerate. This is it. Finally, an opportunity to act instead of react, and, if I'm lucky, this'll be a real lead, a chance to get answers on who shot at me.

I need this to end. The longer it goes on, the longer the threat on my life is out there, the greater chance things might escalate, the greater risk this could impact Tyler.

Determined to never let that happen, I move through the woods. The wailing of cicadas, buzzing of bees, and chirping of birds mask my nearly silent movements. I've always excelled at tracking. I silently make my way over uneven ground, thick with brambles and heavy with vines. Unlike my pursuer.

I hear the man long before I see him. Following the sounds of heavy breathing and cursing, I spot the guy, tall and muscular with a limp. I'm not sure if he arrived with the limp or hurt himself in the woods.

With the grace of a cat stalking a mouse, I duck behind a tree, wait for him to advance, then sneak up behind him. Amazingly, he keeps pushing himself forward, fighting through the woods and never looking back.

Adrenaline spikes and my focus tightens on the man who suddenly seems familiar. I know him. Or I've met him. He's the guy from the bar, the one who I almost ran into when he came out of the bathroom, the one who had glared at me until he'd noticed Dusty.

Despite his poor situational awareness and my near-perfect silence, he turns when I'm nearly there. He startles upon seeing me, then reaches a hand toward the small of his back.

I react as if he'd already pulled the weapon, throwing an elbow punch that snaps into his side and carries the full weight of my body.

He doubles over, coughing, and sucking in air, and I move behind him, kicking hard at his kneecap. He topples to the ground, landing on his knees with a cry of pain.

Securing his wrists behind his back with a zip tie, I search him. He has a gun—which I take—but no cell and no wallet, so not a total idiot.

Pocketing his weapon, I come around to his front and lift his head.

He says, "This is not legal."

"What you're doing isn't legal. You're on private property. There are *No Trespassing* signs all over. My family owns this property, so I'm perfectly within my rights to shoot an intruder who shows up on my property with a weapon."

"I didn't—"

"I need you to answer my questions if you'd like to leave this property without an extra hole in you." Not that I have any intention of shooting this man. He's obviously not the trained professional that came after me at my club, so if he doesn't try to hurt me, I won't hurt him. Well, not too much. "Now, what's your name?"

He hesitates and I jab my gun against his neck. Sweat slides down his face. He closes his eyes and whispers in a fear-tight voice. "Wilkes. James Wilkes."

"You are on private property, Mr. Wilkes. Want to tell me what you're doing here?"

"Call the police." He tries to stand, and I press my gun harder to his temple. "Call them," he insists, panic and worry driving his voice into a higher octave.

He should worry. A woman who fears for the safety of her child has a gun to his head on private property in the middle of rural-as-an-outhouse USA and he's refusing the answers I need.

I pull back the gun and slam it into his kidney. He buckles like origami and curls up on his side with a beet-red face and tears leaking from his eyes.

He sucks in a breath, drawing in a bit of leaf and dirt, then coughs it out.

I'm starting to feel bad for this guy, but not bad enough to let him go without answers.

I squat beside him. "Why are you here, Wilkes? Who sent you?"

"Porter Rush," he wheezes, "wanted information on you."

The shock from his answers nearly causes me to curse, and I never curse. Still, he could be lying to protect someone else. Grabbing the guy's shoes, I drag them around, force him to sit up. He cries out and gasps for breath, slumping over his knees with dirt and leaves stuck to his sweaty face.

I put my hand on his bent knee so he knows that I'm serious. "Why?"

He shakes his head. "I don't know. I swear I don't know. I work for him, for the campaign."

"Rush's campaign?"

"Yeah. I do deliveries and stuff."

"Volunteer or paid?"

"Volunteer. I'm on disability. It's something to do."

Disability? Crud. "What's wrong with you?"

"Bone cancer. Could you take your hand off my knee?"

I pull back my hand like he'd lit it on fire. Cancer. The way he walked... It'd been pain.

I wince with sympathy and the memory of my bio mom, of how much pain she'd experienced at the end of her life before cancer took her. I can't believe this man chased me down, came here, when he's so sick. I can't believe Porter asked him to do this. What an A-hole. "Why did you agree to this? Why not let Porter pay someone? He's got the money, you know."

"You can't trust no one in politics. Everyone's out to get your candidate, prove he's a bad guy. Porter knew he could trust me to look into such a delicate matter because I owe the senator my life. What's left of it."

I'm sure there's a longer story there, and I have to admit I'm interested in any good my father has done, but I can't be distracted by those things. "Delicate matter?"

Wilkes winces. "You being his half-sister and all."

Porter *does* know. "What did he ask you to find out?"

"If you visited anyone. You know, like a boyfriend or maybe someone you cared about seriously."

That's a very bad thing for Porter to want to find about his sister, a thing that means he's thinking about going after those I love, not just me.

Hardening my heart, refusing to think about this guy doing something he thought was good despite his pain, I lean in close and put menace in my voice. "What did you discover?"

He breathes in through trembling lips, past splotchy skin and dried tears. "I know you have a kid."

My heart freezes solid. Tyler. He knows about Tyler. It hits me like an open hand. This is the thing that John worried most about all those years ago. That my family's activities would put Ty in danger. It's one of the reasons I gave Ty up… because I feared he was right. "Did you tell Porter?"

He looks away as if he doesn't want to answer, then shakes his head. "Not yet."

That's good, but it also means I have to make sure he never tells Porter, and I'm not sure I can do that. How did this inept man manage to discover Ty's existence? I'm so careful. "How'd you find out?"

"I've been following you and the girl."

My legs nearly buckle as I let out a breath that vibrates with relief and nearly a sob. "I don't have a kid. That girl is my sister."

His eyes widen. "Oh."

"You suck at this, James."

"I know."

Standing, a little weak in the knees, I flick open my pocketknife, and slice off his zip ties. "I'm going to let you get back in your car and go. You tell Porter to call me. I'm not a threat to him. Let him know that and don't follow me again." I help him to his feet, catch and hold his gaze with my own. "Understand?"

"Yeah." He nods enthusiastically, sending strands of greasy hair flapping about. "I got it. Thanks."

Stepping back, I indicate which way is out and watch him limp out of the woods. Porter will never call me, but at least I know he's interested in me and knows I'm his sister. I can also surmise that his interest in me is not innocent because he's not asking about my reading habits or hobbies, he's asking about those I love. To me, that indicates he's trying to plan something, and that something is likely a threat to me.

What I don't understand is why send a man who is so incredibly sick and certainly incapable? It makes no sense if he's already hired a sniper to kill me.

Unless... could he have wanted me to know that someone was following me? Could he be trying to distract me with James while he actually comes at me from a different direction?

That's really paranoid.

So why does it seem right?

Porter has so much to lose if his father is brought low. The man's whole career is tied up with his father and his family's reputation, and people with a lot to lose are capable of doing almost anything.

Poop.

It looks like if I want to end this nightmare, go back to trying to find a way into Tyler's life and make myself respectable enough to deserve that opportunity, I'm going to have to fight for it.

Chapter 21
Gracie

Thanks to dealing with James, my entire day has been one big mess of playing catch-up.

I hold the door open as Jackie, my chef, wrestles boxes of frozen meat through. We usually have the meat delivered earlier, but my local supplier's delivery truck broke down, so now we're juggling customers and food deliveries.

Normally, that wouldn't be a big deal because I pad my deliveries, but I've been distracted lately by the threat of death, and we're running unusually low on supplies.

After helping Jackie, I return to my office to make a record of what we've received. My cell rings and I recognize the number. *When it rains...* "Hey, Leland."

"Where did you find Cee?" His voice is as rough as stones. Frustrated stones.

"Philly."

He sighs dramatically and I instinctively try to smooth things over. "She regretted running away and wanted someone to come get her. Surprisingly, she picked me."

"She's a handful."

Yeah. Which is why they don't usually adopt that late, but I'm not bringing that up again. "She loves the family."

"I know. Why'd you go to the fields today?"

Considering the bowl of watermelon goodness on my desk, I pick a candy up and twirl it in my fingers. "I needed a break from the club, so I decided to reconnect with nature."

"I also noticed that you've changed security protocols at the club. Is there something we should be aware of?"

Yes. But nothing I can tell you. "I had an incident in the club, but there's no need to worry about it. I've been planning to change things up for a while anyway."

There's a heavyweight of a pause on Leland's end, a pause that weighs as much as Mike Tyson and Tyson Fury combined.

"Gracie, you know we're on your side here, right?"

My heart sinks as his voice gentles. Leland is as much a father as I've ever known. He's Momma's right-hand man and companion. Though they don't publicize it, I've seen Leland leaving Momma's room in the early morning. He's been there for me my entire life and lying to him is not easy. Especially since I know that, if I had any trouble, he'd do anything to help me, to protect and support me.

For a moment, I consider telling him the whole truth, despite the fact that The Guild is still reeling from the drone attack, Tony's betrayal, and the loss of Tony in Mexico, but then my cell buzzes, letting me know my facial recognition software has identified someone from my list. I pull my phone away to read the name.

Toots on toast. John is here. I swallow a ball of panic.

"I know, Leland. Thanks for the offer, but I'm good here. I've got to go." I don't give him a second to respond before I hang up. Just in time as the door to my office creaks open and John steps inside.

My heart jumps into my throat, but I push it back down with a swallow as my fingers fist around the Jolly Rancher.

His eyes fall on me, and I freeze. Not just deer-in-the-headlights freeze, but Neanderthal-trapped-in-ice-for-a-thousand-years freeze. I can't even find words or language right now.

It's the first time we've seen each other in thirteen years, and each of us is looking at the other. He looks so familiar despite the age around his eyes and mouth. He's still thin, with a runner's body, but no longer the wiry teen I'd once known. He's more muscular and dapper in a blue suit that's trendy enough that I suspect his wife purchased it for him.

I'm waiting for the joy, the warmth, the love I'd once felt for him, but I feel... nothing. Not the stirring of lost love, not the longing that held me in its grip for a decade, and not a single spark of lust.

John's perceptive brown eyes travel up and down my black-and-yellow Club When? T-shirt, scholarly bun, and the startled look on my face before narrowing and focusing on my eyes. "Hello, Gracie Divine."

Crud. He's angry enough to say my first and middle name, say it like it's a contradiction, a tactic he'd begun using after I'd first told him the shocking truth about my family's activities.

I unfreeze. In fact, I suddenly couldn't be calmer. I sit forward. "John, I wasn't expecting you. It's been a very long time since you showed up at my club. Is there a reason you didn't call first?" The normalness of my voices steadies me.

He runs a hand over his face and through his hair, then lets out a breath deep enough to dispel old feelings or push them far into the past. "I didn't want to give you a chance to prepare."

Discreetly, I reach down and check the gun attached to the bottom of my desktop. "Prepare for what?"

"I'm here to get you to stop with the computer, stop coming to my house, stop watching my son, stop stalking my son."

My son again. "He's *our* son, John." He detected the backdoor I made for Victor on their computers? *No way.* "I've stopped—"

"After you started showing up, Tyler began researching how to find his birth mother. He's gone from having no interest in you to wanting to know about his own personal stalker. I'm here to tell you to stop."

Stalker? I stopped going by after John's text, even though it killed me, but that didn't stop Tyler. "Tyler wanting to know me isn't a bad thing, John. It's natural. I want to know him."

"No." He shoves frustrated hands into his pant pockets.

"You don't get to see him. That's the agreement we made when I left. I stay quiet and you stay away."

But Tyler wants to know me. He's researching how to get in touch with me. Is it possible for a heart to break with joy? This is it, an opportunity to fight for a chance to be in Ty's life.

A muscle tics in my jaw. "That agreement wasn't my choice. I made it—sent you away—so I could protect you." I don't add that I did it to protect him from Momma and Leland because that feels like too much of a betrayal. Although it's the truth. They threatened to alter John's memory so he no longer knew about The Guild. Back then, M-erasure was experimental. I had no idea what it would do to him to have his mind wiped like that.

"It doesn't matter." John looks truly uncomfortable now. "You asking me to leave was a relief. After you told me about that chip thing under your skin..." An unsettled look crosses his face—disgust? "I planned on going and taking Ty."

The candy I'd been holding drops onto the desk, cracking inside its translucent wrapper. "You planned on taking Ty away from me? But I thought... you loved me."

His dark eyes flash with something—a spark, a memory—and, for a moment, I see the young man I'd fallen in love with, but then he shifts and shakes his head and that young man fades away.

He says, "We were young. Gracie. What did we know of love?"

Like a decade's worth of candles being blown out, my old image of John vanishes in a puff of smoke.

"I loved you and Tyler. *That's* why I gave you both up to keep you safe." *To keep your mind whole.*

"What are you talking about?" His lips thin and press together like the seam on a roll of tape. "Leland and Momma knew I intended to take Tyler and leave. I told them directly that if you fought for custody, I'd reveal what I knew about their illegal activities. If they told you something different, gave you some story to keep you in line..." He motions with his hand. "I'm not responsible for that."

For a moment, my world tilts on its axis. Everything I thought I'd known about giving up John, about being *forced* to give up John, suddenly shifts.

John had decided he was going to take Tyler and go. John had threatened Momma and Leland with exposing The Guild.

If I had known his choice back then?

I have no doubt what I'd have done. I was so young. I've had let him burn The Guild down.

Back then, thinking I was saving John and Tyler from The Guild had made the decision difficult but doable. If I had had the choice of saving The Guild from John? I'd been too hurt, blamed Momma too much. I would never have let Tyler go. The Guild would've been exposed.

So many of my sisters, girls like Cee, would never have had a home.

Momma never told me because of course, she wouldn't let The Guild's fate be decided by two emotional teenagers. Still, Momma did manage to get my input. By telling me she intended to take John's memory, she effectively gave me the decision of what she should do—alter John's mind or give into his demands and let him take Tyler.

I flush a red so hot it's like someone holds a live wire to my skin. I was an idiot. John threw me under the bus, and I sacrificed to save him. He'd made that choice and never looked back. He's only here now to keep me away. I have to know the truth. "What if I'm no longer involved with The Guild and I'm just a woman who owns a club and Ty wants to see me?"

"Come on, Gracie. Even if you aren't directly involved, your family still is. You have to know there's no way I'll ever let Ty anywhere near you and your crazy family and all that stuff they do."

"What we *do*? Rescue people? Stop pedophiles? Stop abuse? Defend those without power?"

"That's not your job."

In a lot of cases, it's not anyone's job. That's the problem. I don't say this because I can't get enough air into my lungs to tell him that or about my creeper-detection software, my work. I finally understand what I should've understood a long, long time ago. It's not Momma or the work that he disapproves of, it's me.

Well, I'm not the insecure teenager I once was, and I'm no longer going to allow him to intimidate or belittle me. "We need to talk about this, John. I'm not going to go away this time. Ty wants to know me, and I want to know Ty."

"Don't say that." He shifts forward from the door. The crisp blue suit, polished and professional, contradicts the impulsive anger behind the action. "I'm not putting up with any of that madness in Ty's life. I have another son and a wife, so don't come around and don't test me. I promise you, you won't like the results. You're not the only one who can operate outside the law."

"Are you threaten—"

"No. No." He puts up a hand. "But I'll do what I have to do to protect my family. Remember that."

"You realize that's a threat, right?"

He jerks back, turns and storms out on me, on our past, and on all the lies.

Chapter 22
Dusty

Early afternoon but the July heat screams against my Dodge's hood. Parked in the back of Club When?, I wipe the sweat from my face, turn the car back on, and answer the call that came in the moment I'd turned the car off.

"Secret Agent Man," I say, as I pick up the call from Mack, "I've actually got something for you."

"Good to hear it, but first I wanted to give you some personal information about your dad. He's been admitted to a hospital in California."

My fingers flex around the steering wheel as the car starts to cool. "That fucker let my mom die when she got sick, but now he's getting treatment."

He'd nearly let me die, too. Not to mention torturing all the followers of his crazy ministry with his *let God heal 'em* policy.

"Yep. He's not half the man you are, Dusty. I'm sorry."

I know it's a reach, but I ask anyway. "Tell me his followers have at least wised up and are abandoning the ministry."

"Some have, actually, but not all of them. Not the ones that have been there the longest. He told them he had a vision. God told him the exact man who would heal him, gave him his name and everything, so it's like God's healing him. Crafty SOB."

Same boat, different river. "Thanks for the update, but from now on, I don't want to hear unless he kicks it."

"Understood." He pauses then asks, "What do you have for me?"

RECKLESS GRACE

Pushing my sunglasses up, I watch a group of people get out of a car and walk around the side of Gracie's club, headed to the front door. "I think Gracie Parish's biological father is Senator Rush from Pennsylvania and the front-runner to become the next president of the United States. I also think he's being blackmailed by Mukta Parish."

Mack is silent for a breath. "Keep going."

I quickly explain what I suspect about the connection between Gracie, Sheila, Mukta, and Rush.

"Did you send me any of this?"

"Not yet."

"Good. Don't."

Don't? "Okay."

"How sure are you about this blackmail thing? What is Mukta Parish getting from Senator Rush? She obviously doesn't need the money."

No, she doesn't need the money, but that doesn't mean she can't find a use for Rush. "It's only preliminary, mind you, but, recently, Rush pulled a bill he sponsored that would've raised the bar on women proving workplace discrimination. His decision came out of nowhere. It's the kind of bill Mukta Parish would've openly disdained."

"That's a bit mild, almost influence-peddling."

"Not so mild. Some of the senator's key decisions have resulted in benefits for her companies and power for her family."

"Like?"

"He supported one of Mukta's daughters, helped get her a judgeship for the Eastern District of Pennsylvania."

Mack whistles. "Okay. You've got me interested. If you're right, this is the tip of the iceberg on what Mukta Parish could be hiding. Her pharmaceutical company asked for approval on a drug that eliminates people's addictions. That's a type of mind control. Think about it. That's what she's showing the public. Imagine what she's hiding. If we get this right, if we expose these crazy bitches…"

"Hey. Dial it back." *And don't call Gracie a bitch unless you want my fist in your face.* "This is still exploratory, Mack, and I'm not convinced that what Mukta has on Rush is just an illegitimate kid. Let me do my job before you try to maneuver this into some political gain."

Mack grunts disapproval of my assessment of his motives. "You think she has something else on Rush? Something dark enough to get him to initiate policy for her for thirty years? Something that made him want to kill his bastard child?"

I do. Because, in this instance, going after Gracie feels personal. Or maybe it's just that I take it personally.

I watch as a familiar man exits the back door of Club When? with fists balled and his jaw set. *John True, what the hell are you doing here?* "Later, Mack."

I hang up, turn off the car, then head into the club. There's no way John would try anything in the middle of the day, not anything violent, but his demeanor tells me he also wasn't here to shoot the shit with Gracie. "

After calling "Hey," to the chef and giving a thumbs-up to the distracted dishwasher, I toe open Gracie's partially ajar door and find her sobbing into her hands.

"Gracie?"

She hunches in on herself. "Go away."

I close the door, walk around to her side to take a knee. I lean in close enough that my shoulder practically kisses hers. "Hey now." I hold out my arms. "I'm right here."

To my relief, she turns, slumps forward, and drops her head onto my shoulder. Her tears are gutting me, and I don't know what I would've done if she hadn't let me at least try to make it better.

She whispers into my shirt, "I'm not sad. I'm angry."

I smooth a hand down her back. "Angry at what?"

She raises her head. "At myself for giving up my son to protect his father."

Her stare is a direct challenge. If I admit knowing she has a son, I as good as admit to investigating her and her family.

Shifting, I reach over to the tissue box and hand her one. Aw, hell. "Tyler. Your son. You gave him up to protect John?"

A small, relieved smile parts her lips and it's about the prettiest thing I've ever seen. I don't regret my honesty one bit.

"Back when John and I were together, he had an issue with my family and some of their business practices."

After saying that, she blushes a red so deep I can feel the heat on my face. "How did John find out about those particular *business practices*?"

"I told him." She spreads her hands as if to stop me from commenting, though I'm too tongue-tied to say a word. "I know it sounds hard to believe, but I was naïve."

"Not so hard to believe. You'd been educated in the Mantua Academy, adopted into the Parish family. All your experiences, schooling, spirituality, had been filtered through that world. You got out and fell in love and wanted to share your truth with someone."

Gracie stands from her chair so abruptly I grasp the desk to keep from falling over.

She retrieves a chair from the front of the desk and drags it over to me. "You look uncomfortable."

Now why does that make me want to hug the stuffing right out of her? I sit. "Thanks."

Back in her chair, she swivels to face me. "You're right. I was sheltered enough that it was almost culture shock to find out what I'd been taught was dogma and not necessarily how the rest of the world worked."

"What'd you been taught?"

"You know, that it's my responsibility to fight for others, to seek out injustice, to right wrongs. The women of the world are my sisters, my responsibility. I was taught a kind of social responsibility that's almost Marvel superhero stuff."

Sounds like she's mocking herself. "So, you get out into the world—to a bar, no less—and see people drinking, screwing around, having fun, and you realize you've been sold a bill of goods, so you said to yourself—this is the teenage you, now—fuck this."

She laughs softly as her tears dry up. "Basically. It didn't seem fair. I'd never been given the option of worrying about my own problems, my own feelings, and doing normal day-to-day things like making money and taking care of my business."

"And then John showed up."

"Yep. An opportunity to worry about me, what I wanted, and who I wanted to be."

"You got pregnant."

"And for a while it was actually good. I got to be Gracie in love. Gracie pregnant. Gracie as a mom. Until, in a hormonal lovefest, I spilled the beans to John." She bites her lip. "I guess you can say I'm not the least emotional of people."

So says the memories of her riding me in this very office, her boldness in Mexico, her email to the FBI, and her tears and confession right now. I'm amazed she's kept such a tight lid on this for so long, but maybe that's why she doesn't let herself get close to people. "So not-the-least-emotional-of-people tells her first love she comes from a family of"—I pause, add secret weight to the words—"*businesspeople.* And all hell breaks loose. Family's pissed. Boyfriend's pissed. And Gracie Parish does what she can to make it okay."

Her shoulders slump. "Not that simple, but yeah. I gave up John and Tyler, and everyone went on with their lives."

"Except you."

She nods. "Ty was two when I gave him up, so I tortured myself with memories of his baby skin, the feel of his hair against my cheek, the way his laugh made the world better. If it weren't for having to take care of my bio mom and this club, I don't think I'd have gotten up in the morning. After Mom passed"—she strangles the tissue in her hand—"I began to distance myself from my family. And the world, really."

She sweeps tears from her eyes with the hand not strangling the tissue. "Then, a few years ago, Ty got sick. He was in the hospital for a month. During that time, I kind of lost it. I couldn't be with him or hold his hand or brush back his hair, and I blamed myself a lot, but I also blamed Momma. I stewed on that anger until I was furious, then I did something to get back at her."

She stops there and looks at me.

I knew it. She sent the letter. She'll never admit it. Honestly, I feel both elated and sad that she's sharing so much with me right now, but I also get it. That John really did a fucking number on her. Anyway, I don't need her to admit it. I nod once. "Got it."

She lets out a breath. "Ty getting sick made me realize I could lose him without even knowing him, and after Mexico, after Tony... I decided to try to live a different life. I thought I could return to being in Ty's life. Not as his mother, but in his life."

I can see where this is going. "John came by today and told you that's never going to happen."

She lets out a long, frustrated breath. "Yeah. Guess I can't blame him."

"I can. I can't square a man who'd keep his son away from a caring and loving mother."

"You don't get it. My life is dangerous."

Like hell. I understand better than most. "More dangerous than a cop, a detective, FBI or CIA, a solider? Lot of parents with those jobs."

She rubs her forehead, but I can tell the truth still hasn't sunk in.

"Gracie, when your biological mother showed up after giving you up for adoption, Mukta, your momma, let you go live with her?"

"Not without stipulations—that I returned for classes, training, Sunday dinner—but... yeah."

"You think that was okay?" I prod her. "Sheila had lymphoma. That wasn't going to end well. And she was taking you away from everything you'd ever known. To a bar, no less."

Gracie sets her jaw. "Wait a minute. Momma let me go

because she loved me, and she wanted me to know my mother. All of that judgmental stuff didn't matter."

"Why the hell not?"

Her wide eyes bore into me as if I'm an idiot. "Love matters more."

I stare back. "Yep. Love matters more."

Hearing her own words echoed back to her, she draws in a shaky breath. As slow as if she's approaching a dangerous animal, she reaches out and rubs a thumb over my jaw. "I really like you, Dusty." She drops her hand. "But I still can't trust you."

"Don't trust me. Don't." I let that hang there a moment, acknowledging that she's right. It's a moment in which the lies, like wisps of an old spider web, fall from me. "Don't trust me, but let me help you. That's why I'm here. To help."

She puts a fisted hand to her forehead; bits of white tissue poke out from her fingers. "I don't need rescuing."

"What do you need?"

Her eyebrows draw in and I can see the debate on her face. She licks her lips. "I could really use a friend."

And doesn't that just break my heart.

I nod, lean forward, and kiss her lightly on the cheek. "Okay, then. We can start with that."

Chapter 23
Dusty

The light show flashes red, white, and blue off of nearly every surface of Club When? Music pulses from the speakers and people crowd the dance floor, bumping and grinding.

Got to admit it, I like working here. A lot. The rhythm of the bar, the way the air begins to buzz as people stream inside. One second prep work, the next I'm running around, like now, exchanging pleasantries with people from all walks. And then there's working with Gracie.

Though she started the night in a haze of gloom, her mood has lifted. Now, as she works, she sways those hips, that ass, in a way that has me certain God Himself would deem it one of the most pleasant sights on this planet.

Damn, being here with her feels right.

It feels right when she bends to get something from a fridge and my gaze finds its way to her fine, round ass. So right, it makes my palms itch.

It feels right when she catches me looking, smiles without reprimand, and, suddenly, all that guardedness, all the hostility meant to ward people off is not there for me.

It feels right, so right, when Gracie, rocking her hips to one of my favorite songs, shoots me a *what-are-you-waiting-for* look, and I forget for a moment those things called *boundaries*.

I put an arm around her waist and draw her back against the front of my body, expecting her to elbow me hard enough to give me second thoughts.

But she moves with and against me, and it feels about as right as anything I've experienced in my entire life.

People at the bar hoot approval, and she turns to me with a blush. Oh, I like how she blushes. I could make a lifetime out of all the ways I can get Ms. Gracie Parish to blush.

It feels right, so right.

Until I remember exactly why I'm here. Then I feel like shit.

The problem is that she opened up to me earlier, and that has shifted something in me I hadn't expected.

Truth is, I'm finding myself conflicted as I finish the martini and hand it to the woman across the bar. I turn to the register and Gracie whizzes by me smelling like watermelon candy and whiskey. Nearly bite my lip in half. Nothing's more irresistible than the smell of this woman.

Too quickly, the evening of laughter and drinks and darting here and there quiets down. The music switches off. The lights come up. And the club goes into standby mode.

I clink bottles and glasses as I clean them from the bar. Gracie sits opposite me with a tablet, taking stock. She looks so damn earnest with not a stitch of makeup, her hair pulled back, resting the tip of her stylus pen against her lower lip.

A server calls goodnight, and I wave.

Gracie lifts her head, gives her customary warning about letting Phil walk her to the car before turning her attention to me. Her bright green eyes are sharp and curious. "Where did you come from?"

Why does the fact that she wants to know about me cause my heart to beat faster? "I thought that was obvious. Kentucky."

"Let me guess. Your dad is one of those typical Southern fathers, super into his family and God and horses."

"Well, I could ride a horse long before I could ride a bike. But my dad's more interested in himself than family or even God. He's a faith healer."

Gracie cradles her chin in one hand. "That sounds pretty religious to me."

I pick up a rag and clean the bar. "The way my dad operates has nothing to do with God. He's a fraud."

"So, you never saw any miracles?"

She's half joking, by the tone, but I answer seriously. "I saw what he classified as miracles. People pretending to be healed because only unworthy or sinful people didn't get healed."

"Pretending? If someone shows up and can't walk, you can see if they've been healed or not, right?"

Funny she should choose that example. "I once saw an old woman who couldn't walk. We're in this big meeting hall. Folding chairs set up, fluorescent lights, incense, and Tiger Balm."

Finished with the rag, I put it in the bucket under the counter, lean against the bar directly across from her. "Dad went over to her. Now, he's a big, powerful guy. The kind of fellow who can intimidate with mannerisms and voice. Dad puts his large hands over hers, and his voice rings out." I raise my hands to demonstrate. "'Walk!'"

I lower my hands. "Moments like that, you could feel his power, feel the tension in the room, everyone standing up from their folding chairs, looking. It was something.

"This lady's feet began to move spastically. My heart starts to pound. It was going to happen. I knew she'd walk. People *ooh*ed and *aah*ed. Everyone praising God. Dad commanded even louder that she rise. His powerful voice gave me goose bumps.

"Her feet went twice as fast and she put her bony hands on the armrests of her wheelchair, tried to lift herself. Her arms shook, her legs gave, and she fell back into her seat with a cry."

Gracie's face follows the story, showing interest, then puzzlement, then sadness. She gets it. Some wouldn't.

"Dad told her, told all of us, it was her fault. She'd done something in her past, some wrong she needed to be forgiven for. If she repented and trusted God, she'd be healed. She began to cry. The whole congregation, including me, blamed her."

"That's awful."

"Yeah, but back then, because I'd never been taught to think any other way, I believed him."

Gracie rubs at her arms. "When did it change for you?"

"When I was seven, I nearly died from a bladder infection because my dad's thinking was that, if he couldn't heal me, or anyone in his *ministry*—and I use that term very loosely—then God had deemed us unworthy."

Her face shows stark disbelief. "That's crazy."

"It seems crazy to me now, too. Back then, trembling and sick and dying, I thought, 'Why did I lie about that cookie? Why did I forget to say *yes, ma'am*? Why won't God let me live?'"

Her face softens with empathy, not sympathy. I appreciate that. Nothing to feel sorry about. That part of my life made me the dogged, determined man I am.

"I've never heard you say *yes, ma'am*."

Can't help but smile at that. "You Northern girls beat it out of me. Nothing harder than trying to explain to some hot thing you're trying to make time with that *yes, ma'am* is just upbringing."

She laughs, but then her face grows serious. "How'd you survive the illness? Did you get better?"

The memory of that time pokes me in the ribs and, for a second, it's hard to breathe. I look past her to the empty bar, the strip-lights along the dance floor, giving myself a minute. Finally, I say, "My mom went against my dad, reached out to my uncle Harvey. He worked in law enforcement. Showed up with his gun and his partner, threatened an investigation if Dad came after us. An idle threat, but the old man wasn't so well-educated. He agreed. Uncle Harvey raised me, helped deprogram me. Thanks to him, I came to see the world differently. Maybe got a bit of a chip on my shoulder for people who try to force their views on others or try to force others into lives based on those views."

She lifts her eyes to me, and I can tell she understands what I'm saying. She opened up to me today, so I feel obliged to open to her. I'm laying it all out there. Why I'm here. Why I'm investigating her momma. Why I care.

Ball's in her court.

Chapter 24
Gracie

Seated at the bar of my empty club with the quiet of afterhours around me and the dim light shadowing Dusty's face, a chill rides down my body as I absorb what he is saying about his father. The guy was a manipulative and abusive man who nearly let his son die to keep the illusion that he was a faith healer. His statement, *"Maybe got a bit of a chip on my shoulder for people who try to force their views on others,"* expands into the quiet between us.

It echoes inside me, sending me a clear message about why he's here, what his motivation is in researching The Guild. I know now that my email somehow found its way to him, and I can't help but wonder at that. Of all the people in the world for my email to reach, it reached him.

Guilt begins to gnaw at my insides. It's not only that my email brought Dusty here, it's also what happened with Tony. Would my brother have been able to plan his betrayal if he hadn't met Dusty? If he hadn't had someone capable of embedding himself with Walid?

Swallowing the ball of sickness churning in my stomach, I push aside my tablet and look into Dusty's sun-soaked eyes. I need to correct his impressions, the false impressions my angry and emotional letter gave him.

"We had similar upbringings, but not exactly the same. Your father would've sacrificed you for his own sense of self-importance. Momma sacrifices herself to save others." I see that more clearly since John's visit. For years, Momma took my anger over John. I blamed her and Leland for forcing me to give up John to save him, but the truth is that John planned to go all along.

Dusty leans over the bar. His face is inches from mine. "I certainly am interested in learning more. Mind if I ask some questions?"

Well, that opened a whole can of worms. "Your breath smells really good. Did you eat one of my candies?"

"Way to avoid the question. And, yeah, I ate one." He licks a too-pink tongue across his lips. "Thought about you as I sucked on it."

Whoa. The statement and the sweet Southern sex dripping from his voice stimulates every hormone in my body. "You have to have sex with me."

His eyebrows shoot up.

Whoops. Did I, his boss for all intents and purposes, just order him to have sex with me?

Lowering my head, I squeeze my eyes closed tight. "I mean, that didn't sound right. Of course, you have a choice."

He says nothing and I raise my head. *Dusty? Where did he—*

I grab the sides of my barstool as it spins. Dusty stands before me, staring down, a little too serious, a little too close, and a lot too hot.

"Got a choice, do I?" He leans in. "Pretty obvious to me the only person here who needs a clear choice is you, so I'm going to ask. Knowing all the things you suspect about me, about why I'm here, are you really, really sure you want to sleep with me, Ms. Gracie Parish?"

Oh. Man. He's not messing around with that question. His breath is warm and sweet against my face.

Gracie, you need to say no. Tell him you don't sleep with the enemy or something equally self-righteous.

"I haven't had sex with a man in eighteen months."

That isn't self-righteous. That's an invitation.

He smiles a smile full of promise. "Got me beat. It's been six months, and I was tested for STDs at my last physical a few weeks ago. Passed with flying colors."

Six months? Why does that turn me on so much? "I'm tested regularly too and on the pill."

I hook my feet behind his legs and pull him closer. He lets out a breath that's part moan as he drops his head and takes my lips. His tongue slides into my mouth, bold and possessive, and I revel in the taste of him.

He angles his head, delves deeper with his tongue, and I find myself squirming in my seat. He tugs my T-shirt free from the waist of my jeans and his hand snake under and cups my breast. We groan simultaneously. The sound vibrates against our tangled tongues.

Now. This has to happen. *Now.*

We come up for air, our labored breaths loud in the quiet club. Dusty moves his mouth up to my ear. "Upstairs?"

Upstairs? Um, no. The servers for my family's operations fill half the space upstairs, not exactly something I want to show him when he's all but admitted he's investigating my family. *Mood killer.*

I shake my head and his eyebrows go up. He's no dummy.

With a shrug, he looks around the bar as if judging the strength of the tables or the softness of the chaises.

That won't work for me. "Not here," I say.

Dusty, as decisive as he is hot, fishes out his car keys and jingles them at me. "My place is real close."

"Text me the address. I'll meet you there."

Chapter 25
Dusty

Driving the deserted streets of what the locals call the Borough, I answer my cell on the first ring. Gracie's voice comes through the car's speakers as soft and sexy as the whisper of lingerie against skin. "I've been dreaming about having you in my mouth."

Holy... I grow hard enough to split denim. "I like where this is going. What do I feel like in those dreams?"

"Thick and hard." She certainly has me headed in the right direction. She pauses, and I know she's every shade of red. Can't wait to see how deep I can get that red to go. "I dream of taking the tip of you in, sucking, and using my hand to stroke you while I go down on you."

Lord. There are way too many lights on this street. I shift, pull at the tight crotch on my jeans. "Just inside your mouth?"

"No, other places, too, but, in my fantasies, I have a fondness for sucking you off."

"Good to know." *Seriously.*

"I have this fantasy about wanting to give you a blowjob on my knees. That's probably kind of submissive and not feminist at all, but I've actually never tried it."

Never? I gun my car through the yellow. Who designed this street? A light every ten feet. "Gracie, hun, I'm all about making your wishes come true."

She laughs, low and pleased. "I'm so wet just thinking about it. Thinking about you sliding into my mouth, sliding between my legs, and then pumping into me fast and hard. I want to see you lose control."

I'm getting dizzy from lack of blood flow to my brain. "Darlin', I'm not sure my insurance will cover collision-by-boner."

She laughs again. "I'm here."

She drives like a maniac. Thank the good Lord. "That's a good sign."

"It is?"

"Yep. I intend to make sure that isn't the last time tonight you get to where you're going before me."

I pull up a minute behind her. There's one major problem I can think of as I lead Gracie up the fire escape to my rental's private entrance. The ducks.

No grown woman wants to have sex while googly-eyed ducks peer down. And the things I intend to do to her required she be comfortable with vulnerability. Not happening if she gets a look at that awful mural.

Checking the alarm I installed hasn't been tampered with, I open the door and don't flick on the lights.

Gracie peers inside, then at me. "It's kind of dark."

I grasp her hand and pull her inside after me. "I'm sensitive about the lights."

She laughs. "I seriously doubt that."

Kicking the door closed with the toe of my boot, I pull her close, and we come together like fire and gasoline. I lay claim to her with kisses as long, hot, and needy as what I'll soon be pushing deep inside her.

Her soft fingers fumble under my shirt. She runs hungry nails along my abs to the waist of my jeans. She startles, looks down, realizing the entire head of my johnson pokes out from the waist of my jeans. "Oh."

This woman out and out murders me. "Impressed?"

She rubs the tip, the moisture there. *Fuck.* My eyes roll back in my head.

"Very," she breathes. "In my office... I hadn't..." She trails off, unbuttons my jeans, unzips them, puts her hand around my length and strokes.

I thrust into her hands and she makes a small whimpering sound. Not the last time I intend to hear that tonight. I nuzzle her ear. "That makes two of us."

"Strip," she says, squeezing me tight. "Hurry."

She lets me go and I spring into action, pulling my shirt off over my head, stripping off the boots, and stepping from my jeans like I'm hot-footing it across a black-sand beach in July.

Not fast enough. She's already naked.

Soft lights from outside filter through the blinds, revealing the curves of a body so ripe and beautiful, I swear the nine choirs of angels themselves sing *Hallelujah* along with me.

Those breasts, hips. Thighs. The gentle V of her... Lord. She is perfect.

I don't even think about it. I simply sink to my knees, wrap my arms around her, palm each round ass cheek, and put my hot mouth against her soft, slick center.

She lets out another soft whimper.

I moan against her hot, slick, and salty opening, growing painfully hard with every flick of my tongue against her clit.

She grabs my shoulders for support and makes soft mewling sounds that quickly turn into sharp, needy demands.

Is there any sweeter sound than the desperate pleas of this woman while I go down on her? Nothing. I want more. I want to have the heat currently against my mouth around my dick.

The thought makes me crazed as I tease and stroke, lick and suck her. Releasing the grip I have on her ass, I slip a hand between her legs, slide one and then two fingers inside her. For a moment, I rejoice in her softness. She's saturated and silky smooth.

"Dusty..." she moans. Her nails dig into my shoulders.

I pick up the pace until her moans grow higher and higher, then I slide the fingers on my other hand back and forth against that smooth skin that leads to her ass. Once, it's slick enough, I slip that finger into that tight opening.

She cries out, rocks her hot silkiness against my eager tongue, writhes against my quick, exploring fingers, bucking like she can't get enough of the sensations. "Please. Oh, please," she begs.

I can feel her tension building, feel as this perfect woman reaches that perfect point, and…

She screams my name as the orgasm takes her.

Warm liquid spills onto my tongue. So sweet the choir surely lift their voices. I lap it up. My dick, hard and full between my legs, is so ready for her I nearly come.

When her tremors slow then stop and I can tell by the way she braces against my head that her legs are ready to give out, I scoop her up and carry her to the bed.

Chapter 26
Gracie

I'm barely able to move as Dusty lowers me onto his bed. My head still spins from the intensity of the orgasm he gave me. My body sings with how he'd touched me, played me with his tongue and fingers. It was like he was everywhere.

I'm boneless and my legs naturally spread wide for him.

As hard as he is, he takes a long, lingering look at me. "You are so beautiful. Perfect, Gracie."

One knee on the bed, his hands explore, caress, and appreciate me, slowly moving up my legs. His touch is a hot worship.

I push my chest up and he answers, fondling my sensitive nipples, lightly pinching.

I groan and he takes one pink bud in his mouth. He sucks on it, moaning as if he's tasted the best dish in the world. I writhe with joy and need as he sucks, squeezes, and teases.

Tossing my head back and forth on the pillow, I beg, "Dusty... Dusty... Now."

Lingering for a moment on my breast, he lets the bud pop from his swollen lips with a hotly whispered, "Perfect," then his hard body aligns over my soft one.

I kiss him. Hungry. Demanding. Imploring. My lips tear at him. My hands drag at him. His cock throbs against me, and I beg him to enter me with a pump of my hips.

He positions himself and pushes inside me, just a little. "It's okay?" he asks.

I want to say *yes, hurry*, but a hiss of both pain and pleasure is all that emerges at the feel of him stretching me.

He groans. His breath is ragged, but he gives me a minute. Sweat slicks his skin. I can see his pulse working in his neck. Hear his heart pounding. He puts his lips by my ear. "Gracie, if this is too hard on you…"

I can't help it, I laugh. "Pun intended?"

"Nope. Not enough blood in my brain right now for puns, but I'm not a small man, so if…"

I wrap my legs around him and squeeze tight enough that he enters deeper into my body.

His eyes spring open, mouth works soundlessly for a moment. He looks down, visibly battling for control. "Grace." His voice is strained and somewhat awed. "You're so fuckin' tight."

I'm pretty sure my tightness has more to do with his size. I arch into him. "More."

He kisses me again. The scent of my own body salty on his lips, he takes me at my word and pushes deep inside.

I grunt. He groans. My slick warmth seems to lock around him. He's right—he *is* big. But I like it. He gives me time to adjust before pulling out slowly then thrusting back in, and again, slow and deep.

The teasing threat of an orgasm builds quickly. So quickly, I'm shocked and blurt out, "Faster."

I'm barely aware of his sexy chuckle or his hotly whispered, "Yes, ma'am."

He pushes fast and hard, sending fire shooting through my body and electric tingles bursting across my nerves. His cock rubs against the sensitive zone of my body just right, so that the coil of pleasure dances through my nerve endings.

The powerful need has me rising to meet him, tossing back my head, then biting him, then digging my nails into his back, shoulder, and bicep.

Each of his deep strokes meets my rising hips and rising voice. "Yes, Dusty, yes. That! Don't stop."

With each slam of his powerful body, tremors of desire climb higher and higher until, with a burst of blinding speed, the orgasm explodes, expanding through me in a thrumming level of electric bliss I didn't even know was possible.

I'm mindless with my response, babbling and frantic. He seems to revel in it, pushing his body into mine at breathtaking pace. I rejoice in the power of him, the way he fills me, takes me like he's making a point, like he's found his home, like this is the start of something that will continue every day from here on out.

The fury of my orgasm is met with his own cry, his lost rhythm, his mad thrusts. He curses then breaks inside me with a warmth that soaks into me as his hips buck then slow while he whispers a pleading, "Grace, Grace, Grace," into my hair.

After a moment, he rolls off, palming my hip. The wetness of him drips between my legs, and the feel of him spent is warm against me. I snuggle into him.

It takes us both a moment to catch our breath, but he seems to recover before me. He kisses me, wipes the tears that have slipped down my cheeks, then whispers in my ear, "I have no words for you, Grace. None."

I open my mouth to respond, but he kisses me silent, probing my mouth again with his commanding tongue, sending my blood to boil. I moan into his mouth. His big thumb finds the still sensitive nub at my core and begins to press hotly. He's taking control of me, working me up again.

"Dusty," I breathe.

"I want to see you come again."

"I can't," I say because I've never come three times in a row, ever.

"Pretty sure you can," he says as he works my clit with a pressure that's so delicious, I raise my hips and grind against his hand.

"Oh. Oh, God. Dusty."

"That's it, now. Look how beautiful you are." He increases his smooth pace while inserting two fingers inside me. He slides those fingers in and out quickly while increasing the lovely pressure against my clit.

I'm undone, dizzy with the onslaught, and completely under his control, so when he says, "Give it to me now, Grace; let me watch you come," I break apart under his hands.

I'm keening and throbbing and completely lost to the pleasure. The orgasm goes on twice as long as any I've ever had, with me moaning and writhing under his authority.

When he finally does release me, I'm so sensitive down there a brush of his breath against my clit could set me off again. I had no idea that was possible either.

He settles in next to me with a smug, "You can sleep now, Grace."

I'm unable to utter a word in response. Still throbbing between my legs, I'm pulled into a deep sleep.

#

I can't help but grin when I wake to Dusty looking down at me with soft eyes. Nothing could've prepared me for how good having sex with him would feel, how quickly I'd climax. I've never come that fast and hard in my life. I can't help but marvel at the way our bodies fit together to cause that reaction. As he said, it's perfect.

I want to say a thousand things. Two thousand, but all I can manage is, "Are those cartoon ducks on your ceiling?"

He laughs and says, "Ignore the ducks, Grace. Me, I'm still seeing stars from the best sex of my life." He kisses me, presses his hard cock against my thigh, traces the tattoo on my hip, the apple and the hand holding the apple out. "It's beautiful, like you. When'd you get this?"

It's been a long time since I've thought about the crazy two weeks that had led to my tattoo. It'd been only a short while before my bio mom had shown up. It'd been a testing of boundaries when Justice and I had run away. "I was young, still fifteen."

"That young? Tell me more."

I smile as he nuzzles my neck. Dusty, it turns out, likes to cuddle. Usually I'm not a cuddler, but, with him, it's different. "At fifteen, a bit of a wild child, I snuck out with Justice, and I wanted something that symbolized how dangerous I felt. Dangerous enough to change the world with one bad decision. With one wicked offer."

I turn to meet his eyes which are filled with wild need and honest interest. We lay face-to-face. "And since, in fairy tales, a hand offering someone an apple always seems to start the most trouble, that's what I wanted for my tattoo."

He kisses my nose. "Thank you for sharing that with me, Grace."

Grace. Not Gracie. I'd noticed the change. "I like when you say Grace. It sounds... nice, but why the change?"

He exhales a steady stream of air, fanning hair across my cheek, and even this little connection brings me joy. "Because I don't know any other way to show my gratitude for the bounty you shared with me last night than to say Grace."

Oh. Wow. I take back anything I've ever thought about not liking puns that involve my name. "If it's possible to be completely comfortable and utterly keyed up all at once, that's how I feel right now."

"Keyed up, huh?" Again, he presses his hard-on against me. "We'll get to that, but first, I need to set some things straight."

"Okay. I'm not sure I like where this is going."

"I need you to know that, right now, this is more than sex for me, so I don't think it's right to let this go further without me giving you the truth."

The truth? My mind perks up and begins pacing the inside of my skull. I know what he's going to say and I don't want to hear it.

Chapter 27
Gracie

In the dark of Dusty's rented room, I'm cradled in his arms, completely comfortable, but starting to panic. How do I get him to shut up?

Oblivious to my panic, he says, "Some time ago, I received an email at the FBI, an email I'm fairly sure you wrote."

Nope. No. No. No. I hold my breath as my mind screams for him to stop talking.

He runs a hand affectionately up and down my arm. "Read that thing a thousand times. Got it memorized."

Oh. My throat grows tight. I'd sent that letter in the hopes of reaching someone, sharing a pain that seemed too great, and the fact that he'd gotten it should be amazing, but it puts everything in danger—whatever this is between us, my relationship with Momma, my siblings, and the important work The Guild does. All in danger.

"I guess you can say I became a little obsessed with taking down the woman who would train children to be vigilantes."

My eyes widen. My heart lurches. He's after Momma? Not The Guild, but *Momma*?

"I worked on the case for a few months, set myself up with Tony, gained his trust, and tried to work my way inside your family so I could get the information on Mukta."

For a moment, I think I'm going to be sick.

"Grace? Are you okay?"

I try to focus on my inhale and exhale, but my heart is

pounding, my chest feels tight with terror, dread, and a loss of control. I manage, "You're after Momma." Heavy breaths. "You're trying to lock her up." Panicked breaths. "Take her away from my siblings—from me—based on an unfair and emotional email?"

"Whoa. Slow down." He slides his arm around me. "Grace, are you okay?"

Okay? I'm not okay. My vision starts to dim. Of course I'd known he was investigating my family, but that he's specifically after Momma is a punch to the gut. I've been lying to myself by thinking I could control all the horrible things that might result from that stupid email, and now it's so obvious I can't.

"Grace, calm down now. Your heart is beating a mile a minute."

"Calm down? I've risked my family, Momma, and if that isn't shameful enough, I slept with the man determined to destroy my family."

Will I ever learn? Forget about trusting someone else, I shouldn't trust *myself*.

"I don't want to destroy anything. Listen to me."

"I have to leave."

"What? Grace, please don't leave."

I try to slide out of bed, but his arms tense around my waist. He lets out a troubled breath. "Grace, please. I messed up. Said things out of order. Look, I need to tell you something about your dad. You know him, right? Rush?"

He knows about my father?

"I believe Mukta is blackmailing Senator Rush." His voice quickens. "I think she's using your existence to control how he directs government funds and votes on legislation, among other things."

Blackmailing? Over me? "Is this how you'll set up Momma? Is this your case?"

"Stop that now." He puts his other hand under my chin, turns my head so that I'm looking directly at him. He brings his face close to mine. "That's not what this is about. I want to help you. Whoever is after you hasn't gone away. They let things cool off, but they'll come back. Hard." He leans his forehead to mine. "And here's the thing I should've said first. I want to protect you, stop whoever is after you. So much so, I'm willing to give up my case, to trust you, trust that your momma isn't who I think she is, but I need to see for myself. I need to talk to her, ask her some questions. Okay?"

My stomach rolls so fast I'm pretty sure it twists into a knot, a complicated Gordian knot. "Are you seriously using this moment between us, my fear over the fact that someone is after me, to try to get in to question Momma?"

I know I should be cooler than this, better at controlling my emotions, but I can't be, not when it hurts this badly.

He shakes his head. "Don't do that. Don't write me off that way. I'm willing to trust you. Are you willing to trust me? Trust that that isn't my motivation here?"

"Trust you? You just admitted to a thousand lies."

"To tell the truth, Grace. I admitted to a bunch of lies so I could tell you the truth and tell you that I want to help protect you. Please settle down. Take a breath and think about what I'm saying, what I'm risking here. If you think about—"

I push away from him and climb out of bed. "I can't march a fudgin' FBI agent into my fudgin' family home like it's no fudgin' big deal."

Especially when I'd sent the email that launched his investigation. I begin finding and putting on my clothes.

Dusty sits up. "Come back to bed. Let's talk about things."

"Talk? You threw everything but the kitchen sink at me. No, Dusty, I need to—*"to get away*—"think."

He climbs out of bed, walks over, and intertwines his fingers with mine. "Let's not be reckless. Stay with me. I can't help if you won't let me in."

"Being with you is reckless." I shake him off, push him back, then finish putting on my clothes. "You can help by giving me space."

A moment of pain, of rejection, flashes across his face, but he quickly schools his features to FBI-empty. "Okay. So, maybe we can talk if I show up early for work next?"

Work? I slip into my shoes. "You no longer work at my club, Dusty. I'd think that should be painfully obvious."

Chapter 28
Gracie

I pull into the gravel lot behind Club When? feeling confused, worried, heartsick, and tired. Thanks to a night of great sex followed by a morning of hard truths, I didn't get a lot of sleep.

I drag my body toward the club as the sun begins to warm the air. It's going to be another hot one, just like yesterday, but that's the only thing that's the same since yesterday. So much has changed.

First, John told me it wasn't me who sent him away—something I'd held against Momma for a decade. He'd always intended to leave. Momma lied to me so she'd know what to do, if she should take John's memory. All the time I'd sacrificed for John, he'd thought I wasn't good enough to be in Ty's life. Well, we'll see about that.

Then Dusty... Oh, I put a hand to my heart as I walk across the lot. Dusty *had* to tell me he's not trying to take down The Guild in general, but Momma specifically. He wants to destroy my family. I really hope no one else decides to tell me any more truths today. I have an honesty headache.

Waving a wrist over the security pad, I put in my personal code so the florescent lights blink awake as I enter. The lingering smell of fried food and booze envelopes me. Home sweet home. Boxes from yesterday's delivery line the hallway. It's going to be a busy day, but, first, I need food because I'm sure I burned two thousand calories last night.

Inside the club kitchen, I drop my purse, collect the

ingredients for an omelet, and take out a frying pan. My cell rings. My heart picks up its pace because it's too early for a casual call.

I check the screen. Not Dusty.

"Hey, Victor." I spray cooking oil into the skillet, then turn on the burner.

He hesitates. "Roja, I'm going to want every salacious detail of last night's sexcapade, but, first, we got a problem."

Only Victor would hear my stupid moaned-sore throat and make the correct assumption. "What problem?"

"Another fifty thousand went out of John and Ellen's account and into another offshore account."

I will do what I have to do to protect my family. Remember that.

"Sugar." I turn down the burner.

"That's not all. I've gone through security footage outside your club and spotted Ellen sneaking around, taking photos."

My empty stomach rolls, and I have to swallow sudden moisture. Could Ellen know about my family? I've suspected. If she does, is she looking for intel on us? I say, "Momma could be blackmailing Rush," and break a few eggs into a bowl. "Perhaps using my existence as his illegitimate child to get him to support legislation that mirrors her agenda." An agenda that often clashes with big businesses with deep pockets.

"Mierda. Looks like we have a winner in the explosive news department, but that's not to say your news rules out John and Ellen. Rush has obviously been putting up with this for some time."

"No. It definitely doesn't rule out Rush either." Not after that confrontation with John. "But I agree Rush has been putting up with this for a long time, so why go after me now? Also, Porter had me followed. I confronted the man he sent after me and sent back a message to let Porter know I'm not a danger to him."

"Coño. Porter coming out of the woodwork kind of blows away everything else I was going to say about the lower half of the Rush kids."

"Tell me anyway."

"Well, the youngest male, George, has a sick kid. IMO, he spends too much time in the hospital, at a support group, and researching to bother with you. Plus, his motivation is low. He doesn't seem to care about his father's politics. The second oldest boy, Quincy, is a heart surgeon. He's mega-rich and married with two kids and two mistresses. He's got no time for murdering you. Oh, I have some great sex tapes of your half-brother, by the way."

"Gross. The first two Rushes on my list aren't likely either. They're close and have built their own digital design business. Their politics actually lean away from Rush."

"Interesting. Lots of computer geeks in that family. The daughter is some kind of celebrity in the geek world. Two million followers for this hot chick who works artificial intelligence."

So far, I've only dipped a toe in the AI waters. "On a side note, I'd love to know more about her work. It's a fascinating field."

"You two would have a lot to talk about. She's the queen of geeks. She has a once-in-a-generation talent for AI, and she's the Rush I'd most pick to change the world on her own. Again, not a huge interest in Poppa Rush's work, and her personal life suggests a more progressive bent."

"In what way? I thought she was in a traditional relationship, engaged, right?"

"Yeah, but rumor has it that her bodyguard is part of the equation. Not only sleeping with her, but with him. There a throuple on the DL."

Cradling the phone against my shoulder, I break some eggs one-handed, whisk them in the heated pan. "So, she's playing by her own rules in her own world and living large."

"Sí. From what I can tell, Porter has the most to lose if Rush goes down."

"That's my take, too," I say. "The other family members all have their own lives. Even Rush's wife, Carrie, has her career as an interior designer."

"Exactamente. And if the blackmail is true, Porter definitely won't want the fact that his father plays ball with Mukta Parish in the news. Their donor base would go nuts. Your mom isn't exactly beloved among the rich and greedy."

"Understatement. I also found out from my investigation of Porter that he's had some personal issues, including a recent ugly divorce, so his career might be the only thing going right for him."

"We're getting closer on this," Victor says.

After what Dusty said about the killer hitting harder when things die down, I'm anxious to have answers today, but narrowing our suspects from ten to three isn't nothing. "Yeah. Having only John and Ellen or Porter to look into makes it essential to go hard on the intrusion of privacy."

"Verdad, Roja. I'll plant a bug and see what I can hear from John and Ellen, but we shouldn't risk that with Porter."

"I'll take Porter. I have a few cyber tricks up my sleeve. Let's touch base tomorrow.

"Un momento. There's something else."

"Something else?"

"Yeah. Since you're sleeping with that FBI guy—"

"That's none—"

"Be careful. He's not playing straight with you."

The hair on my arms stands on end. "What are you saying?"

"I spotted something in the club security footage you sent me. It's blurry, but, right now, my Spidey sense is tingling. Can you let me see footage from farther back?"

"Why?"

"I'm not ready to share with the class yet because I might be wrong, and, if I am, it's not something I want you near, trust me on that."

"My trust factor is a little off right now, especially when it comes to Dusty."

"I get that. But let me investigate my suspicions first."

"Fine."

"Gracias. See you tonight."

"Tonight?"

He hangs up. I flip my omelet. He expects me to let him upstairs to look at the security footage tonight? Victor is one of the busiest people I know, especially with Sandesh distracted with his new wife, my sister Justice. If he wants to expedite his search... this can't be good.

My ears perk up at a sound in the club. Not the normal *click* and *whoosh* of club fridges or ice makers, but something definitely human. No one should be here this early. Plus, my alarm would've told me if someone had come in. Turning off the burner, I remove my gun from my purse, then slink along the dim corridor that connects the kitchen to the bar.

I peer around the doorway, gun raised, and spot her at a table, eating a bowl of Cheerios, judging by the big yellow box. I lower my weapon, then step out from behind the wall. "Cee. Are you crazy? I could've killed you."

Her eyes widen and she freezes with the spoon halfway to her mouth. "Sorry. I didn't want to interrupt your call."

Yikes. Did I say anything important? "When did you get here?"

"Around four."

My annoyance ignites a fire under my cheeks. "How do you keep getting out of the school?"

"Friends in low places."

That's a telling answer. No wonder Momma showed such an interest in me spending time with Cee. She's trying to juggle a rebellion among the younger kids. "Wait. Why didn't my security system alert me that you'd entered? I should've gotten a text. How'd you get in?"

Cee waves her wrist. "I used my chip and the code I saw you punch in last time I was here."

No she didn't. "I change the code every week as protocol demands, and only Leland and Internal have access to the codes. Who programmed your chip?"

Cee's eyes grow wide and guilty.

I press. "The only person in your class who has those kinds of cyber skills is Rome."

She bites her lower lip. "I'm not a narc."

This is turning into a ball of wax. Cee's unit, Vampire Academy, isn't only the largest unit with six kids, it's the most aggressive, testing every boundary, and Cee seems to be leading the charge. If my sister Justice was here right now, I'd be able to tell her that I told her so, because I did.

"That answer's not going to work for me." I hold up a hand to stop her protest. "We're going to unpack all of this, but, first, I have to finish making my omelet. I'm starving."

"I bet, after such a long night."

Smart mouth. "Wait here."

I take my good old time getting my breakfast ready, and it's not because I don't want to fight with Cee and uncover more truths. Okay, it is exactly that. It's been a year-long morning.

With my omelet plated, I return to Cee, sit down opposite of her, and decide to hand her an ultimatum. "You and Rome have to stop messing with the security chips or I'm going to inform Leland of the Philly job, and he'll come down on you like a ton of bricks."

Cee slams her hand on the table, causing the silver spoon in her now empty bowl to jump. "They already have. I'm practically a prisoner. They won't let me do any research!"

Whoa. Angry much? "League operations are shut down because of the drone attack. We have to protect our people, too, and it's not like we're doing nothing. We're doing a lot in other areas."

Like blackmailing a senator to support our agenda.

"That doesn't help me." Cee fidgets. "When I can't forget them. When I think of them every night. When I worry about them."

Swallowing a bite of omelet, I take the bait. "Who?"

She sits forward. "The other girls like me—they're scared,

uncertain. Not understanding how men's desires reduce us to just a body. As if we have no souls." Her lips tighten for a moment, then release. "Please. Allow me to do the work. Please."

The tug on my heart is immediate and strong. This is the first time Cee has shown a motivation that isn't prompted by anger or revenge. As someone who grew up safe and loved, I've always felt protective of my adopted siblings. And, right now, with Cee's eyes slick with tears and fierce with intensity, I'm a goner.

"I know what it's like to believe that what you're doing, what The Guild does, is the only way to fight back, but the best way for you to help right now is to train and go to school. One day, you will be able to do the work."

She frowns at me. Truth. As much as I complain about The Guild, my time in the world has only made me believe more in the work we do. Yes, sometimes Momma's tactics are questionable, even hurtful, but her intention is to help, to free, to rescue others, especially girls like Cee, and intention matters in this world.

Fudge buckets. "Let me drive you home. We can talk more on the way." I scan the chairs close to us, then search the floor. "Do you have a bag or anything with you?"

Cee nods, looks away. "Yes. Upstairs."

Upstairs? A finger of foreboding sweeps down my spine. "You managed to get upstairs? That requires a completely different set of permissions, Cee. You and Rome have got to knock it off. That's unacceptable to me and an invasion of The Guild's protocols since the servers are up there."

Angry again, Cee stands up and stomps her foot. "Do you want lions or rabbits in The Guild?"

"Neither. We want foxes. Cunning. Not rage. You need to stop being so angry."

"You need to stop being so afraid."

What? "I'm not."

"Yes, you are. You lost your son and gave up your courage and your heart."

I stand up and point a finger at her. "Don't you dare."

She dares.

"Now, you're afraid of being one of us, of coming out from behind your computer screen to do the work, of finding out that the family you still have,"—she pauses, swallows what seems to be a genuine emotion—"is worth getting to know."

My face flushes with heat and, to my horror, tears prick at the corner of my eyes. *She's kind of right. But I can't stomach that right now.* "Look, I get how tempting it must be to do Guild work when you have so many resources behind you, but The Guild doesn't let teens run operations. It's my job as your older sister to make sure you complete your training in a place that is safe and secure before you get anywhere near the field."

Cee shakes her head. "No place is safe." She gestures around at the club. "You think you're safe? This place can't protect you. It won't. Nothing will."

Gooseflesh rises across my skin. Why is it this particular sibling can be both a needy child and the scariest human on the planet? That almost sounded like a threat.

I pick up my plate and napkin. "Let's get your stuff."

Chapter 29
Dusty

Not much can ruin a stroll through the charming sidewalks of Bristol, PA along the Delaware River, with its antique stores, mom-and-pop coffee shops, bookstores, and taverns. Cute as all hell... but too bad my brain won't let me enjoy it. Keeps replaying Grace's reaction this morning and hammering me with it. The way her face had heated. Her eyes had watered. Her body had shaken at my confession. That image pretty much obliterates cute as hell. Makes my chest hurt, and I can't text or call her because she asked me for space.

Space sucks when I want to be holding her.

After skirting an timeworn washboard and a pram carriage in front of the antique shop next door, I enter the restaurant where Mack and I are meeting. It's an old timey diner—rectangular booths, steel-poled barstools, and a long Formica countertop.

I automatically note the number of people inside and where they're sitting. Not too busy. Practically empty. There're two women in a booth and three guys at the counter. There's one waitress and one fry cook visible through the serving window.

Swinging into the last booth, I put my back to the wall with a view of the front door, kitchen door, and reflection of the restroom doors in the mirrored glass at the other end of the diner.

The waitress, a middle-aged woman with a been-there, done-that smile, hands me a menu with a, "You let me know when you're ready, handsome."

"Thanks. Coffee for now," I say, "I'll order food when my friend gets here. I'm a bit early." By design. I like to arrive early to take in the surroundings and make a note of things. Recon never hurt anyone, and it's saved my ass on multiple occasions.

It's a good twenty minutes before Mack shows and I'm on my second cup of coffee. He's wearing a suit as trim as his lanky frame. In all the time I've known Mack, I've never seen him put on an ounce—not of muscle and not of fat. He's immune to both, apparently. In his dark suit, with his *Mission: Impossible* shades and his G-man swagger, Mack couldn't look more Fed if he had a bard following him around singing about his Quantico exploits. Gracie would hate him on sight.

Must not think of how my spy lover would feel about my spy boss. Or about anything that happened with her last night. I push *those* hot images of her away, far away.

I semi-stand as I shake his hand.

Mack slides into the booth. "You look distracted."

No shit. "No more than usual. How's the fort?"

"Still secure. How's the investigation?"

Here we go. "Investigation stalled. No leads. Getting nowhere with the asset."

Nowhere I can put in a report, anyway.

Mack's eyebrows go up high enough to qualify as UFO, but before he can ask, the waitress shows up, drops off two glasses of water, then fills my coffee again. She tries to hand Mack a menu, but he shakes his head. "Burger. No bun. No fries. Black coffee."

"You're going to live to be a thousand, Mack. And not one day is going to be even a tiny bit fun." I hand the waitress my menu. "Give me the same with cheese fries and a sesame bun."

She smiles at me before leaving, and I take that smile as approval for a healthy appetite.

Once she's clear, Mack's dark eyebrows pinch together at the bridge of his nose. "Kind of surprised you admitted that about the investigation, Dusty. That's part of why I asked you to come today."

"It is?"

"Yeah. I think you should let this case go."

I open my mouth to object, to talk about the sacrifices I've made, to talk about the Parish kids, to talk about… things I thought I knew, but ain't so sure about anymore.

But I close my mouth instead.

Mack just rolled a girder off my shoulders. After the last year working my way in with the Parish family, getting to know their business practices, getting to like them—more than like some of them—I've been fighting a growing sense of wrong. Judging by Grace and Tony, those kids were raised to care for others and themselves, and, honestly, what they do outside the law is a drop in the bucket compared to some—a drop that weighs toward justice.

Still, I find myself clenching and unclenching my hands.

"I know what you're thinking," Mack says. "You put it all on the line. Your job, your life, your own money, and ended up with the same results. Could've just stayed home."

"Way to cheer me up."

He grimaces. "Sorry. But I think you've got to face facts. We're never going to get them on the vigilante stuff. Whatever they were doing, they're not doing now. They're spooked from the drone attack, from having our guys all over them, and they've gone underground."

True. Plus, Grace pegged my cover the day I'd strolled into town. I bite back a smile. Might be at loose ends for a little while… which could give me time to find out what this is between me and Grace. Will she agree to see me? She has to know, way down where it matters, that there's something between us that's more than sex.

Mack twists his water glass, sizing up its cleanliness. Satisfied, he removes the paper from his straw and takes a sip. "Look, all the doom-and-gloom silence isn't necessary. It's not a total loss. I still want you in town so you can concentrate on the blackmail."

I sit up straighter, as straight as if someone shoved a steel pole up my ass. "What?"

"I know what they have on Rush—or pretend to have. Mukta Parish has an old video of Gracie's mother claiming Rush drugged and raped her."

"Rush drugged and raped Sheila Hall?" Does Grace know? "How'd you—"

"Digital copies were anonymously sent to the Chester office last night. No sooner did I hang up with you than I had that proof in my hot hands."

"You were sent digital copies of Grace's biological mother accusing Rush of rape?"

"That's what one recording said. Turns out Mukta has been extorting multiple government officials, not just Rush, with different information. She's been doing it for ages."

I lean forward. My heart rate picks up because anonymous copies of this blackmail scheme appearing in Mack's lap while I'm investigating the Parish family doesn't seem a coincidence. "Explain how Mukta orchestrates this bribery."

"Take, for example, Rush."

"Yeah. Start there."

"Rush sleeps with that woman—"

"You mean Gracie's mom, Sheila? The woman he raped?"

"What if it wasn't rape? What if she lured him to sleep with her? Then the Parish family makes a tape with Sheila, looking so young and innocent, claiming Rush drugged and raped her."

Looks like Mack has already condemned Sheila. I want to argue, but I'm smarter than that. I feel him out. "Who's to say he didn't?"

"Exactly, and he wasn't the only one Mukta set up this way. I don't know how many men have been blackmailed, but I've seen a couple of these recordings. Same girl, Sheila, but each recording accuses a different man."

"So, you have recordings with Sheila Hall claiming different men drugged and raped her?"

"She never mentions them by name. There's someone asking her leading questions. She answers the questions."

"The interviewer asks leading questions like was it this guy, was it that guy?"

"Exactly. It's bullshit, but might be enough to kill a political career."

I'm still trying to wrap my head around this so-called scheme. "Let me get this straight. You're in possession of different videos questioning Sheila Hall, and each one has a different politic or VIP's name that she accuses as she answers?"

Mack nods.

"And you have proof this was sent to other men besides Rush, proof the Parish family blackmailed them all? Along with men who were blackmailed willing to say so?"

"Not yet. The videos are thirty years old. Out of the recordings we have, Rush is the only person still in government and the only one who apparently produced a kid. Two of the blackmail victims are dead. One had a heart attack six months ago and the other shot himself in the head two weeks ago."

That's suspicious. "Anybody else?"

"That we know? There's a federal judge who's no longer on the bench. He's got Alzheimer's. I went to see him this morning. Saddest shit ever. Kept asking for his wife."

He'd been to see the judge? Investigating on his own? "So, except for Rush, none of these recordings are currently in use. And there's no way of corroborating the other stories? Sounds like a convenient way to get Rush off the hook for something pretty damn heinous. Who's to say he didn't alter the blackmail recording sent to him, then send the altered recordings to you? He had to suspect the truth might come out, so maybe he's trying to muddy the waters. Have you had the recordings digitally verified?"

I lean back as the waitress puts our food on the table, asks if we need anything else. I smile at her. "No thanks, darling. This'll do for now."

She looks at Mack in question, but he waves her off and picks up his fork and knife. "Give me a day or two, Dusty. I know this isn't what you originally wanted, but you're being a little hostile considering I'm giving you the Parish matriarch. She's been controlling government, changing laws, diverting government funds to support this crazy women-centered agenda for years. We only need more proof. As you pointed out, so far, this is weak."

"Meaning, the answer to my question is no, you haven't authenticated the recordings."

Mack slices his burger, delivers a bite to his mouth with the fork. For such a dainty action, he doesn't seem to care about talking with his mouth full. "The recordings are copies. I got the lab on it. We'll see. But I'm pretty sure we'll need the originals to determine that shit."

I push away my plate since my stomach won't accept food right now. I know Mack, know he's ambitious and that he feels he has walked into something big, something that could get him in good with the future president. I ask, "Any other proof that she was bribing officials using these doctored recordings?"

Mack gestures with a forkful of meat. "Years ago, someone filed a lawsuit worth tens of millions against one of Mukta Parish's companies. The case was thrown out by the same judge—Judge Roberts—I mentioned. Months later, Roberts was photographed at a fundraiser with Mukta Parish. It shows her and the judge in what looks like an intense conversation."

"That's light beer mixed with water. Weak."

"Yeah. Well, like I said, we're just getting started. Things will unravel quickly once we start pulling the threads. Mukta Parish is devious, but we can get her on this blackmail scheme."

"You sound pretty sure."

Mack cuts another triangle of meat. "Last night, I reached out to Rush's son, Porter. I spoke with him on my way over. His father might be willing to testify against Mukta."

He reached out to Porter? The guy, along with his father,

might be trying to kill Grace. "He's willing to testify? Admitting he's been Mukta's puppet will ruin any chance at the presidency."

Chewing, Mack shakes his head. "Not necessarily. He never played ball with her. Any decisions he made for legislation aligned with his values, but also protected his family. It wasn't until she tried to secure a cabinet position that he came to us."

I lean back in my seat. Of course, Rush and his son would love to play victims fighting back. Standing up for what was right even if it might cost him the presidency. Mack knows that. Has to. "And you think his constituents will buy that?"

"Buy what? Rush is taking on people like Mukta, women who would use and abuse the system, claiming victimhood in order to gain money and extraordinary rights. He's standing up to them. Let's face it, his base will eat up the idea of Mukta getting her comeuppance."

Fuck. Mack is all in. People always imagine informants as lowlifes, but it's the assets in high places that rate. No higher place than the presidency. "Mack, tell me you aren't trying to free up a candidate for president." *At the expense of Mukta's family.* "A guy who, once in office, would be beholden to the Bureau?"

Mack stops with his fork halfway to his mouth. He lowers it. "If it helps our reputation, gets us a friend in the White House, maybe more funding, and takes Mukta and even a couple members of her family off the streets, I see no down side."

Looks like Mack has found a way to go from a so-so career to being upwardly mobile. "Hold on a sec. What do you mean a couple members of her family? I thought this was about Mukta."

"Mukta and anyone else involved in the bribery."

The hairs on the back of my neck stand on end. "Are you trying to tie Grace Parish to this whole thing?"

"Tie her to it? She *is* tied to it. It's her father. We have evidence that she has hacked into the senator's home computers and his campaign. Among other things."

I lean into the space between me and Mack, my arms resting far over what can be considered the table center. "What things?"

"Don't worry about it."

"Who's looking into who sent you the recordings? Is it you?"

"Leave it."

"No. I won't. You're putting Grace in more danger. Ignorant people might hate Mukta—she wears a hijab, is overly educated, wealthy, and ferociously outspoken—but Grace isn't so easy to hate. She's as sweet as apple pie, beautiful, and runs her own business. No matter what evidence you have, Rush won't want her out there speaking for herself, speaking against him. You just made her even more of a target."

Mack's eyebrows rise. "You seem to be getting a little agitated and paranoid."

"You're the reason, Mack. You're the reason people don't trust us, don't trust us to do our job, don't trust that we're making decisions based on our roles as defenders instead of what's best for our institution or our careers. You're what's wrong with this country, the Bureau."

Standing up, Mack throws down a ten-dollar bill. "Why don't we touch base after you've had some time to digest?" Head full of steam, he walks out of the restaurant.

I see him texting as he walks. A moment later, my cell beeps.

You're off the case. If you do anything to jeopardize this investigation, I will have you arrested.

A fistful of angry strides later, I find myself back on the pleasant streets of Bristol, delivering my resignation to the swell of Mack's too-straight nose. And jaw. And thick skull.

The sizzle of a Taser hits my ears a blink before fifty thousand volts squeeze my body down to manageable. I drop to the sidewalk with my jaw tight and my body rigid.

Fucking Mack. Can't throw a punch to save his life.

Chapter 30
Gracie

Music pumps through Club When?'s speakers in a pounding rhythm that gyrates through the bodies that bump and grind on the dance floor. Behind the bar, I mix a mojito. Even the wild abandon of my customers can't lift my mood. It actually makes me miss Dusty more. Work is a little duller, a little lonelier, without his good-natured humor and easy-going manner.

Yikes. I have to stop thinking about him.

I force myself to focus on making the servers' drinks. At least I managed to get help behind the bar tonight. My re-hired bartender is dealing with the people leaning across the bar to order drinks while I handle the servers' requests.

She's a good hire. Hard working and quick, but not as fun as...

A little niggle in my awareness alerts me to his presence, and I try to push that sensation down as a wave of desire and heat light up my insides.

Forcing myself to finish the order, I pour a draft beer, then put it on the tray before glancing up.

Dusty leans against the end of the bar where I'm working. "I need to talk to you."

The little butterflies in my stomach wing up my throat to flutter and dance.

Dang, he's so good-looking. Heat kisses my cheeks as a memory of him entering me, seizing me and bringing me, shaking and writhing, to pure bliss surfaces. This is a problem. When someone can make you feel as good as he makes me feel, they have power over you. I refuse to be powerless.

Wait. Why is he here when I asked for space? Rude.

I pick up the next drink order. "You'll have to wait."

His honey eyes flash. "Grace."

My breasts perk up and pay tight attention. *Way to go, tatas, why not send up an I-want-you-bad signal flare?* One that matches the hot patches of red now marching across my face and down my neck.

Control. Make the drink. I turn to the blender and ignore him. When I'm done, I finally give him my attention and find... *What the what?*

A beautiful young woman with dark hair stands at Dusty's side, slides him a beer, and points to his bruised and scraped knuckles. How did he hurt his hands? Was he in a fight?

The girl runs a finger along his injury. Classic pick-up. Got to admire her tactics. Not shy. Not fawning. A direct get-the-guy-to-talk-about-himself-and-see-if-he's-interested move.

For his part, Dusty looks like a deer in headlights. I watch with growing amusement as Agent Leif McAllister tries to find a graceful way out of the conversation.

He hesitates over a few pleasantries, smiles, sweats, and then, seeing me watching, motions toward me and says, "I'd like you to meet my good friend, Grace."

The brunette with a killer tan—or great genes—looks over. Finished making a pina colada, I put the slip on the waiting server's tray and approach Dusty and the woman. I smile at her. "What can I get you to drink? On the house, because if you've had to deal with this guy, you deserve compensation."

Dusty puts a hand to his chest. "Now, Grace, I'm a little hurt you wouldn't give me a higher recommendation."

Ah, stupid fair skin. I can feel myself turning lady-you-have-no-idea-how-good-he-is red. Followed by angry-emoji-face red.

The brunette's eyes bounce between me and Dusty, but she doesn't seem embarrassed or uncertain. She shrugs. "I'll have a gin and tonic."

Wow. A straight shooter all the way down to her drink. I quickly make her order and slide it over to her.

The straight shooter takes the glass, raises it in *thank you*, then clinks it with Dusty's bottle before walking away.

I watch her go. How cool would it be to never turn all shades of red in a somewhat awkward situation?

The light plays across Ms. Cool's shimmery silver cocktail dress as she skirts the dance floor.

Her drink hand comes up, and there's a flash and boom that lifts her and drives her across the room.

Chapter 31
Gracie

Everything changes in a second. The blast sends not only the cool chick but dancers and debris flying across the club.

I am frozen in horror. Me. A person trained, with quick reactions times, who studied martial arts, who likes to run, and I can't move a muscle.

Shock keeps me rooted in place as fire and noise and smoke punch through the air.

And then I'm on the floor, behind the bar, under Dusty's heavy, protective weight.

I struggle to get up, feeling ice cubes under my back and his heat on my front. He doesn't let me up. His voice insistent in my ear growls, "Stay down."

I'm about to argue, to complain, because now that I've had a moment, I realize I need to do something, to help. There's another explosion and another. Shards of glass beat around me like hot spikes.

Dusty has me so locked down, I can barely turn my head, but I see the roadway of smoke driving across the ceiling, and, after a moment of anguish, I push against Dusty's chest. "Fire."

He rolls off and helps me to my feet. Blood runs down his face and neck from the shards of glass from the explosion behind the bar. There was more than one explosion.

Dusty's expression is calm and his eyes are dead serious as he quickly runs hands up and down my body, stopping in places where I've been cut. "Are you okay, Grace?"

Surprised to see buds of blood rolling down my arm, I can only nod while, beyond the bar, the entire club is in a panic.

Their panic is like another blast wave, sending people racing, stumbling over bodies, shoving toward the exit.

The club's front doors quickly became choked with the pressing mob. Smoke begins to compress the air. I consider a thousand options in a thousandth of a second. Soon the sprinklers will go off, increasing panic, and people will push harder to escape, trample, and die or kill in their fear.

The emergency system has already called 9-1-1, but they won't get here in time to stop the crush. There's a back door, but I have no idea how bad the fire is back there. Besides, trying to get the attention of a panicked mob to give them instructions on how to get out the back will be impossible. I need to create another way out, a place people can see, so they go that way and ease the crush at the front door.

The stained-glass windows! Handcrafted and specially made for the club by my bio mom, they are large enough for people to get through and close enough to the floor that no one has to climb or jump too far.

Tiptoeing, I reach Dusty's ear and shout, "We need to break the stained-glass windows, create a way out that panicked people can see and access without us having to tell them."

He nods and shouts back, "I'll get the big window by the front."

The big one. The one that will be harder to reach with the mob surging to the front door. Before I can object, he vaults over the bar, grabs a barstool, and makes his way through the layers of smoke and humans toward the front of the club.

Climbing over the bar, I land on the other side, almost on top of a guy and a woman curled on the floor. A tug on the woman's slender forearm gets her to look up, eyeglasses broken, nose cut. I mouth, *You okay?*

The woman nods, and I pull her to standing. Together, we grab the man's arm and haul him up. He staggers against the bar, latching onto it for support despite the glass all over it. Is he tipsy or concussed? It's hard to tell.

Coughing, eyes burning, I follow Dusty's lead and pick up a barstool. I know it's heavy because I bought it, but I am frantic and filled with adrenaline, and the chair feels like nothing as I lift it over my head.

Shuffling through the debris, I nearly fall, but I make it to the window, haul back, push out from my hips, and toss it with a cry at the colorful image of my mother working behind the bar. The stool smashes the glass but doesn't break through. It gets hung up on the leaded frame. *Fudge.*

Hacking, tears streaming, I rush back and grab another barstool. My heart is pounding, but I can't feel anything other than my need to succeed.

With a burst of energy that starts as much in my desperate heart as in my right leg, I let the power and the scream rise up and out and hurl the chair.

The barstool tears clean through, dragging the first stool with it. Quick as a flash, a patron scrambles up to the windowsill and begins kicking out the remaining glass. When he has it clear, he begins helping people through.

I thank God for him when more people seeing the opportunity begin scrambling out. My tug of relief is short lived, because the sprinklers go off.

Water soaks people in seconds, making things slippery as I fight my way through overturned tables to the people still struggling to get out the front door. I turn people around, wave at the window, and get them to head in that direction. Once enough people begin to see a clear, easier way out, the tide turns, easing pressure on those at the front door. *Good.*

Dusty has cleared the window by the front, so people begin to disperse more, easing even more the panic. I grab two women with cuts on their foreheads and send them out, and suddenly realize I haven't checked on my cook staff, Jackie and Leigh, or, for that matter, poor Victor. I'd let him go upstairs earlier to check security footage.

My heart pounding a thousand guilty fists against my chest, I move back behind the bar and run through the walkway. I jerk to a halt in the kitchen.

It isn't on fire. Smoke drifts about, yes, but nowhere near as bad as in the main club, and the sprinklers aren't on back here. Something isn't right.

Jackie and Leigh aren't anywhere in sight, and it's easy to see why. They would've had no problem going out the back door, and, considering the smoke out front, would've had little choice.

Victor. I sprint through the kitchen and crash open the swinging doors into the back hall.

The light pad by the upstairs security door blinks with an error code. The door is programmed to unlock during a fire, but that shouldn't produce an error code.

Something is really wrong.

Removing my Beretta from my ankle holster, I shove the heavy door open and run full-out up the stairs.

At the top, I glide through the hallway. Calling on the smooth and measured training of The Guild and the deep and pointed focus that has been instilled in me since childhood, I note every blinking security pad, including the ones by the servers.

How did three layers of backup fail? This is not right.

Awareness locks on every shadow, split-second analysis of potential danger while dismissing the throb of alarms against my ears.

I enter my office, moving through the pristine space to a side door. Victor is on the floor of my computer operations center. A well of panic tries to overcome my focus as I move over to his prone body and check his pulse. A small sound of relief escapes my lips. He's alive.

I gently run a hand against the bump on his head. Someone hit him hard, but he'll be okay.

With a flash of regret at having to leave him, I squeeze his hand and continue my search. The server room across from my office is empty.

That leaves one area left unexamined.

My mouth grows dry as I stalk down the hall to the door that leads to my apartment. My teeth are clenched together. My breath gusts loud through my nose.

Cracking open the door, I spin through the doorway and scan. The bookcase that hides the elevator is open. Something hard catches in my throat. It's never left open. I would never leave it open.

Moving deeper into my apartment, I head toward the kitchen. It's an open floor plan, but someone could be hiding...

Someone jumps out at me from behind the breakfast bar.

He's low, trying to tackle me by my waist, but all my shock has gone now. Operating with skill and training, I use an Aikido avoidance technique and slip to the side.

He lurches past me, and I take in the fact that he's masked, taller and wider than your average person, but it's hard to get a feel for his height.

He recovers quickly, turning to me in a half-crouch.

I bring my gun down across his masked face. It should've been easy to knock him out, but my sprinkler-moistened grip slips and the gun glances off his temple.

He leaps to standing, latches onto my gun hand. Wrestling me for control, he twists viciously.

Pain radiates through my hand and my weapon falls.

He tries to grab the weapon, giving me an opportunity. Using my free arm, I send an elbow into his nose, fast and hard.

He drops back to his knees and grabs me by the waist. I jab my thumbs into his eye sockets. My fingers slip against the moist eye and an obvious contact lens. He lifts and smashes me into the breakfast bar. My back seizes with the sharp jolt of pain and air leaves me in a rush.

Fighting for breath, it's all I can do to focus on the one chance I have. I shove my thumbs deeper into his eyes. Something squishy gives way with a pop. He cries out, drops me, and slaps a hand over half his face.

Back on my feet, I grasp him by the exposed neck and drive his head down, hammering my kneecap into his hand and face three times before he goes boneless.

I let him drop to the floor.

Staggering away, the excruciating pain in my back making me feel queasy, I forget to stay alert, forget there might be someone else until I hear a whoosh of sound.

I shift a second too late and the solid and unexpected whack of metal slams my neck followed by the sharp sting of a million volts of electricity. The stun baton convulses my body.

Chapter 32
Dusty

After leaving Grace, I'm wading through water and a crowd of panicked people with a barstool held over my head. Shaking water from my face like a dog, I cough and hack up phlegm through an already aching throat.

Shouting, smoke, water, and people driven by survival instinct force me to use my size and strength to try to get through. Someone grabs my belt from behind. Chair still aloft, I look down at the woman. She's using me to help her get through the crowd, the way someone might follow an ambulance to get through traffic.

"Hold on," I tell her and keep moving.

By the time we make it to the front window, I've got a mini conga line trailing and my legs are like Jell-O. No time to waste, I heave back and pitch the stool as hard as I can through the large stained-glass window. The shattering noise is lost to the alarm, screams, and gush of water, but the window breaks like an egg.

My conga line needs no more help from me. A few take-chargers begin directing everyone out the window. The crush at the front lessens as people turn for the new exit.

Red lights from a firetruck bounce off the open window. Cavalry's here. Firefighters start to haul people through the broken window as other firefighters with axes work to free people trapped at the front door.

Hacking into the crook of my arm, I push back through the crowd and into the club to help Grace. It's amazing how quickly things turn now that we've opened other ways out. Smart idea on

Grace's part. I don't even have to fight my way back inside. I do have to watch my step. Thick globules of wet drywall drop from the ceiling and onto couches like burst piñatas.

Why would the ceiling fall apart? I look up and can see clearly that marks of some kind of explosion. I'm no fire expert, but I am observant. There was a decoration in that spot, a fighter jet that was surely big enough to hold an explosive device. Question is, how did someone get inside to place the device?

Better question, where the hell is Grace?

She's not near the bar or anywhere in this part of the club, and there's no way she'd leave until everyone was out. Not while her staff and customers need her.

Her staff. The kitchen. Wiping water from my eyes, I vault over the bar just as a splintering crash sends another decoration slamming onto the spot where I'd been.

In the kitchen, smoke drifts around like fog, but it's clearer here and damn easier to breathe. Nothing like the nostril-burning quality out front. And there're no sprinklers spouting water. What's going on?

Wiping soot, snot, and water from my face, I remove my Remington .380 then make my way through the kitchen to the back hall. No one around, but the security pad on the door leading upstairs is flashing and the door is open.

A couple of burly firefighters rush inside through the back entrance.

Before they can spot me and order me out, I slip through the doorway and climb the stairs on the balls of my feet. At the top, I scan the empty hall.

I begin to check rooms and find a body. Male. It takes me a moment to place the guy as I check his pulse. I pat his cheek. "Victor?"

His brown eyes open, then widen with recognition. "Got a thing for Latinos?"

I help him sit up, lean him against a wall. "I got a thing for redheads and one in particular. Seen her?"

Victor shakes his head, groans, then closes his eyes. He whispers, "Stop fucking with her."

Guy is out of it. "We'll talk later. I'm giving you a pass."

Victor's eyes shoot open. He punches weakly at my upper arm. "Did you give Tony a pass?"

What? A slight press on Victor's shoulder keeps him from swinging again. "Settle down. You hit your head."

There's a swish and clink of metal followed by a booming voice, "Fire and rescue. What do we have here?"

I hide my weapon and answer. "Looks like a concussion."

Victor curses. The firefighter muscles his way into my space and I'm happy to retreat and leave him to help Victor. Back in the hall, I make my way down it, searching a room with computer servers before coming to the end of the hall.

The door, like every door on this level has a blinking security pad. Unlike the other doors, this one is ajar.

I enter and realize instantly this is Grace's apartment. I scan the room and spot her struggling into a seated position from the floor.

"You okay?" I ask, helping her up even as I continue to scan with my gun raised.

She asks, "Did they leave?"

Fuck. "Stay here," I tell her. After taking a hot second to make sure no one is in her bedroom or the bathroom, I rush back over to her. "Where are you hurt?"

"I'm not. I was tasered." Her eyes begin to clear. Her hand latches onto my forearm she squeezes. "Dusty. The escape route, behind the bookcase. Quick. Close it."

I look over to the bookcase opened to reveal a secret elevator. Not bothering to argue with her or ask about it, I walk over and shut it. There's a snap as it sinks into place, seamlessly integrating with the wall.

An elevator and an escape route hidden in the wall. Fancy stuff. Is that how those who'd attacked her got in? If so, how in hell did they know it was here?

I turn back to ask her when two firefighters appear in the doorway.

#

The lights from emergency service vehicles, police and fire and ambulances strobe across the back of Club When? The madness from inside has switched to the outside.

Injured people sitting on the ground, being tended at ambulances, walking around aimlessly. Less injured people crying, hugging, talking at each other as much as to each other.

Some people standing around in shock. There's local news held back by police and a few local lookie-loos gathered at the edge of the parking lot, still in their pajamas.

I guide Grace over a fire hose as we exit the back of the club, then try to steer her toward an ambulance. She shakes me off. "I don't need help. I need *to* help."

There's that upbringing of hers again. "You're going to be looked at first."

She begins to argue and walk away.

I catch her by the forearm and hold her for a moment. "Watch."

Her head swivels, noting the ambulance as it comes to a halt in the parking lot, squeezing in between the fire truck and another ambulance. Two techs climb out, rushing to meet a man carrying an injured woman. She has a tourniquet on her bleeding leg.

Grace makes a sound of grief so heavy and unexpected my stomach sours.

I look closer at the woman and recognize her dress and dark hair. *Shit.* The woman at the bar, the one who'd been flirting with me. The one Grace had given a free drink to.

Part of her right leg is missing.

Tears run down Grace's face, even as her brow scrunches in anger. "This is my fault."

She's breaking my heart. I put my arm around her. "Steady. It's not your fault."

"I should've known something like this might happen," she rasps. "That's my job."

"Grace, you can barely speak because you were in the thick of it, helping everyone you could. I know because I couldn't get you to leave until it was only firefighters left inside. Violence happens and it's not always easy to predict when, so don't convict yourself over something you had no control of."

She looks at me with genuine pain pinching her face. "But how can I fix this?"

Fuck.

I fold her into my arms, gathering her up in the hope that my strength might muffle some of her pain. I'm so damn grateful she's okay, so damn grateful she lets me hold her. I kiss the top of her head, swallow over the bricks of anger stacking like a barrier, the Great Wall of China, in my throat. "We are going to find whoever is behind this. It's that person's fault, and they will pay."

That's my out-loud promise to her. I've got another that I say silently to myself. I'm done chasing heroes like this woman and her mother when there are real villains out there. I know now who it is I need and want to protect.

One Ms. Grace Parish.

Chapter 33
Dusty

I walk through the surgical-white hospital corridor certain the smell of smoke has taken up permanent residence in my nostrils. Probably better than the smell of antiseptic.

With an, "Excuse me, ladies," for almost crashing into them, I veer out of the way of a woman with an IV bag walking with a nurse's aide in a candy-stripe uniform.

I'm tired from being up all night trailing Grace. A night in which I grew to admire her more with each passing hour.

Never seen a more determined person in my life. She helped out with the ambulances, talked to the injured, consoled those in shock, dealt with the police and emergency services, got names and information. With an equanimity that blew me away, she even handled a couple of accusatory and angry dudes outside the club. I'd been one second from handling them in a very different way.

After all that, I made her come here to be checked out—took nearly every bit of charm and convincing I had, stubborn woman. The moment she was cleared in the ER, she began to check on people here and recheck on her staff and Victor.

I'd been by her side through all of it, but since she went to speak with the hospital administrator about taking care of the bills, I'm on my own. And since I wanted to talk to Victor privately because of what he'd said when I'd found him and because he'd acted funny when I'd visited him with Grace, I'm back at his hospital room.

I knock on the door and walk inside when Victor shouts for me to come in. He's sitting up in bed with his keen brown eyes pinned to the TV news, currently showing clips from the club fire.

I purposefully keep my eyes off the screen. "You'd think that'd be the last thing you'd want to see."

Victor squints one eye but keeps watching. "I'm trying to catch up on what happened. I was knocked out through most of it."

He'd been knocked out after fighting back. Turns out, not only does he have a concussion, but he has a broken clavicle, a couple of broken ribs, and one hell of a shiner. According to him, there'd been two men, and they'd wanted into the computers that Victor had been working on.

Another thing I want to find out about. I got a fuzzy answer from him and Grace on what he'd been doing up there. "Is it helping any?"

"Mostly, the news is speculating on the Parish family's bad luck. They're bringing up the drone attack earlier this year, but no one's asking the obvious questions yet."

"Obvious questions?"

"A series of explosions without a raging, out-of-control fire isn't amateur hour, so who would go through the trouble and why? It seems this person didn't want Gracie dead, but he or she sure wanted her to suffer."

"You and I are thinking along the same lines. Which is one of the reasons I'm here while Grace talks to the hospital administrator."

"Grace?" Victor picks the corded remote off the guardrail, cringes in pain, then flicks off the television. "What's that in your hand?" Now that he's given me his full attention, he's noticed the flowers.

I shrug. "Wasn't sure of the protocol."

"I would've preferred a naked picture of your girlfriend."

Huh. This guy wants to wave a red flag in front of a bull. "You're a lot less friendly now than when I was in here with

Grace. Heck, less friendly than the guy I remember from Mexico. And you were in a lot more pain."

"Pain is a chronic condition when you get involved with the Parish family. You might want to write that down, tattoo it on that generous bicep, and walk away now."

Instead of taking any of that to heart, I walk to the windowsill and shove the flowers into a vase that's already pretty full with other flowers. I sit on the vinyl burgundy chair by the hospital bed, resting my elbows on my knees as sunlight heats the left side of my face. "Why are you so pissed at me?"

Victor's eyes hold the glassy sheen of medication, which might explain why he's a tad slow to answer. He says, "You need to be honest with Gracie. She might seem tough, but she's—"

A spark of anger rides up my spine. "She's not anyone I want to mess with. You don't need to warm me off. She knows why I'm here. She knows everything I'm about."

Victor lifts his head from the pillow, then lets it drift back. He closes his eyes. "Everything? She knows about Tony?"

Not the best way to start any kind of relationship with a woman—using her brother to get in with the family so you can investigate the mother. Can't say I blame Victor for his anger. But, to be fair to me, I started this investigation for the right reasons—or so I'd thought at the time.

The relationship thing with Grace kind of came out of the blue. Like a volley of lightning bolts thrown by Zeus, accompanied by a flurry of arrows from Cupid. I never had a chance. "I've been totally honest with her and now I'm going to be with you. I'm no longer working at my job or interested in pursuing her family."

Victor blinks at me. "Then why are you here?"

I'm cut off from answering when a nurse comes into the room to take his vitals and ask him a bunch of head-injury questions. Victor flirts outrageously with her, and she tosses a *maybe* smile in his direction before leaving.

When she closes the door behind her, I pick up our

conversation. "I'm here because someone is after Grace. She tells me you've been helping her out, and I'd like in on whatever details you can provide."

Victor picks up a Styrofoam cup of water, misses his mouth twice with the straw before managing a sip. "You know the players?"

"There's some reason to suspect Rush and his family, specifically Porter."

Victor puts down his drink. His eyes seem to clear. "Specifically Porter?"

He's trying to feel me out, see what I know. "Yeah. Mukta has been using Grace's existence to bribe Rush for thirty years, but from where I'm sitting, he's got no reason to balk now. It's more likely the son, the campaign manager, found out about it."

Victor presses the button on his bed and sits up straighter. "I don't trust you, and until I can talk to Gracie alone, I'm not giving you a pass on this Tony thing." He's like a dog with a bone. "Still, I'm not going to be much help to her here, and you are an investigator, so I'm going to trust you on that."

"Great. Sounds like we have an understanding. What you got?"

"John and Ellen True have a money market account. One of them took out fifty thou last week and put it into an offshore account. A similar transfer of money happened right before Gracie was shot at, 10k."

That was an odd coincidence the first time and even odder on this second attack, but I don't buy them as perps. Still, a niggling voice is telling me not to ignore this information. There's something there. "Anything else on them?"

"I spotted Ellen taking pictures outside of Gracie's club."

"The wife? Isn't she some kind of respectable news anchor?"

"Yes, but she has a history of jealousy. Twelve years ago, she got into a fist fight with another girl over her boyfriend. She broke the girl's nose."

Seems like a stretch on its own, but with everything else…

"You're telling me not to focus too much on Porter and Rush."

"Yeah. Don't." Victor shifts, makes a face that lets me know he's clearly in pain.

I stand, reach out a hand. "Thanks. I'll get out of here."

Victor ignores the hand. "You better have told her about Tony. I don't care how big you are, I'll kick your ass if she tells me otherwise. And if you *are* telling the truth and you aren't investigating her family and you do care about her, then don't you dare ask her to choose between you and her family. That decision is all you. She's a package deal."

I drop my hand and swallow the fist of anger that maybe doesn't need to hear all of Victor's opinions right now. For Grace, I nod and say, "Get some rest."

Out in the hall, I consider the brick of truth Victor lobbed at my head. It hurts, but I have to admit he's right. I can't ask Grace to choose between me and her family. She's already lost her brother, and I know how much her family means to her. The choice needs to be mine. The question is, can I stand by not just Grace, not just her family, but her mother?

I honestly don't know.

Chapter 34
Gracie

Dusty's driving my car as I rest my head against the window and watch the wind whipping the late-blooming white flowers from the olive-barked Amur maackia. They drift across the road like petals cast before a bride on her way down the aisle.

I usually love this time of year, the magical drive through the flower-strewn country road that leads to campus, but, today, those petals remind me of ash and lost limbs.

Including Victor, eight people were injured badly enough to require hospitalization, though none as seriously as Delilah Mojang, the woman who lost part of her leg, the straightshooter all the way down to her drink.

Pain presses like a boulder against my chest when I think about her. I wasn't permitted to see her, but as soon as I can, I'm going back there. Until then, I'm doing all I can to get her the best possible care.

"Why don't you close your eyes?" Dusty says as he drives steadfast and intent behind the wheel.

"I'm not sure I'd be able to sleep if I do close my eyes. It feels like we've been awake for a week not just a day."

"That's because we've shared a lifetime of emotion in those awake hours."

He's not kidding. We've shared a heat like nothing I've ever experienced when we made love, a real connection before his honesty and my crash to reality.

The anger and sadness when he'd admitted the focus of his

investigation crushed me, but he's sworn off all that. Sworn it off, he tells me, even before the explosion where he threw me to the ground, saving me from worse injury when the second and third explosions occurred.

He's a good man, a man who risked himself not only for me but for all the people in the club who he helped rescue.

"I'm glad you're here," I say, shifting my head so I look at his profile, at the already healing glass cuts along his handsome face.

"I'm glad I'm here," he says, catching me looking at him. He winks. "Looks worse than it is."

He's trying to make me worry less. "It looks as bad as it is, but it could've been worse if whoever had set the explosion, whoever used that mess to break in upstairs had been intent on hurting more people."

"Any idea what they were looking for?"

"I would've said the servers, but then, why fight Victor for access to my personal computer?"

Dusty reaches out and grabs my hand. He squeezes. "We'll find out more when we're able to get into the club. Give it a rest now. You're exhausted."

True. He pulls to a stop at the elaborate wrought-iron gate of the Mantua Academy campus. A security guard comes out, checks the trunk, takes our weapons and Dusty's service belt, checks his credentials, does a pass under the car, then finally waves us through.

Dusty looks over at me as he accelerates through the gate. "Hate to think what happens when someone who's not family shows up."

I smile at that. "They don't mess around."

We stop at the first stop sign and we both look right, toward campus, lined walkways, spires, and brick buildings. It hurts to see it so empty. Even in summer it's usually busy with activities, but since the drone bombing a few months back, students haven't been allowed to return.

"Which way?" Dusty asks.

I suddenly find my tongue stuck to the roof of my mouth. Honestly, I didn't really process how big this moment was until right now. I'm bringing Dusty to my home, to meet my family. My mother. Sure, he's no longer working on his case, but still... this is really happening. "Left here, right at the next stop sign, and then up the hill."

He follows my directions up the steep drive with the large house at the top. It's not a McMansion or even a regular old mansion—it's the size of a palace.

It has to be to hide the operations center for The Guild deep below ground, something Dusty has no idea about. Even if he, along with the government, tried to scan the place, The Guild is hidden by a stealth technology that sends a false signal to any thermal imaging. As Momma says, the idea behind The Guild—to help women—is simple, but the means to help them is often complex.

Dusty's eyes widen as we crest the hill. He says, "Bigger in person."

I should laugh, but I can't. What am I doing? Has my lack of sleep impaired my judgment? Isn't this how things ended with John? Me inviting my love interest into my secret world?

Pulling around the fountain, Dusty parks in one of the many empty spots opposite my family home. Disconnecting my cell from the car charger, I get out. Dusty grabs the bag that I hastily threw together under police supervision, since the entire place is under investigation by police and fire.

I can feel him following me, but I've somehow forgotten to be nervous. At the top of the stone steps, both massive front doors are thrown open. Between them stands Momma, with her sturdy body in a light blue business suit and matching niqab, and her arms spread wide in invitation. Something in me breaks, and I run up the steps.

Until this exact moment, I'd never experienced what it felt like to arrive here, like so many of my sisters have, broken and in need of respite.

For the first time, I understand exactly how this home, these grounds, would appear to my siblings, to children like Cee. It's a sanctuary, a place that calls out, *Here, you can put down your burden, because, here, you are safe and welcome.*

I rush into Momma's waiting arms, which come around me soft and secure. She smells like Une Rose and home.

She whispers to me, "It will be all right."

Until she speaks, I don't realize I'm crying into her shoulder.

A second set of arms, Leland's arms, come around me and Momma. He holds us tight and, in a heartbeat, there are more arms, more family surrounding me, holding me at different heights and angles.

A sob breaks from my throat as I lose myself in the comfort of family.

I can't even see them with my eyes shut tight, but I don't need to. Feeling them is enough.

And then reality breaks in.

"Stop stepping on my toes." A scuffle. A shove. And some angry words in a couple of foreign languages. Mandarin and Cambodian.

I can't help but laugh as the hug breaks up and everyone piles back into the house. I sense Dusty walk through the threshold behind me and realize it's time for introductions.

But Momma has already turned to Dusty. Her dark eyes, mysterious when framed in her niqab, are narrowed at him.

She says, "Aren't you the young man who is investigating me?"

Sugar. She knows?

Chapter 35
Dusty

Have to admit it's a mite awkward, standing in the lavish entranceway of a multi-million-dollar mansion, while a family of rescued kids hover on the stairs, my lover puts a shocked hand to her mouth, and the woman I've been intent on taking down for the last few years rightly accuses me of spying on her.

Grace's head spins between me and her momma, but she doesn't seem to have any words.

My hand grows sweaty against the handle of Grace's suitcase. Guess it's up to me. "I'm not investigating anyone right now, ma'am."

"What's that mean?" a twenty-something woman with a blue stripe in her shiny black hair and a tattoo on her neck asks from the steps.

Shouldn't come as a surprise to me that Grace's siblings like to turn up the heat. Not a lot of shrinking violets here. Surely not that woman, who stares at me angrily, brazen as all hell. I don't answer her. Can't really.

Grace spins toward the stairs and hisses out, "Not now, Troublemakers."

Momma also turns to the woman who spoke. "That is a good question, Elisaveta, but not yours to ask." With that mild rebuke, she waves her hands as if shooing everyone up the stairs. "Please find something else to occupy your afternoon. I will see you all at dinner."

Once they take off, Leland says, "I'm not sure I like him

being here at all. There's a lot we need to discuss with Gracie and he complicates that."

Dude's voice is as rough as his attitude. And though I know him from photos, and from the file we have on him—he's Mukta's right-hand man, best friend, and lover—we've never been properly introduced.

"Nice to meet you, Sir," I add *sir* to be respectful, but I square my shoulders in an I'm-not-budging way. "And you, too, Ms. Parish. I'm here for your daughter. She invited me, but, to be honest, even if she hadn't, I'd probably still be here. I don't like to leave a friend when they need me."

Mukta and Leland exchange a long, wordless glance. They have a whole damn conversation with that glance, and I can't tell what's said, but I can tell something's decided when Leland nods and steps back.

Grace's momma smiles winningly at me. "You both look exhausted, Agent McCallister—"

"Please call me Dusty, ma'am."

"Of course. Dusty, why don't you help Gracie to her room? I assume you'll be staying together. We can talk when you've had a chance to rest." With that, she puts a hand on Grace's cheek, then takes Leland's arm. They disappear together down a long hallway.

After they go, Grace whispers hotly, "How do you think they found out about you? Do you think they know about the email?"

I kind of wonder, too, but I'm not going to get into that with her right now. She's wearing all her worries and her lack of sleep on that beautiful face. I say, "Why don't we follow her suggestion and get some sleep before we go kicking at a hornet's nest?"

She leans into me, tiptoes, then kisses me on my chin. "I'm glad you're here."

We start up the elaborate staircase, an absolutely stunning piece of artwork with a wrought iron railing decorated in gold leaf. The woman I'd made love to under the judgy gaze of cartoon ducks grew up swanky.

Somewhere above, hidden by the sweeping turns of the stairway, kids chatter in differently accented voices that echo. Probably aren't many places in the world where this is possible. They've got a regular Tower of Babel, but I can already tell by the way Grace was embraced outside that they make it work.

At the second landing, we turn right then down the first hall on the left. "This," she says, "is known as Spice Girls Corridor. It's where Dada, Justice, Bridget, Tony, and I grew up."

"Your unit was called the Spice Girls?" Tony never told me. Not that he said a lot, but he let a bit slip now and again. "I bet he loved that."

"He hated it, but we'd already had the name by the time he arrived. Momma had planned for our unit to have five and no one could've figured the last one would be a boy."

Planned? This was a bit of Parish culture I've never heard before. "She plans the group size before adopting the kids?"

"Yep. Momma is big into details. Of course, sometimes it doesn't work out. One unit, known as the Troublemakers Guild—the dark-haired woman with the blue streak is of that unit—was supposed to have five, but it turned out those three were enough to handle on their own."

"Units are divided by age, not when you're adopted, right?"

Something crosses her face, but I can't decide what it means. "Does it bother you that I know that?"

At her door—marked with her name in scrolling calligraphy on a pink-and-white plaque—she shakes her head. "No. Actually, it makes it easier. The answer is yes. The unit you're assigned upon adoption goes by your birth year. I was the first in my unit."

Her voice sounds smaller, as if she's reaching into the past to retrieve it. "I was five before any siblings in my unit were adopted."

I can almost imagine her, someone with all these kids around but still a little lonely, still someone who didn't quite fit in. I want to reach for her but keep my arms at my side as she continues.

"Dada was the first. And, at twelve years old, she was old enough that she could've gone into the A-Team, but Momma put her with me."

"It made all the difference," I say to her, because I somehow know.

"It did," she says. "Two years later, Bridget came and, a few months later, Justice. A year later, Tony was adopted. He was twelve. The day he came marching down this hall with a new backpack, we were all waiting outside our suites. He looked so angry, but I was so excited, so happy. I told Justice, 'We're complete now.'"

My breath comes faster than it should at hearing this story. My head begins to hurt and, for a moment, I'm assailed by memories of Mexico. Tony standing over me with some kind of needle and... What? I shake myself. *Leave it be, man. Leave it be.*

Must be more tired than I even knew. I shake off the nauseous feeling and thoughts of Tony that don't make any sense as we enter Grace's bedroom.

Actually, it's more of a suite. There's a sitting area, a wall of windows, and a round table with a colorful mandala painted on top. The suite has been freshly made up, but still has the feel of a teen. Posters, teenage memorabilia, and photos, and a series of inset bookcases filled with books, model planes, and Muay Thai trophies.

Grace walks down a hall in the suite almost in a daze. She's growing quiet, and I can feel her starting to shut down.

I follow her.

She strips off her clothes, socks, bra, and tosses them willy-nilly onto the floor. Grace making a mess? She's losing it.

I place her suitcase in the closet and pick up her clothes as I trail behind her. By the time I get into the bedroom, she's curled up on her side in her undies on top of the blankets.

The bed is an exact match of the one I'd seen in her apartment last night after the explosions. It's a huge bed with a wood canopy that makes me a little claustrophobic, but for her...

Diana Muñoz Stewart

I take off my own clothes and put them, along with hers, on a chaise by the floor-to-ceiling windows. There's a great view of her backyard with shrubs crafted to look like animals, walkways lined with flowers, and multiple seating areas.

I tug the blankets out from under her, climb into bed, gathered her to me, and kiss the tears from her cheeks.

Soon, she's breathing soft and easy.

Chapter 36
Dusty

I wake from a dream charged with fire and fighting. For a moment, I'm absolutely lost. Where the hell am I?

Grace moves against me, and it all comes back in vivid color. Not only where I'm at but who is curled up in my arms. I hold her tight as relief sweeps over my shaking body. Just a dream.

I'd dreamed Grace had been trapped in a burning building. I'd broken down door after door to get to her only to find myself faced with another door. Unable to reach her, I'd rammed fists against the walls, trying to beat them down.

It had felt so real.

Now, with her warm and tucked up against me, I breathe her in and say a prayer of gratitude to my Lord. I made the promise before, but I make it again now. I'll do whatever it takes to keep Grace safe. Even if that means allying with her vigilante family and the head of that family, Mukta Parish.

I kiss Grace lightly on her warm cheek, then on the side of her hot lips. This woman has no idea what she does to me. She does enough that I'm going to go downstairs and ask her momma straight out about the digital recordings of Sheila. I need the whole truth before I tell Grace.

I roll out of bed with infinite care, but Grace is still so tired, even though the sun tells me we've slept through the night and into the next day, she barely stirs.

After getting cleaned up and grabbing an apple from a giant

breakfast spread on the round table in Grace's suite, I head downstairs to find Mukta.

Technically, I've never been here before, but, thanks to the thoroughness of the Bureau—they took extensive photos and videos after the drone attack—I know nearly every inch of this place. Well, those inches above ground.

Though I have no proof, I'm convinced there's something under this place. Where else would Mukta, who spends so much time here, hide a secret operations center?

Have to admit, I like the hallway Grace grew up in and all the intersecting hallways. The interior of this home is what my mother would've called a hodgepodge. Some folks call it eclectic. Mukta has done her best to incorporate a little from each of her kids' cultures in the decor. There's an almost colorful mix of artwork in the wide hallway, also large floor lamps, ornate furnishings, and tapestries.

What I hadn't known from those photos and reports and what I now find most interesting is the smell of the place, clean and floral. And the way all these cultures and personalities mesh into one family. Not sure how Mukta did it—got them to feel such loyalty and kinship—but the way the group of them hugged Grace... It makes my throat go tight.

As I jog lightly down the front stairs, the sound of kids playing drifts up from the indoor gym. Though Grace's room is a quiet oasis, the main part of the house is filled with laughter, teasing, and games.

Kind of love the fact that they have a gym off their front corridor. I stop by the four open doors and watch the two teams playing a game of dodgeball.

The one male Parish—if my memory serves, his name is Rome—plays the role of referee. He has on an eye patch and is doing a fair Steve the Pirate from the movie *Dodgeball*, saying things like "Bollocks," and "Gar, this sucks."

Funny kid. I push off and keep going, heading down the corridor with its hand-crafted red-velvet gold-filigree wallpaper. The kind of money here is insane.

A little girl comes running down the hall with her hands spread wide. There's plenty of room, but I still step to the side as she passes me.

I call to her, "Where can I find Momma?"

She answers, "In the library," and keeps going.

Russian accent and cute as a bug. Can't help the smile. Yep, some things all the intel in the world can't tell you.

Marble pillars mark the grand entrance to the even grander library, with its two-tiered walkways and books from floor to ceiling.

As I enter, Mukta rises from a long table with a bank of Mac computers and moves toward me with her hand outstretched.

I shake her hand, jingling the many bracelets she wears. Today, she also wears a pastel pink business suite and matching niqab. The color makes her dark eyes stand out.

"Welcome, welcome," she says, and if she's a liar, she's a good one because she sounds genuine. Maybe it's something in her voice, a sort of whiskey and syrup, a sweet and strong flavor.

"Thanks, and thanks for your hospitality."

Her direct eyes never waver from my gaze as she says, "It's the least I could do to repay you for being there for Gracie. Come, sit." She directs me to the computer table that looks like it was made for people a lot smaller than me.

Okay. I sit, and, yeah, the chair is comically tiny for me. My knees jut up. Awkward. Seems to be a family trait—keeping a man off-balance.

She seems to take no notice of my predicament as she folds her hands comfortably on the table and says, "You work for the FBI, are investigating me, and are sleeping with my daughter."

A lot of awkward. "That's your idea of an icebreaker?"

She laughs and the brush of air flutters her veil. "Being direct saves time. Time is precious to me, and who I share it with greedily guarded, as that person takes from my family. Something I despise."

Well, that clears it up. "You're worried about Grace."

The edges of her eyes crease. "Yes." She slows as if counting her breaths, this pause in time, and finding it worth her while. "Grace."

The heat rising in my body kicks me in the face. Calling her Grace and not Gracie was stupid. Might as well have told the woman that, for me, it's more than sex. Something I've barely admitted to Grace. Well, quitting my job for her and punching out my boss for her might've given me away on that score.

Nothing for it, but to go with the truth. "My uncle always said there's no greater waste of time than an inauthentic person, so let me state, flat out, I'm not here for you. That part of my life, my work, is done. I'm here to protect Grace, and if that means protecting you, so be it."

She doesn't answer me. My statement, what I offered her, gets no reaction.

Not put off, I move on to my demand. "I've been told you have a tape of Sheila Hall making accusations against Senator Rush. I need to authenticate it."

This gets a reaction. She shifts back in her chair in obvious surprise. I'm guessing this isn't how she thought this conversation would go.

She composes herself quickly. "Why?"

No denials, no questions on how I know this. She really doesn't like to waste time. "Because there are altered digital versions of that tape that suggest you have been blackmailing multiple officials with the same ruse. I need the original to prove it's real and, hopefully, prove that you didn't make the other versions."

She doesn't even blink. I laid out how I know she's blackmailing one man, a senator, but that I want to prove she's not doing it to others, and she doesn't blink. She'd make a great poker player.

She leans forward. "We obviously have a lot to discuss, but I have to ask first if you've told Gracie about what her father did."

Aw. Hell. My body washes with warmth. She didn't even

ask about the charges against her on Rush. She wants to know about her daughter. I have no idea how Grace will react to finding out that she's a product of rape, but I know she needs to be told. "Not yet. I wanted to talk to you first, so I have the facts straight."

She leans back, nodding in a way that seems to indicate it's this information she needs time to absorb. "We can discuss what kind of access I can allow you to the recording after I speak to Gracie and let her know the truth. I don't feel right giving you information before she has it."

Honestly, this woman is winning me over. "That makes sense to me."

"Good. If you don't mind, I'd really like to ask you another question."

"Okay. Shoot." Probably not the best colloquialism to use with a vigilante. *Suspected* vigilante. *Wink, wink.*

"What sparked your investigation into my family?"

Whoa. Lady knows how to strike at the heart of a matter. "I think that's Grace's story to tell."

Her eyes widen. "So, it's true. Gracie sent an email to the FBI about our family."

I close my eyes against the humiliation of being played. Grace isn't going to like that I accidentally ratted her out to her momma. I say, "I've got nothing to say about that."

She takes me in for a full breath before saying, "She must trust you an awful lot. You realize that's a gift, correct?"

"Yes, ma'am. And if you forgive me, I'm not foolish enough to keep risking that trust, so I'm going to go now."

She smiles. "You're a quick learner."

She says that like she's impressed that I realized she'd played me like a fiddle, and I smile back, because she's right, I *am* a quick learner.

I tip my head in her direction. "Ma'am."

Chapter 37
Gracie

When I wake at home in my childhood bedroom with the sun streaming inside and comfort all around me, I have a moment of deep ease. I stretch in bed then remember the explosion at the club. I barely make it to the bathroom.

I've never been so sick emotionally that it's caused me to throw up, but there you have it.

After brushing my teeth, showering, and dressing in The Guild uniform of black workout pants and top, I nibble at the breakfast laid out while I reach out to the hospital to check on the injured and make sure all their bills are covered. Delilah still isn't taking visitors, but I send her some flowers. It feels almost wrong to do so because it's so small a thing, but I can't stand the thought of her thinking I don't care.

I also call the police, fire marshal, and my insurance company. Repairs might not take that long because there's mostly smoke and water damage, but, right now, my club is off-limits due to the investigation. Not that I think that stopped my family. I'm sure they've been to the club and can't help but wonder what they discovered while I was sleeping.

Maybe I'll go find out. And find out what happened to Dusty. He's not a shy man, so I can imagine he's made himself quite comfortable around my family. Still, this can't have been an easy morning for him.

As I descend the front staircase, I realize what I've missed most about this place and why I enjoy the nightlife of my club so much. It's the noise.

In total, fifteen of my siblings still live here, though we have whole families of siblings visiting at any time during the year. The house is always filled with love, laughter, and arguments. Usually, the arguments are between girls. After all, Momma only adopted two boys and one of them is gone.

Oh, Tone. Miss you.

But when he'd been here, Tony had rarely argued with anyone loudly, so it's weird to hear a guy arguing with someone at full volume. I spot Rome in the center of the gym openly arguing with Cee. I stroll toward the high-pitched conversation.

Rome's voice strays higher. "No. I think this has gone too far."

"What's gone too far?" I ask.

Rome's head shoots up. Cee spins around, a hand-in-the-cookie-jar look on her face. Seriously, that's Spy-craft 101: watch your back.

Rome and Cee automatically move to stand side-by-side. Wearing the uniform—black workout pants, black tees, and bare feet—they couldn't look more like a team if they had a lacrosse stick in their hands. Even though I also wear black—force of habit—I suddenly feel like the outsider. "What's going on?"

"Nothing."

Both at once. It must be something, and I can't help but have a twinge of suspicion. I know Cee was working on one case because we escaped said case together. I also know Rome was involved in some way. If I hadn't been juggling my own investigations, I might have delved deeper into theirs. I didn't. Could there be more cases or more to that case these two are looking into?

They're up to something, but is it only the two of them? Even though their class has six kids—the most of any unit—they've naturally divided themselves into younger and older kids. These two are part of the older ones. "Where's Jules, the third of your dynamic trio? She's not involved in this?"

They stare at me with thin bodies and thinly veiled guilt. I don't like it. "Come on, guys. I'm not the enemy here."

"Es nada," Cee says.

Nothing? Sure. But I can't get them to open up to me, not when I haven't built a rapport with them. That was Tony's gig and an opening I intend to help fill because Cee was right; I *do* need to come out of my place and realize people are worth it.

"Let's go," I say, beckoning Rome with a crook of my fingers.

Rome casts a glance around the gym as if hoping for understanding. "What? You mean training?"

"Yep. Tony and I were the most advanced Muay Thai instructors, but Tony, our dear brother, is gone." I swallow the pain of it, hard and choking. "So that leaves me."

To my utter shock, Rome bursts into tears. *Crud on a cracker.* I shouldn't have mentioned Tony. He and Rome had been so close. Not only had Tony mentored him, but when Rome had first come here, he'd been Tony's shadow. Of course, Tony had loved it. He'd taken it as a compliment and had seen the need in the kid, a space he'd tried to fill.

Fudge. He is really crying. He needs a hug. I suck at hugs, at comforting. It's all the walls I put up over the years. They not only keep others out. They've kept me in. Not for nothing, as Tony would've said.

I reach out and walk two steps forward, like a short, redheaded Frankenstein's monster.

Why didn't Shelley name the monster?

Cee snorts something that sounds like, "Tin Man" under her breath.

It's awkward all around as I wrap my arms around the tall, skinny boy. Someone with a good sound effects machine should definitely start making rusty-hinge noises.

But my lame attempt doesn't seem so lame to him judging by how he bends into me, putting a weight on me I hadn't expected. I take it all. I'm strong. And he reminds me so much of Tyler. I hug him tighter, gripping him as tears spill down my face.

"I'm sorry," I say. "I miss him, too."

He sobs harder. It's all I can do to keep from joining him.

My throat is tight with tears, but I hold it down because this is about Rome. He needs my strength.

I rub his back and whisper over and over, "He loved you. He loves you still. It's okay."

For some reason, my words only seem to make him feel worse. Or maybe he just had all of that inside him for so long that he can't control the flood waters.

What have we done by telling these kids Tony was dead, but never having a funeral? When all of this is cleared up, I'm going to insist Momma have a memorial service. These kids obviously haven't processed their grief, and, honestly, it's not only them. I'm going to include me and Justice, Bridget, and Dada in that, too.

After a cry long enough to have us both sweating and my back aching, he pulls away and wipes the tears. His eyes are red ringed as he wipes them and says, "It means more because you suck so bad at it."

I burst into tearful laughter. "Tony would've loved that you're quoting him."

Tony used to say that all the time as encouragement, as if the thing that we're worst at, because we have to try harder, is worth so much more.

I've been wrong not to come here, wrong to distance myself from Momma—who I blamed—and the family—who I feared because being around kids reminded me of my loss. Of Tyler.

I wipe my eyes. By staying away, I'd made everyone accountable for my pain but me. No more. "I love you guys."

Their turn to look shocked. Cee's gaze drops to the floor as a soft red rises in her cheeks. "I'm sorry about your club, Gracie. I really am."

That's so sweet.

Rome claps a hand over his eyes, obviously embarrassed that he turned to me with his grief after everything I've been through. "Me, too," he says. "I mean, I'm sorry about your club, too."

These kids… I want to get to know them well enough that they trust me with their secrets like Rome trusted Tony. "I appreciate that. The club can be repaired, but the fact that people were hurt is really hard for me to accept. But you know what? The fire brought me home and I'm not going to pretend like it didn't teach me something. Life is too short not to make time for the people you love."

Cee perks up at this, smiles in a way that seems triumphant, rushes over, and gives me a fierce hug.

I hug her back. "Two hugs in one day," I say. "I might be getting better at this stuff."

Cee pulls away. "Definitely better the second time."

We laugh and the tension melts away like the dusting of snow on a sunny day. "Okay. Let's get to work. It's not Muay Thai, but I'll show you a move Tony taught me years ago. It's saved my life. Twice."

Chapter 38
Dusty

I creep back into Gracie's room feeling like I owe her a big apology. Not only for spilling the beans with her momma, but for misjudging Mukta so badly. After spending the morning with her and wandering the home, I can better understand why Grace left me that morning. Kind of feel like an ass for the way I presented it all to her. Yep, I owe her an apology.

And I see from the laptop, cell, and stack of papers on the round table we saw when we first came in yesterday, she's also been up and busy. I call out to her, but there's no answer. I check the bedroom part of her suite, but she's not in there either. Looks like she's somewhere in this huge home. I might have to send out a search party.

Doubling back, I pick up the unexpected sound of water running. I follow the sound through the hoity-toity closet to the back wall of mirrors. I place my ear against the glass. Yep. Water. Another bath?

Feeling a bit foolish, I knock on the glass. The answer comes quick and clear, "Dusty, if that's you, come in. Anyone else, go away."

Makes a man feel special. I push against the glass mirrors, and the wall glides open to reveal a large sauna and hot tub room with black-and-white marble floors and pink octagonal tiles. And who should I find sitting up to her perfect pink nipples in jetted bubbles but one Ms. Gracie Parish.

I close the door and inch closer to the stairs leading up and into the hot tub. "God, you're beautiful."

"Take off your clothes and get in. This is going to make your day."

Pretty damn certain of that fact. I set the land-speed record for undressing, then climb the stairs and drop into the water.

Thing is so deep it's almost a pool. The heat and bubbles loosen my muscles. The sight of Grace, head against the cushion and eyes closed, tightens my cock.

I drift across the water to her. Settling on the seat next to her, a view that has me as hard as the marble on this tub, I kiss her cheek, run a tongue against her ear, lick water off her neck, collarbone, and suck her earlobe.

Feeling a bit dizzy from the heat and lack of blood flow, I whisper, "How was your morning? Everything okay?"

Eyes still closed, she doesn't answer, but her hand goes between my legs and begins to stroke.

I gulp in a breath and buck into her tight grip. Obviously, she doesn't want to talk about it right now. I'm all about respecting that.

I moan as the pressure and the pleasure increase. "Nice way to change the subject."

She laughs, opens her eyes, and, with a curious tilt of her head, asks, "How long do you think I can hold my breath?"

"I..." Might have died and gone to Heaven.

Before I can form an answer—again, lack of blood flow—her head dips under the water. Her hair and her lovely ass float up as her mouth slides around my cock.

Holy hell.

I grunt and arch into her mouth as she works my hard-on. My breath quickly outpaces my heart. My moans echo across the room. My vision... hard to see with my eyes rolling back in my head, as I rightly tell her, though I know she can't hear me.

"Your ass, Grace. Damn near irresistible."

Make that completely irresistible. I give it a nice, sharp slap. And beneath the water, my little mermaid goes wild, dipping and sucking and rolling that talented tongue.

I have to fight to keep from coming. Walking the line between pure bliss and ecstasy, I fist my hands and work for control.

She comes up for air. Just in time, because I wouldn't have lasted much longer.

The moment she surfaces, out of breath, her bottom bearing the red imprint of my hand, I'm on her. I grab her by one ass cheek and press her to my raging cock as I devour her mouth.

I'm breathless and aching, but I make sure she knows how incredible she is. "That ass, Grace, there is none finer. None. It's all I can do to keep from reddening it properly."

She inhales sharply, rubs her core against my hardness. "Yes, to that."

Half-crazed with her go-ahead, I lift her so her fine ass breaks the water and land a heavy-handed slap against that firm, round cheek.

She yelp-groans into my mouth, so I do it again.

Harder.

Chapter 39
Gracie

I've had sex in a shower, but never in a hot tub. I can't imagine experiencing this pleasure with anyone other than Dusty.

He's sweet and commanding, with dirty talk for days. And when he stripped down to climb into the hot tub earlier, I'd nearly swallowed my tongue. He has a build like Thor and what's between his legs is large enough to make you do a double and triple take.

Not that I let him know I was looking. I'd kept my eyes slitted so I could visually grope him in private. But when he'd sat down next to me, I hadn't been able to resist feeling all that manhood. Which, naturally, had led to me having to taste him.

Now he's spanking my bottom with a heat that has me throwing back my head and groaning.

He switches from devouring my neck to devouring my mouth, kissing me like he will literally eat me alive.

Can't wait.

"Oh," I breathe as he delivers another stinging slap. My need for him suddenly overcomes everything else, and I push him back until he's seated.

My impatient hands travel the prominent muscles of his arms, thick deltoids, biceps, and traps. I straddle him and, with barely a moment to consider, grab then slide down onto him. My breath *whooshes* out of me in one startled rush as my body first protests his erection, then stretches to accommodate him.

"Careful there, Grace," he whispers into my mouth.

I don't want careful. I want him. Bracing my hands on his shoulders, I began to lift and lower along his hard length.

We moan in unison as I rise up and down, and each time my butt breaks the surface of the water, he gives me a solid, stinging slap. The sound echoes in the room and sends heat dancing along my cheek. I moan in approval. "Oh. That feels good."

"Goin' to make me come," he protests.

But he doesn't stop and neither do I. Pumping faster, my breast bouncing, I watch mischievously as his handsome face fights for control.

"Grace. Please."

His words are far away now. Now, there is only the tight feel of him, the coiling energy, the building pressure, the bubbles and the sighs and the sharp gasps. I moan against his forehead, into his ear, against his cheek, until the building energy releases and my voice rises into sharp, grateful cries.

Despite how loud I am, I still hear his serious and earnest proclamation.

"Watching you come, Grace, is breathtaking."

My head slumps forward onto his shoulder. My body is paralyzed for a moment by the intensity of that orgasm. I'm as malleable as clay.

He kisses my cheek, rubs my tender backside. "You good to keep going, darlin'?"

"Mmm," I manage, which he takes for the agreement it is. He lifts me up as easily as a feather, turns me, and positions me so that I'm kneeling on the seat, facing the large window.

I brace my arms on the cushion that the rims the tub, resting my head on my forearms, I look back as he positions himself to enter me.

I'm thrilled when I see the serious look on his face. Not a hint of playfulness.

He says in a voice both rough and sure, "That apple on your tattoo, I'd bite it a thousand times without a moment of guilt. You're worth damnation."

Brushing away wet strands of hair from my back, he bends over me, kisses the back of my neck, and moves a strong hand around my hip, down my stomach, down.

I gasp as his confident fingers tease my sensitive clit. I arch back, pump my hips.

He pushes a finger then two inside.

And because he's Dusty, and probably could talk a stone to dust, he tells me how hard he is, how deep he's going to enter me, how fast he's going to take me, until I'm gyrating against his fingers and begging, "Yes. Please. Do that."

He chuckles, but it is deep and predatory. "Happy to oblige."

Removing those skilled fingers, he grasps my waist and shoves himself deep inside me.

I shift to keep from falling as he begins to pump hard into me, proving he's a man of his word.

My body responds instantly, and my need becomes urgent with every forceful stroke. I moan my approval as he takes me.

The *slap, slap* of our bodies, the splash of water, the whir of the jetted bubbles can't drown out the cries that break from my mouth with every thrust.

The fever builds so high inside me and breaks so quickly that I'm panting and moaning and lost to the squeeze and release of all that energy riding between my legs.

Dusty doesn't stop or slow for one second. If anything, my moans and gyrations drive him faster. Harder. His thrusts are deep and long, thick and possessive.

I can feel every inch of him with each frantic push of his body as it rocks me against the tub. He braces me, holding me up, by snaking a hand under my stomach.

I'm lost to him, lost as another orgasm breaks in me, so sudden and strong, I can't even move. All I can do is delight in the overpowering pleasure delivered by each hard stroke. He is in complete control.

Gripping me, he comes with a fierce growl, a sound so

animalistic I feel like we've gone back in time, all the way back to his caveman roots. And I love it.

He pumps until his hips slow, then he drops back onto the seat and drags me into his lap. I am quaking and subdued and awed.

He doesn't ask if he hurt me and I'm grateful. It would be a natural question considering how hard he went, but it would be disingenuous. It's obvious to anyone with half a brain that I enjoyed myself thoroughly.

He snuggles into my neck, and I tilt my head to give him access. I'm pretty sure that saying, "in like a lion and out like a lamb," best describes Dusty right now. He sure is cuddly after breaking over me like a storm.

"Grace." He breathes hard against my forehead. "Didn't just make my day; you made my life."

Mine, too. I kiss his swollen lips. "Where did you go earlier?"

"Uh…" He stops kissing me. His eyes open wide. He clears his throat, hesitates. "'Bout that…"

Dusty at a loss for words? This can't be good.

Chapter 40
Gracie

There's practically a line drawn down the middle of Momma and Leland's Mantua Home office. There are two desks, two sitting areas, and two minibars.

One side of the room is designed with Momma's whimsical, bold color palette—purple chairs, teal side tables, and rose desk. The other side is Leland's no-nonsense cowhide, brown leather, and earth tones.

I expected Leland to be here for this conversation with Momma, but only she and I are inside their large, shared office.

I sit opposite Momma, who's seated at her desk. She hangs up the phone. My sister Zuri, a scientist and one of Momma's prized pupils, called with an emergency from the lab. If it hadn't been one of my sisters and an emergency, Momma would never have taken the call. I respect how she offers herself for her daughters.

Momma gives her attention to me. "Are you sure you don't want anything to eat or drink?"

I cross my arms and hold onto my elbows. "No. I need to finish telling you this."

Cupping her chin in her hands, bunching the blue silk fabric of her niqab, she says, "You were explaining about Tyler and his illness and his hospitalization."

"Yes. After finding out about it, I was despondent. It seemed... It's hard to explain, Momma, but, even now, I can still feel the ache of those painful days. It's like that moment of helplessness, of utter panic lives in me."

She whispers, "I know this feeling. I know how it can linger." Her veil flutters with her words.

For a moment, we simply look into each other's eyes. Two women who have known pain and loss and regret. I understand her in this moment more than I ever have. She has chosen a complicated life based on her desire to help others.

"Angry and hurt, you wanted to end The Guild." In true Momma fashion, she cuts right to the chase. "You figured that, if it was no more, you would have nothing standing between you and Tyler, so you sent an email to the FBI alerting them to our family's clandestine operations."

I close my eyes, guilty and hurt. "Yes. I see now that what you did with John was a way to protect The Guild. But I didn't know that then, and I was so hurt and so angry." It sounds like I'm excusing myself, but I only want to explain. "I shouldn't have sent the email. I'm sorry."

She makes a noise of protest. "You had every right to send the letter."

My eyelids spring open and I look directly into her serious brown eyes.

"Gracie, I sacrificed Tyler and you for The Guild, for the family and the work we do. It is *I* who am sorry."

She's apologizing to me? "No. No." I shake my head. "You did what you had to. If The Guild had been exposed, I likely would've lost custody to John and might've ended up in jail myself."

Momma tilts her body closer to the desk, to me. "I ask a lot of my children. I ask them to risk much in the hopes that we can help balance the scales, help those in need. Sometimes, I worry that what they are given in return isn't enough to compensate for what they are asked to do."

I slap a hand onto her desk. "No. That's not true. What we're asked to do is the reward, Momma. Helping others the way we can is a gift." I see this now more than ever. It's not Momma who taught me this, though she tried to. It was Cee. "When I talk with

Cee, someone who desperately wants to do the work, I understand what a privilege you've allowed us to have. If not for you, for the opportunity of The Guild, Cee would never have a chance to heal herself through service to others. That's the gift, Momma."

Grabbing a tissue from the box on her desk, Momma comes around to me.

I stand automatically, uncertain of her intent until she reaches out and dabs the tears under my eyes.

"My daughter, you are the gift. All of you are my gifts."

I walk into her embrace. She holds me so tight that I know I'm not only forgiven, I am truly loved. "I'm sorry," I say again.

"Shh," she whispers in my ear. "We can't change the past, but we can do our best to make our present better. So, I am going to promise you, right now, that you will be reunited with your son. I will move Heaven and Earth to see it happen."

She pulls back from the embrace. "But, before that, we need to deal with the information your young man has brought us. The recording of your mother speaking of Senator Rush is real. Any other recording of her is unequivocally false."

I never had a doubt. "I want to see the recording."

#

Dusty and I are seated on Momma's side of the big office she shares with Leland. Leland and Momma sit across from us on a multicolored couch that resembles a quilt, sewn together from dozens of bright fabrics. Kind of like my family.

Since I'm the only one adopted as an infant, I feel like I have a unique perspective on Leland and Momma. One that's different from Justice, Bridget, Dada, and Tony. To me, Momma and Leland are my parents. They've been in my life since my earliest memory and I love them.

But there's also Sheila, my biological mother and the woman I came to know as she struggled to ring out every bit of joy from life while battling cancer.

She won that battle. Up until the end, she won the battle to keep living while dying. The young and healthy woman on the retractable television screen isn't the woman I remember. The woman who'd been sick.

As a nineteen-year-old, Sheila had had a healthy glow, blonde hair, a thin, girlish body, and a guileless look. She also had a heavy burden to carry even then.

The long-ago recorded interview started with how she'd first become involved in politics, and how she'd met the would-be senator, Andrew Rush. An off-camera female interviewer asks her to describe the night of the "incident." It's a leading and unprofessional interview, but it's obvious this is difficult for both of them.

The story comes out haltingly and has already brought me to tears multiple times. I'm clutching the tissue in one hand and Dusty's hand with the other.

My heart aches hearing the details of how my biological father tricked, then drugged, a naïve Sheila.

As devastated as I am for Sheila—and for myself for being a product of such a vile act—the logical part of my brain can't miss how easily this tape could've been altered by having the questioner ask different things. Still, you'd have to be blind not to see the honesty of it. There isn't a question in my mind as to Senator Rush's guilt as the interviewer very gently asks, "Were you a virgin?"

Sheila lowers her head, nods and breaks into sobs.

I cry with her, putting the tissue to my mouth to muffle my own cries.

Dusty puts his arm around my shoulder and squeezes me close.

I wipe my eyes, then lean into him. He is solid and warm, and I'm so glad to have him at my side.

The tape winks to black. When it starts again, Sheila has a tissue balled up in her right hand and the interviewer asks her, "Why didn't you go to the police?"

"It would've been his word to mine, and I didn't even have citizenship. I wouldn't matter to them."

"You matter to me," Dusty says to the girl on the screen, and my heart opens even more to him.

She matters to me, too. All of them do. All of the women and girls discounted and not believed matter to me and to Momma. It's why The Guild exists. We might not be able to change things overnight, but we can't not try every day to help.

The playback stops. There are long moments of silence broken only by me slowly getting control of myself.

"Dalia was so young and inexperienced when this was recorded," I note about my sister, who'd recorded this interview with her friend, Sheila. Dalia is one of my older sisters, a person I see more on television than in real life. She's an international reporter, but, back then, she'd only been a teen, like my mother.

"Yes," Momma says, wiping the corners of her own eyes where a part of her niqab has gotten wet. "She and Sheila met at a nail salon and became fast friends over the next year. After Rush raped her, Sheila confided in Dalia, who took it on herself to record the facts. It wasn't well done, but Dalia refused all my attempts to redo the recording. As you can see, it was difficult for both of them."

I say, "After Sheila told Dalia what happened, Dalia told you, and you did what you do."

There's no heat in my voice, but Momma asks, "You're disappointed in me?"

"No. I'm not even mad. And not only because you've been so understanding and sweet about my indiscretion with the FBI." I blush to the roots of my hair and Dusty squeezes my hand. "Mostly I'm glad that Rush was made to pay, at least, in this way. Honestly, I hope all this time he's doubted his safety, doubted his choices, and regretted his decisions. I hope he spent years looking over his shoulder, checking the locks on his home, terrified of what might happen."

As my bio-mom Sheila had surely done.

"He has," Momma says. "But now that you know, you must have many more questions."

I do. Questions about why she adopted me, questions about who else knows, questions about how the blackmail worked, but, right now, my biggest questions is, "How do we take Rush down? Not just stop him or whoever is after me, but stop that creep from becoming president?"

Leland's face, which up until now had been creased with worry and concern for me, breaks into a slow smile. "That's my girl," he says, and his voice is tight with emotion.

Darn tootin'. Questions will come later when I can go back to fixing the things I broke, when I can make it up to Momma for sending that email. She might not blame me, but I do.

Momma looks to Dusty. "And what of you? Are you interested in joining us in this endeavor?"

My heart rockets into my throat. I'm stunned by this question. More stunned, if I'm being honest, than when I'd found out about Rush being my father. Still, I shouldn't be surprised. Momma needs to make some quick decisions about Dusty, and she's all about seeking opportunity. What better way than to put him on the hotspot before he really knows too much?

Mouth dry, I turn to Dusty. His face is uncertain and confused, as if he wishes he were anywhere but here. A sharp ache stabs me in the chest. Why does his reaction hurt so badly? It shouldn't be a surprise. After all, he came here to stop The Guild, not to join it.

Leland, ever the protective father, makes a disparaging sound. "Even if he said yes, we can't trust him."

Dusty meets Leland's straight stare with one of his own, then squares his broad shoulders.

I can't help but wonder if Dusty knows exactly how intimidating that gesture looks on him.

"I appreciate your concern, Leland, I do," he says, crossing his arms and making himself even bigger. "But if I wasn't already all in, I wouldn't be here, revealing company secrets, breaking the law. I'm hesitating because I'm not sure you will let me do my job my way."

"Your job as an agent investigating my family?" Leland's tone has as much bite as growl.

Dusty's legs are slung out in front of him and crossed at his ankles. He'd appear casual, except for his crossed arms, squared shoulders, and the storm in his eyes. "Already told you that's not's an issue."

"What *is* the issue?" Leland asks with not an ounce of give in his tone.

This is getting beyond tense, and I'm not sure of my role here. Part of me wants to back Leland up, press Dusty, but part of me trusts Dusty and wants Leland to leave him alone.

Basically, I'm a mess.

Dusty says, "The issue is information, Leland. If you want me to help out, I'm gonna need everything you got on Rush and on the blackmail. Anything that will help me identify the real threat to Grace. Something tells me y'all aren't prepared to give me what I need."

I tighten my hands into fists so hard that my nails dig into my palms. Dusty is asking not only for information, but for proof of the family's activities.

This information is exactly what he'd need to create a case against Momma. This is the very thing he was looking for when he'd first contacted Tony.

Chapter 41
Gracie

The sticky ball of tension now filling Momma and Leland's office seems to press on my every nerve. Dusty is asking for proof of family activities in order to help me, and Leland isn't taking it lightly.

Leland glares. "We have a whole organization of trained and capable people who've been on hiatus and are itching for work. In short, what you're demanding is out of the question. Moreover, we don't need you."

"You're wrong." I say, and I even I'm a bit shocked at my response.

Momma and Leland give me their stunned attention.

I relax my fists and take a leap of faith. "We need Dusty. He knows more about this case, the players and details, than almost anyone. He has the contacts and skills, and, unlike someone from The Guild, he won't need to be brought up to speed. He's already given us valuable and actionable information, and, more than that, I trust him and want his help."

An awkward silence crashes into the room. It thuds down, kicks up dust, and sends Momma's and Leland's eyes rapidly blinking.

I chance a peek at Dusty.

He smiles at me like a kid on Christmas morning. His heart, as the saying goes, is in his eyes.

"See there," he says softly, "always knew you had good instincts." His smile drops as he addresses Leland and Momma.

"And I think a good family, so if you can't offer me the same trust as Grace, maybe you can trust the facts. Facts are, I've got no reason to go against you right now. I'm off the case, punched out my boss, and I'm sleeping with the enemy."

He winks at me, and I shake my head, biting back a smile.

Leland and Momma exchange a long look, and though it's subtle, I see a signal pass between them, a tip of Leland's chin, an acceptance.

Momma clasps her hands together in an all-business way that isn't diminished at all by the jingle of the bracelets on her wrists. "We can extend you the courtesy, as you have, of facts. This is what we know so far."

For the next forty minutes, the exchange of information is breathtaking. The flow of facts and ideas sets the energy in the room buzzing. It reminds me of why The Guild works and why I need a team and why I should've come to Momma sooner.

My fear of what I did with the email, my unfounded fear of what Momma would do to John, all of it had tied me in knots. For all the wrong reasons.

No one person can do this on their own, and, now, I'm not alone. My throat closes and my heart melts at the realization. Though, of course, that doesn't mean the *team* is always going to say things I want to hear.

"Although I dearly respect Victor," Momma says after I tell her that he'd been helping on the case, "how focused could his investigation be when he's still recovering from severe injuries from Mexico and simultaneously picking up the slack for Sandesh who's now overseas with Justice?"

The implication is obvious. *He isn't Superman. We need to reevaluate his research on the Rush family.*

"Let's not get stuck on the Rush family," Dusty says. "I do think Victor makes a good point about John and Ellen, too. It's odd that they moved money around before each incident. There's something there. My gut says it's tied to this."

"Maybe," I say, "but my money is on Porter."

Momma nods. "Both are viable avenues to explore." She fiddles with the series of gold bangles on her wrist. "But Dusty's point has my attention, because…" Trailing off, she looks at Leland.

He says, "All of this feels very personal."

"Exactly," Momma says. "The attempts on Gracie's life feel… personal, not professional. And who would have a deeply personal reason for these attacks besides John?"

Leland cocks his head to the side and meets Momma's gaze. After a look that seems to last a full minute, they simultaneously blurt, "The sister."

"Layla?" I ask, the shock in my voice obvious.

Dusty whistles like he's had an epiphany. "She has multiple degrees in computer engineering, including as an artificial intelligence programmer." He's already incorporating information we shared moments ago. "She would've been able to mess with the security at the club, allowing those guys who broke in access through the tunnel."

True, but how would she have known about the tunnel?

"She could have altered the video and sent that to the FBI," Momma adds. "Maybe her brother gave her the original, the one we sent to Senator Andrew Rush years ago. Maybe Layla is doing this alone or maybe she and Porter are working together in multiple pronged attacks."

Layla or Layla *and* Porter? They kind of make sense together. He definitely wants his father to be president, but could she be that angry over being ousted from her role as the one and only Rush girl?

"I don't know," I say. "She has her own life. According to Victor, she's engaged to one man, happily involved with her bodyguard in a secret throuple, and has millions of followers on social media."

"Two men willing to stand by her side and a community of people at her fingertips with a bit of hero worship?" Dusty says. "Could be enough for one woman to be happy or it could be a sociopath's starting point."

As soon as the idea of Layla as our would-be killer is out there, we begin to build on it, on how Porter and Layla or Layla and her partners conspired to kill me. The ease with which we toss out different hypotheses drives home the fact we've grown comfortable with each other in the last hour, if not certain of each other.

In the end, my head is swimming. "We have some theories here, but not anything concrete. If Layla did cause the explosions at the club in order to hurt me and/or get information, she made a big mistake. The servers dump anything incriminating automatically when 9-1-1 is called."

"We can't know what she wanted until we get into her own computers and into the club computers," Dusty says.

"True. I'll take a closer look at my computers and Layla. If it is her, I'll find her weakness, a point of attack for us to exploit in our response."

If Layla thinks she can out-hack me, she's dead wrong. Emphasis on *dead*.

Leland, typing madly on his tablet, says, "Evidence that she doctored those videos would come in handy."

"So would a confession, Leland," I say. Sheesh. "Wait. Is it possible for me to use the computers down in Internal Security to do this deep dive into Layla?"

The computers inside The Guild, the underground operations center, are unrivaled in speed and ability. They'd make it so much easier to hack Layla.

Leland eyes Dusty, then shakes his head. "No. Much too risky right now. Not only because of the FBI investigation, but we have reason to believe the NSA is directing satellites toward the house."

"They are," Dusty says, putting out information that raises every eyebrow in the room. "Or, at least, they were. If you've got something to hide, you should take all precautions."

"Thanks," Leland says.

It's one word and simple, but what happened in the last few

moments is momentous. I feel it, the shift. Dusty isn't John. Dusty is here for me.

"Okay. I'll have to use the club computers tonight to—"

"Tonight?" Momma says. "But what of dinner?"

I cringe. It's not like we don't have a dinner together nearly every night, but it is a new thing for me and for Dusty to be here. Momma is big on family, big on unity, and big on dinners that unite family.

Seeing as I have no choice, not after she was so gracious in her response to my letter to the FBI—even going so far as to take partial blame—I say, "Tomorrow then."

Chapter 42
Dusty

Wearing a borrowed suit from what Leland calls *stock,* I hang back at the edges of the dining hall, taking in the immense Parish family eatery. A giant table long enough to bowl on, wood beams cross a fifty-foot-high vaulted ceiling lined with a sparkling array of chandeliers. The table is set with blue crystal goblets, gleaming blue plates, and vases of blue roses running down the center. *Swanky* doesn't cover it. Neither does *crowded.*

There's a lot of laughter and conversation as people file into the room, but I've been given the stink eye by more than one person. That chick with the blue streak in her hair, for one. I'm going to wait right here for Grace because I'm friendly, not suicidal.

The same little girl I'd seen earlier runs past me into the dining room, shouting, "Gracie's here!"

My heart echoes her shout as I spin to greet my woman.

Holy—

Blood explodes through my body like a hot, painful grenade. Good Lord, that isn't fair.

Grace has dressed up.

She wears an off-the-shoulder sapphire dress that swathes around her hips like a second skin. Her hair is down, kissing those bare shoulders. The swing of her stride in heels shows off every sleek muscle and sets my heart racing.

She comes to a stop before me and my gaze travels down her body. I am dumbstruck by her beauty.

She runs a hand down my suit. "You look handsome all dressed up."

This is the point where language should come out of my mouth, something spectacular that lets this woman know exactly how gorgeous she looks—and how I'm going to worship every inch of her later tonight. And every single night thereafter. But all I can manage is a restraining hand to my chest because she has shot me dead center.

Her face warms with heat. She swings her hips. "You like?"

I like. If only I knew sign language, I could tell her just how much I *like*.

Aw, hell. Maybe, this isn't the right time for words. I put my hands on her waist and pull her close. The heat of our contact draws a hiss from my mouth. I kiss her, a slow torture that speaks every phrase I really wish I could say right now.

I draw back and she says, "I hope that's a promise."

I find my voice. "It's the start of a promise." A bit rough, but I did find it. "You get the rest later. Eat up now. You'll need nourishment."

She blushes a heart-revving red as we turn to find every eye at the table is now turned on us. Including her mother's and Leland's. Damn. I'd forgotten where I was. Completely unfair.

With a dip of my head, I let Grace drag me into the room.

She introduces me to her siblings in rapid fire before quickly trying to pull me away. I resist and repeat every name while pointing to each one—rude in some instances, but not this one—ending with the kid I remember from our adventure in Philly. I point at her. "Cee, right?"

She nods a bit suspiciously at me.

I say, "You ever consider being a pole vaulter? You got some mad fence-jumping skills.

She covers an unexpected laugh, but the kid next to her, Rome, gives me a hostile look. He can join the same club as Elisaveta, AKA Veta of the blue hair streak, also giving me the stink eye. Can't win 'em all.

Grace pulls me away and I whisper to her, "I feel like Veta is warming to me."

She laughs loudly. "No doubt you're right, but I wouldn't let her lure you into any dark alleys."

My turn to laugh. "Noted."

Grace takes me to the head of the table where we sit near Leland and Mukta. Much to my surprise, after we greet them and settle in, Leland and Mukta spend dinner acting like regular parents, talking with kids, telling others to take a seat, keeping people in line, helping Bella, the little Russian kid, cut her steak.

Bella made a good choice with the steak. Mine's damn good. I take another bite of the perfectly tender, perfectly rare bit of meat. The whole night, so far, has been damn good. Though no one from Gracie's class is here, and I had hoped to get to know Justice, Dada, and Bridget better, I'm enjoying myself.

Being around a whole bunch of Parish kids—though far from all of them—is a totally enlightening experience. The thing I'm noticing most, besides the sense of unity and inside jokes, is the casual swearing. It has me wondering.

Swallowing a sip of water—seems a sin to wash down even the memory of that bite of steak—I lean over and ask Gracie, "Your whole family cusses." I nod toward Bella. "Pretty sure I heard her swear in Russian. Your momma doesn't mind?"

She shakes her head. "Each of the kids here has come from a difficult and sometimes nightmare situation. Getting them to heal and feel trust and feel accepted is a higher priority for Momma than raising a bunch of proper ladies."

Makes sense. "Sounds like she's got her priorities well set."

"She does."

"So why don't you ever cuss?"

She scoops up a forkful of French fondant. "Growing up, I was a multilingual curser." She lowers her voice. "Except for the b-word, of course."

Does she mean bitch? "Help me understand that 'of course.'"

She swallows the potatoes. "A lot of my sisters came from situations where that word labeled them. It described their femaleness as lesser, a wrongness. For us, it's taboo because it was used so often to hurt and control."

I look around the room at the kids eating and laughing, teasing and joking. Yeah. I'm never using that word again. "Okay. That makes sense to me. So you used to cuss, but not that word."

"Yep. Until I had a baby. John hated my cursing and wouldn't let a *damn* pass without comment." She pauses with her fork midair. "And, really, he was right. I mean, who curses around a baby, even if it's in another language?"

"Practically every adult I've ever met, but I'm still having a hard time figuring out what you're saying. Why don't you curse?"

She looks down at her nearly empty plate. Red rushes up and over her cheeks. "It's my way of still being a mom, I guess. And my penance for letting Tyler go."

She means her way of never forgiving herself. Damn. Hurts my heart. "Remember that story I told you about me getting sick and my uncle coming into my dad's ministry to get me out?"

She puts down her fork, then wipes the corners of her mouth with a blue cloth napkin. "Yeah."

"My mom called him. She called him to come get me and take me out, even though she knew that if she'd tried to go with me, my dad never would've let me go."

Her eyes widen.

"Yep. She gave me up so my life would be better. That's what you did for Ty. Given the choice, you sacrificed yourself to keep someone you love safe."

When a tear slides down her face, exposed and raw, I brush it away for her. "I know you wish you could take back that time you weren't there, but you have to realize that what you did was out of love."

This time, she wipes aside her tears, then tips up her head and kisses me.

I jolt. Not from the kiss which was nice and sweet, but from the pinch. I look down at the pincher.

Bella. The corners of her dark eyes are squeezed in anger. "Don't make Gracie cry."

Grace laughs.

Aw, hell. These kids tug at a man's heart. "Yes, ma'am. Sorry 'bout that."

Chapter 43
Gracie

After dinner, I'm ready to skip dessert and head to bed, but the dessert trays are brought out and Dusty's eyes go wide. There's nothing like dessert at the Mantua Home. The servers carry the artful cakes with various frostings and layers and intricate decorations around the table as my siblings *ooh* and *aah*.

Dusty leans over to me. "I had a grandmother who could make a mean pecan pie, but this is *Cake Boss*—type material."

I kiss him on his cheek because his appreciation of things I've forgotten to appreciate makes me happy.

After everyone has had a chance to appreciate the cakes, they're taken to a serving station. One of the servers, a big guy with an easy grin and a Pacific Islander tan, takes out a gleaming silver knife, and, with a flourish that sends the kids clapping, begins to cut slices.

I decide on the Mantua Home's world-famous cheesecake, but Dusty has the red velvet because he's never had it before. That newbie statement, made loudly to the table, means that while he eats his first bite, the kids around him watch his reaction intently.

Okay, I watch, too. With a raise of his eyebrows, Dusty hums his approval, then closes his eyes and declares it, "Good enough to make the angels sing."

It touches my heart because his vulnerability, showing that he might be big and tough looking but that he doesn't know everything and isn't afraid to say it, is a gift to these kids.

With the addition of sugar, the conversation at the table

quickly reaches earsplitting levels. Dusty keeps up without a problem. When Momma claps her hands twice, though, the room goes silent. She stands and nods in approval. "It's time for us to share a story."

I grab Dusty's hand, ready to get him out of here. "Let's go to bed."

"You don't like stories?" he asks.

Passing behind us on her way into the story room, Momma stops and puts her hand on his shoulder.

He looks up at her.

She says, "I'd like you to hear this. It's my story. The way this all"—she waves around—"came to be."

Fudge. Dusty looks to me and I smile my acceptance because I have no choice unless I want to create a scene.

He tells Momma, "Looking forward to it."

My hand tenses on his forearm and he looks down. I let go, not wanting to clue him in to my distress. I don't think he'll react well to story time. I don't think he'll understand the importance of it.

Everyone rises from the table in various levels of casual, heading through the archway to the room with the large hearth.

My mouth is suddenly dry.

Dusty and I enter the room hand-in-hand. All around us, my siblings take seats, plopping down on blue-and-gold pillows to form a circle around the enormous brick hearth. Unlike at the table where everyone sits with others their age—their units—here, older kids call the younger ones to sit beside them, so it's a mixture of ages.

I point to a spot, and Dusty and I settle on the floor. My shoulders rise almost to my ears and my jaw aches as I clench my teeth. Dusty puts one arm behind me, leans on it, so my entire left side is by his strength and warmth.

He leans close to my ear. "I take it by your tension that this is a big deal?"

I whisper in his ear, hoping I can mitigate whatever damage

is about to happen, "Look, given your history, this might not be your cup of tea, but you have to understand that sharing stories is a way for us to become close. Each person here has a story that tells us about them, where they came from, what they've endured, even me. Our stories are told in second person, read by one of our older sisters, and are shared at different times throughout the year. Sometimes, we hear stories about people who aren't even at dinner because it helps us connect with them."

"Read in second person? That seems"— he pauses, and I can tell he's becoming uncomfortable with this— "to unnecessarily personalize it."

"It does, but the idea is that you feel the others' stories."

He frowns. "Tonight, it's your mother's story? I know she was attacked with acid as a child. Are the kids here, the younger ones, okay to hear that?"

This, at least, I can answer. "They've lived this or worse, Dusty." I place my hand over his, which rests on my knee. "Please keep an open mind. This is a big deal. We don't ever let strangers hear these stories."

"Never?"

I nod and gesture at the room, which has emptied of the caregivers. "Not even the care staff is allowed."

He shifts uncomfortably. "I'm not sure…"

A soft female voice whispers out from audio speakers, and everyone falls silent.

You walk into the Red Cross tent with feet chalked white from the dust and dirt of the road. The ruined skin on your face pulses with a thousand painful fires.

Rejection. Regret. Injustice. Shame.

Sliding onto the hot stool by the entrance, you wait to be noticed. It doesn't take long before a woman gasps, grabbing at the loose-sleeved olive shirt of another woman.

"Karen," she says, forcing her to turn around.

Their colored eyes, specks of blue and green, float over you like flower petals adrift in a bowl of water. You can't help but be drawn to them as they bloom with pity at the destruction of your aching face.

The second woman, Karen, comes to you without hesitation. She scoops you from the chair, murmuring words you cannot understand, and, yet, they comfort your ragged thoughts, tucking in grief with their plush softness as she places you upon a plain, narrow bed.

You groan as the shift in position pinches your wounds. Her words seem kind, soothing, but under that softness rests a pallet of ripe anger, a frustration born of centuries. You recognize the sound. It has been with you since that far-off day.

That day, your mother whispered to you, "They will cut you here," and placed her warm hand between your legs, "because we must pay the price of desire. No charm comes without a chain."

"Who did this to your face?" Karen asks, speaking English now. Her oddly accented words sound clipped and tight.

You say, "A man I refused."

The story continues, recounting Momma's pain, humiliation, and being rejected by her family after the acid attack. I watch every emotion that crosses Dusty's face. I see the sympathy, the disbelief, and empathy, but as the kids around him begin to cry, I see him change, grow tense and angry.

The story finishes with Momma being adopted by the women in that tent—a lesbian couple, one of whom, Karen, happened to be the daughter of the wealthy Coleman Bell Parish. It stops with that happy ending.

Dusty's face looks anything but happy as the lights come up to reveal older siblings comforting the younger ones. He squeezes my hand and says, "I'm gonna get going."

He stands and I stand with him. I know now why my heart is racing, why this pain feels so very familiar. He's leaving like John, and, like John, he will never come back.

Around us, in the quiet aftermath, my siblings talk about details from their own life stories and a wave of love for them envelopes me.

How can he not see that Momma's story helps them share their own pain? Can't he see how children from all over the world suddenly come together as one loving unit, a family? Momma's story has become their story, just as each of their stories became the family's story.

But his eyes are shocked and bothered, and I know he doesn't see this aspect of story time. He sees the manipulation, the force-fed story that shows Momma as a sympathetic character, something that might make it harder for these children to question what she's asking them to do, training them to do.

I understand, but I don't agree, so I harden my heart to him. "Can I walk you to your car?"

His eyes settle on me, on my tell-a-tale face, and he opens his mouth then closes it, swallowing whatever he'd been about to say. "Sure."

After saying good night to Momma and Leland, Dusty takes me by the arm, and we walk in silence through the hallways to the front doors. He turns to me. "Grace, I don't actually have my car."

"I know. You said good night to Momma, told her you weren't staying. Trust me, by now she's directed someone to bring a limo around for you."

He looks toward the front doors. "Kind of her."

"That's Momma."

He shifts. "Grace—"

"Don't," I say. "I can see it in your face. You don't approve. Trust me, I've been there. You're not the first person I've cared about that I've introduced to my family."

That gets a reaction. His eyes widen. He leans close to my face. "That's not this, not what I'm experiencing. That's John. Not me."

"You're leaving, and I saw your reaction during the reading. I saw it."

"What you saw is complicated. Not so much disapproval as—" He runs a hand through his hair. "Fine. It got me. I'll admit that. Reminded me of my childhood, of the way my dad would manipulate people into feeling empathy with him, for him."

He's wrong. "I know the storytelling feels manipulative, but it's not. We can't understand each other's story, each other's pain, unless it feels like we are experiencing it for ourselves. Why are you so bothered by our truth?"

"Fuck, no." He shakes his head. His honey eyes are angry now, intense. "It's not about wanting you to keep all that inside. It's complicated. The way I'm feeling is complicated because of the fucked-up way I was raised. You get that? I need time to process, to sort out all this…"

He doesn't say anger, but I hear the word.

He says, "Can you give me that time?"

Of course, I understand what he's asking, but it still hurts, and it still feels like that familiar ache that happened with John, like rejection. "Okay."

He bends and kisses me on the lips. "I'll see you tomorrow."

I watch him leave, knowing there won't be a tomorrow for us. I don't believe that, not for one minute.

Chapter 44
Gracie

Wearing a charcoal-gray pantsuit buttoned up over a white cami, my hair in a tight bun, I speed walk through the hospital corridor. The click and pound of my shoes echo across my jangled nerves. Delilah is finally ready to see me. I'm so nervous that my heart keeps time with my sharp-heeled footfalls.

I'm almost there when I get a text from Victor: *Roja. Came back for a follow-up and noticed your car. Can we talk?*

I really do want to chat with him and check up on his injuries, but I don't want to rush this meeting. And I promised to meet Dusty at my club when I was done. He said there's something he wanted to tell me. I'm not sure if that's good or bad. Probably bad.

I text back: *I'm meeting with someone. I could be a while. Another time?*

He answers right away with a ping of his location and: *I'll wait for you here.*

He's going to wait? It must be important.

I text *okay* to Victor, then text Dusty that I'm meeting with Victor after I speak with Delilah and might be a little late to the club. I put my phone away. Taking a deep, fortifying breath, I knock lightly on the door using a single knuckle.

After a moment, it swings open. An older man with thick black hair, still black eyes, and a sun-lined and tanned face stands there.

His heavy eyebrows bunch together. "Can I help you?" He has a soft Middle Eastern accent.

I hold up the flowers in my hands. "I'm Gracie Parish." I swallow over regret and shame. "I'm the owner of Club When? I'm here to see Delilah. Is she available?"

Someone inside answers. "Let her in, Papa."

The vase suddenly feels heavy and slippery in my sweaty hands as I walk into a room packed with flowers and people. It reminds me of a poem I once read about bringing a cup of water to the ocean. Flowers. What a meaningless gesture.

I've never seen so many people squeezed into one room, and considering my family, that says something.

Reclining in the bed is Delilah, the woman from the bar, the straightshooter all the way down to her drink.

Her leg is missing below a heavily bandaged knee. She also has bandages around her head. Her eyes are sunken and bruised.

The people in the room silently watch me as I awkwardly hold the flowers. "I wanted to come and say how sorry I am," I say, licking dry lips. "And to see if there is anything I can do to make things easier for you."

One of the men in the room speaks to one of the women in Arabic, and because I know enough of the language, I understand him saying they'd left Iraq to avoid losing limbs while dancing.

Delilah eyes flash at the speaker. A warning? Agreement? She shifts forward in her bed. "Could you all leave us for a moment, please?"

My face grows hot as the people begin to rise and move from their positions holding up the walls, and exit.

"You understood him?" Delilah says.

She's observant. I nod and change the subject, saying what I came here to say. "I'm so sorry that you were injured. I'm going to do whatever I can to help you, including paying any hospital or rehabilitation bills. And I want you to know that I would've been here sooner, but I wasn't allowed to visit before today."

Delilah shakes her head. "The timing of your visit and what happened to me are not your fault."

She's wrong. Her injury is my fault. I should've closed the club.

She holds out her hands. "They're beautiful and my favorite."

"Mine, too." I hand her the vase.

After smelling the lilacs, she slides over the hospital phone and a Styrofoam cup of water and places the vase on her nightstand. Her eyes crease with concern. "Don't look so miserable. Honestly, you're making me uncomfortable. You didn't do this."

I didn't do it, but I'd suspected someone was after me so I should've anticipated that they might go after the club as well.

"I'm taking care of all of your hospital bills. I'm working with your attorneys to get you the money you need to..." I swallow the word *recover* and instead say, "rehabilitate."

Delilah closes her eyes. "I know. You and your family have been very generous. I would not be eligible for some of the technology, especially for my home, that you've been able to get for me, and I really appreciate it."

It wasn't enough. Not nearly enough. "Is there anything else I can do for you? Anything?"

"Anything?" She opens her eyes.

"Name it," I say, hopeful in a childish way.

"You can tell me about him."

Confused, I say, "Who?"

"Your man, the one at the bar. He's so hot."

"Dusty? You want to hear about Dusty?"

Hearing my tone, Delilah flops exasperated hands down by her sides. "I'm just so tired of conversations about pain and fear and lawyers. About interviews for television news and calls for justice. My leg hurts, my back hurts, and I'm simultaneously bored and anxious. My family barely leaves my side. I had to have the nurse throw them out yesterday. They mean well, but they're making it worse."

She wipes a tear from the corner of one eye. I get it. With one single act, Delilah's life has completely changed. She wants to feel like herself again, to talk to about everyday things, like hot guys.

Sitting in the closest chair, the burgundy vinyl seat still hot from the last person, I say, "I met him in Mexico."

Delilah's gaze sharpens. "On vacation?"

Um. Well... "A wild trip, for sure."

#

After visiting with Delilah for nearly an hour, I find Victor exactly where he said he'd be, on a bench outside the main entrance. He looks good, as usual, despite his arm being in a sling. He's wearing black-and-white checkered slacks and a violet shirt, unbuttoned enough to see his naturally tan skin. His dark eyes are bright and alert and his smile wide.

I sit beside him on the wooden bench, lean over and kiss him on the cheek, avoiding his hurt arm. "You waited. I can't believe it. What's up?"

He pulls nervously at a ring on his hand. "Sorry I didn't return your last call, Roja. I've been a bit overwhelmed with the injury and handling the business."

"I completely understand. I was only calling to check up on you. How are you?"

"Good. Fine. Look, I was so out of it the last time we spoke, I forgot to ask you about the Tony stuff, about what you intend to do about him? Whatever you decide, I'm with you."

"Tony stuff?"

Victor's brow drops low over his eyes. "FBI didn't tell you?"

"Tell me what exactly?"

"The security footage you gave me." He makes a fist with his good arm. "You know how I'd been looking through it for anything suspicious?"

"Yeah."

"Well, after I'd spotted Ellen taking photos outside, I kept looking. That's when I spotted someone else. At first, I couldn't believe it was him, so I asked to see more footage. Sure enough, I spotted him twice more lurking around your club, and I zoomed in close, so that there was no mistaking him."

Chills run down my spine. "What does this have to do with Tony?"

"It was him, Roja. Tony."

"No. Tony's dead. I saw him die."

Victor shakes his head. "Where's his body?"

I open my mouth and shut it with a snap. "Dusty... buried him."

"Did he?" Victor says. "How would you know? None of us were there when Dusty took care of Tony. We didn't see any wounds on Tony."

More chills slide down my body. It feels as if I'd plunged into Lake Michigan in November. "There were no wounds. He was poisoned."

"Yep. Poisoned. I know enough about your family to know they probably have access to some extreme medications through Parish Pharmaceuticals."

He's right. My sister Zuri is a scientist. I have no doubt she's invented something that could mimic death.

Victor says, "Everything was so chaotic and emotional in Mexico, he could have easily fooled us."

My heart leaps high into my throat, and I throw my arms around Victor. "Tony is alive!"

He one-arm squeezes me back as joy overwhelms me and tears slide down my face. I don't think there is a word for the relief I feel. I don't think that many people in the world get to experience it, to know what it feels like. It's like waking up and finding your worst nightmare was just a dream. I have to tell Momma. I have to... "You found this out before the fire?"

"Yeah. And Roja, I confronted Dusty. He knows. He swore he'd already told you."

I gasp. "He told you that?"

He nods. "Lo siento. I shouldn't have believed him. I should've told you sooner."

My hands fist at my side and my heart takes a dive so fast and hard, I feel a kick in my chest. "Don't do that, Victor. You won't put up with me blaming myself for the club, and I'm not putting up with you blaming yourself for this. Dusty did this. Dusty and Tony."

"Why do you think he did it?"

"Tony? To get away from the family and the retribution that was coming his way for betraying Justice."

"I meant Dusty."

Oh. My mind starts to race over the possibilities. Is Tony working with Dusty? Is he providing the FBI with information on Momma? Is the family in danger? Was Dusty collecting information on the family, on Momma, on me, last night?

"I don't know." I'm so confused, but Tony is alive, so anything seems possible. "I've been an idiot. Dusty asked me, in bed no less, if he could meet Momma, so what do I do? I bring him to the house."

Victor puts a hand on top of my hands which are clenched in my lap. "He's charming as hell, querida, so don't blame yourself."

No wonder Dusty had shown such disgust when he'd listened to Momma's story.

Stupid, Gracie. So f'ing stupid! I pull my hands away. "Can you let me be the one who tells my family about Tony and Dusty? It's my responsibility."

"Claro." He squeezes my knee. "Pero, if you want, I'll kick FBI's ass for you."

Standing, I sling my purse over my shoulder. "I'll kick it myself. Thanks."

Chapter 45
Gracie

I pull into the parking lot of Club When? with my mind racing over Dusty's betrayal and what I'm going to tell Momma about it, about Tony—not to mention telling my unit. Justice is going to be so happy she'll punch Tony in the face. Once we find him.

As much as it sucks to have this information, I'm keeping it to myself for now. I can't afford to wait any longer on discovering who did this to my club.

Momma was able to get quick approval for the remediation company to come in. Judging by the construction trucks in my parking lot, they've already gotten to work.

I pull into an open spot by the back door, turn off the car, then head inside with a squeak of hinges, no code necessary. It takes my eyes a moment to adjust from going to the light into the dim club, so I hear him before I see him.

"Grace, just in time. I was about to go over some of these—"

Dusty's words cut off as I stalk toward him. He puts up his hands. "Who do I need to murder to take that look of pain off your face?"

"You," I say, letting the tears fall from my eyes. "You did this."

He blinks in surprise. "Don't cry. Please. I'm sorry for leaving last night. I realized this morning when I longed to be holding you that I'd made a mistake. I should've stayed so we could talk. I'm so sorry."

"You're sorry for leaving? What about for lying?"

"What? I didn't—"

The door creaks open behind me and sunlight streams inside. Dusty's head goes up and his eyes widen as if the devil and the grim reaper had walked in.

I spin on my heels, ready to fight or flee.

John?

Entering the corridor in a black suit, black as his mood, the hard set of his jaw a clear rebuke, John stops a few feet from me. "I need to talk to you."

His eyes travel to Dusty, whose Lyle's BB*Q* T-shirt is snug against his huge chest.

Dusty squares his shoulders. Yes, he definitely knows how intimidating that gesture is.

John's eyes bounce from me to Dusty. He says, "This is private."

Dusty crosses his arms, biceps bulging.

I can feel the weight of him, the weight of his protection. It's as if he's saying to me with the absolute strength of his body that he is the one I can trust.

Liar. Liar. Liar. Trust no one.

I say, "What's this about?"

"Gracie Divine..." John cracks his neck as if he has the weight of the world on his shoulders. "It's about Tyler."

Tyler? Where is privacy? My ground-floor office is still a hazard, but the upstairs one is safe, and thanks to the fire marshal's request to leave all security doors open, accessible. "Let's go upstairs."

We move to go. Dusty follows. "Grace."

I stop him with a glare, anger surging through my chest. "No. This isn't about you."

He jerks back, looking sincerely hurt and confused. But he's an *f'ing* special agent of the F.B.-tootin'-I. so I've no doubt he'll figure out why I'm so angry.

Pulling a Jolly Rancher from my pocket, I slip it into my mouth and lead John upstairs. In the hallway, I spin and ask him, "What's going on?"

He glances down the row of open doors. "Where's Tyler? Is he here?"

"Ty? Why would he be here?"

"Stop it, Gracie. I know you were supposed to meet him today. I've read all of your correspondence and really don't appreciate you trying to recruit my son into your family's bullshit."

He looks over my head and down the hall again. "Is he down there? Is he in your apartment?"

"I haven't been talking to Ty. I wouldn't go behind your back like that. Now tell me what's going on."

"You wouldn't go behind my back?" His eyes are mean and angry. "You lied to me for years about who you were and who your family was, and I know you're lying now. I read the emails and texts. You've been messing with us for weeks. El even started her own investigation into you, and now Ty is missing."

Ellen started an investigation on me? Was that why she was taking photos? "Wait. Hold on. Tyler is missing?"

"Stop pretending you don't know."

For a moment, as his dark eyes drill condemnation and anger into me, panic washes through my body, but that's quickly replaced with training. A detached calm that coolly focuses my screaming mind and sends me into action.

"Come with me into my office." We walk through my office to my computer operations room. I kick the chair out of my way, sending it spinning on its wheels. I boot up the computer. I can track Ty's cell from here. I've done it before.

The sound of fans and technology coming online fills the room. "How long has he been missing?"

"El went into Ty's room early this morning to ask him if he wanted to hang out at the station while she performed her new radio show, but he wasn't home."

It's after noon. He's been missing for hours. "Is that normal behavior? When was the last time you saw him? Did he have his phone?"

John gives me an odd, almost panicked look, then says, "What's normal? He's a teen. El dropped Henry, our other son, off at daycare and went to work, figuring Ty would show up eventually. She called him a few times, but no answer. She came back around ten to check on him and found his cell in a drawer. That's when she really started to panic."

Why would he leave his cell? "Have you called the police yet?"

"If you cooperate, I'm hoping it won't come to that." Again, he focuses his rage on me.

The space between us suddenly feels too small, so I take a step back.

He steps forward. "I know what's going on, Gracie. After El found his phone, she opened it and read his texts. Ty has been communicating with your sister Cee on your behalf, telling Tyler he can be part of your family, luring him in with your wealth and media image. She even set up a meeting between you and Tyler for today."

"Cee? My Cee knows Tyler?" No. That makes zero sense. And... "I'm going to need his phone to access those texts." Tyler wants to meet me? The thought sends a surge of panic and hope through me so quickly, I sway on my feet. *Focus. Focus.* "If Cee is involved in this, I know nothing about it."

"If?" He looks mildly nauseous. "Don't you have some kind of tracking system for your people?"

He's right. I turn back to the computer and its still-dark screens. Is this due to the fire? Has something been damaged? Leland had someone out last night and they said the security was working, but I didn't ask to have the computers checked because I wanted to do it myself. *Crud.*

"As soon as the computer kicks on, I can access family GPS information from here. It should only take me a minute or two to figure out where they are. Until then, anything else you can tell me?"

Now John looks uncomfortable. "Years ago, Momma set up

a money market in my name for Tyler. I don't really think about it except at tax time. Today, El searched Ty's room, looking for clues as to where he went and found bank statements he's been intercepting."

Ice rolls down my spine, straight over my feet, freezing me to the spot. Never once had I considered the idea that *Tyler* had been taking money out of that account. "There was money missing from the account and you think Tyler took it and gave it to Cee?"

"It makes sense, doesn't it? Cee is…" He trailed off.

But I get his meaning. Cee is a Parish, a broken kid from the streets who doesn't play by all the rules.

Pushing aside my annoyance, I review what he's told me about Cee's communication with Ty and the money. Cee doesn't need money. Unless…

"Please let me do the job. Please." Was Cee trying to fund her own shadow Guild? If so, how does Tyler fit into this mess? Was it only for the money that she contacted him or for something else?

Crud. I lean back over my computer, check the connections, and one of the screens finally blinks on. I type in my access code to bring up the GPS locator.

Nothing changes on the screen.

A thread of panic works its way through my heart as I try again. The screen pops to life and a video of Sheila, *the* video, begins to play. It's my bio mom giving the exact same testimony she'd given about Andrew Lincoln Rush, except the voice asking the questions isn't asking about Rush.

Isn't this what Dusty had told me about? He'd said there were multiple versions of this interview, but how the heck is it on my computer and playing right now?

"Gracie?" John steps back from the monitors. He looks like he's getting ready to run straight to the police.

I'm starting to sweat as panic bubbles up from my chest. Tyler. I need to focus on finding Tyler and Cee.

I fish my cell from my pocket to call Leland, and it rings in my hand. Victor is calling. I send him a *Can't talk right now* text and dial Leland.

He picks up on the second ring. "Gracie, how'd it go today?"

How'd it go? Oh, the hospital. "Leland, I've got a situation. Can you ping Cee and tell me where she is?"

He must hear the anxiety in my voice, because he doesn't even question. "Hold on. Let me get to the right computer."

As he does his thing, I continue to try and get control of my own computer system. Leland comes back on and says, "She's here on campus and in her room."

Thank God. But where is Tyler? "Are you sure? She couldn't have taken her chip out?"

"No. We've finally figured out a way to program the chips to go off if removed without making them vulnerable to hacking or easily destructible."

I let out a breath and mouth to John. "She's there." And then to Leland I say, "I need to talk with her. It's an emergency."

"I'll have home security run her down."

"Thanks."

The video of my mother is now on every monitor, playing over and over with each one showing a different time stamp, and each one having a different voiceover. The dualling voiceovers run into and against each other through my speakers.

I squeeze my cell between my chin and shoulder and continue to type commands, but nothing is happening. I can't even lower the sound from my keyboard.

The click of a call coming through my cell buzzes in my ear, and I let it go to voicemail. Someone has taken control of the system and blocked me. That's impossible. My system would've alerted me to…

Unless… someone was working on my computer from inside this room.

A lightbulb goes off inside my brain. The fire wasn't set so someone could search for something. It was set so someone could plant something, this video on my computer. *Fudge.* This is bad. "Leland."

"Hold on." I hear him talking with Momma before he comes back on the line with a gruff, "Your mother just walked in. She says security searched Cee's room and found a chip but no Cee."

"You said it couldn't be removed."

"This one was clean," Momma says, and I realize I've been put on speakerphone, "There wasn't a speck of blood on it, which indicates she somehow had a duplicate made."

"But if there are two chips with her ID on it, wouldn't there then be two signals for her?"

"Not if she's wearing a device that blocks one of those signals," Leland says. "In that instance, the signal on the first chip might drop for a moment in the control center, but then we'd have pinged her and picked up on the second chip."

"What about pinging her cell?"

"That was also in her room," Momma says.

My heart hammers as John eyes me warily, the monitors play, and my mind skips over possibilities without landing anywhere. Why would Cee do this? What game is she playing? Could she have anything to do with the attempts on my life, the club fire?

Yesterday, I'd have said no. Yesterday, I'd have thrown down with anyone who suggested this about Cee, but, today, Tony is alive and Dusty is a huge liar and anything seems possible.

I can't help but realign the details to this new reality about Cee. The morning of the fire, Cee had gotten into the club when I wasn't here. She could've planted explosives, and she could've used the money from Tyler to get them made.

Could Cee's need for payback extend to me? Did she lure Tyler away to hurt me and get back at The Guild?

"What's going on?" John asks.

"Gracie?" Leland says. "What's this about?"

I say, "Tyler is missing, too. John is here and he says Ty and

Diana Muñoz Stewart

Cee have been in contact." I hear Momma's sharp intake of breath and feel that same ache of betrayal in my own chest. "Do either of you know why she might do this?"

Momma says, "I can't imagine why."

Leland says, "I don't think we're going to get an answer on that unless it's directly from her, so now that we know about the second chip, let's work on the how."

"You think Rome has some part in this?"

"I do, and we're going talk to him right now."

"Thanks. I'm on my way over."

I hang up and my cell rings immediately. I ignore it and face John, bracing myself to tell him I have no idea where our son is and to tell him that part of the family he's feared—has rightly feared, it turns out—has taken Tyler.

Chapter 46
Dusty

Standing in the debris-strewn corridor outside the kitchen of Club When? I watch as Grace and John head up the stairs without me. I can't get the image of her angry and tear-stained face out of my head. This makes no sense. Why would Grace be so hurt and angry she'd shut me down to talk privately with John?

And what the hell does John have to speak to Grace about? Whatever it was, his face said it wasn't good. This is the last thing she needs today after having met with Delilah. I know it had to have been rough on her, which is why I'm here. I thought she'd need me, but that look of pain she'd given me, the ache written all over her sweet face when she walked in... it nearly killed me.

Why is she hurt and angry at me? It can't be about last night. Yes, she was upset last night, but when I texted her this morning and asked to meet, she'd responded. She said she'd meet me at the club later because she was going to see Delilah. Afterward, she even texted that the meeting went as well as could be expected and that she was meeting with Victor before heading to the club.

Victor.

Could he have said something, made some comment against me that pissed Grace off? I take out my cell, find Victor's number, and call. I put the phone to my ear.

A couple of the construction workers come in through the back entranceway carrying equipment. I nod to them and step out of the way.

"Cops are here," one of the guys says as he goes past.

I turn to find Mack in the back doorway.

Victor answers the phone with an, "Hola."

I have a half second to make the decision and make it in half the time. I shield my mouth from Mack's view and hearing and whisper, "Call Grace. Tell her to take the escape route. Now."

Wearing a black suit and sporting a nose brace and dark circles under his eyes, Mack walks the hall like he owns this place. He's flanked by two police officers and has what I assume is some kind of warrant clutched in his hands. This isn't a friendly visit, and I know it means trouble for Grace. Not hard to put two and two together, not after that last conversation where Mack told me he was going after Grace.

I flex my slow-things-down muscles and reach out a hand to Mack like we're old friends. "Mack."

He ignores the hand. "Dusty."

I shove it into the pocket of my jeans. Casual-like. "What's going on?"

Mack holds out the folded paper. "We have a warrant to search the upstairs and confiscate evidence."

My hackles rise, along with my temper, but I set it to simmer. "What's that all about?"

"You wanted proof, so I'm here for proof." He hitches a thumb toward the steel door that leads upstairs. "I have reason to believe proof that Gracie and her family are involved in blackmail and extortion is contained on a computer upstairs."

Grace told me whatever was left on the servers was harmless. "What proof specifically are we talking about?"

"I have the location of a file that will show that Gracie Parish has taken part in a series of blackmail schemes against elected officials and business leaders."

Evidence? The obvious answer hits me all at once. The evidence was planted during the fire. "Don't do this, Mack."

He shakes his head. "We follow the facts where they lead, Dusty. You know that."

"DNA, evidence, facts—none of it will make a lick of difference if you've decided to toe Rush's line. And he doesn't need your help. The kind of control people like him have over information—whole media empires dedicated to his spin—isn't likely that facts will ever play too large a role."

Mack smooths the lapel of his suit jacket. "You laid the road for this drive. Now, is Grace Parish here? Because I also have a warrant for her arrest."

I square my shoulders, not to intimidate, but to fight. "On what grounds?"

Behind Mack, the two officers tense and exchange a get-ready look. They don't stand a fucking chance, but no reason to make them wary.

I unhitch my shoulders, give them both an all-good-here nod of my head.

Mack takes it all in stride. Actually seems to be enjoying himself. "The exact things your investigation uncovered: blackmail and human-trafficking." He gestures around with that paper clutched in his hand. "Add to that, arson."

Bullshit. My stomach churns. Mack is determined to shield Rush even if that means fabricating evidence. "You have evidence of her involvement in *human-trafficking*? Arson?"

"The fire marshal has plenty of proof it was arson. It's not a stretch to tie it to Gracie, because, as the marshal said, it would've taken a very long time to set those devices. Hours. It's not something some bozo can come in and do on his lunch hour. She lives and works here, has plenty of off time, and there's no way she wouldn't notice the devices. Anyway, I wouldn't be surprised if we found evidence of purchases to make those devices when we search."

"Why would she want to destroy her own club?"

"She obviously knew we were onto her and tried to burn her club down to destroy the evidence. A lot harder to get evidence off a burned computer than a wiped computer."

Oh, sure, and the area upstairs where the evidence is just happens to be unharmed. "This is my case, Mack. I'm not going to let you railroad her."

"As we've already discussed"—Mack runs a finger over the wrapping covering his still-swollen nose—"you are no longer on this case."

Bastard. Although I know the records show why I'd started my investigation, I also know my reports could be misconstrued to support Mack's theory. Especially if Mack has other information to guide the narrative.

If Victor told Grace to run, she should've gone, and John should've come down. He hasn't. I've got to buy more time. "I think Grace's in the front of the club."

"Not here," one of the construction guys says, carrying a halogen work light and an extension cord through the hallway. "Maybe upstairs."

I close my eyes, count to three, and try another tactic. "Let me go up and get her. There's only one way down." I point at the door. "It'll be easier. After she's down, you can go up and search for your evidence."

Mack shakes his head. "You've gone too deep on this one, pal, so take a step back and save what's left of your career." He waves up at his nose. "Because of our history, I didn't turn you in for this. You still have options.

Mack pivots to head up the steps, and I cut him off. Every trace of cool and casual has fled my posture and my mind. These accusations are deadly. "You've got Grace's life in your hands, Mack. Rush will know exactly where she is and how to get at her in your custody. He's already made one, maybe two, attempts."

A tinge of disappointment seems to weigh down Mack's shoulders. "Give me some credit. I checked it out. He wasn't even aware of any attempts on her life. Besides, I intend on taking her someplace no one can get at her."

"Did you check Porter out, too?"

Mack steps past me and starts up the stairs, cops in tow.

Following, I try again. "If you bring Grace to jail, you'll

make her a duck in a shooting gallery. It'll be easy for Porter to get her there."

Mack's loafers make gritty sweeping sounds as he ascends the steps, and he shakes his head. "Trust me. No one will be able to get her. It's a secure location."

"I'm going to fight you on this, Mack. The Parish family will, too. You're going to look like a fool."

Mack stops and glances over his shoulder. "Not if I get Mukta to confess."

Confess? "Why would she do that?"

"I'm pretty sure she'd do just about anything to get her daughter out."

He continues up the stairs, but I'm frozen in place at the implication of what he just said. He's right. Confessing to the blackmail—a white-collar crime—would get Mukta a few months in a cushy Club Fed. Mukta might do that if it got Gracie out of the more serious charges—and if she had no other choice. But she would have a choice. She could send a team of lawyers today and have Grace out of jail in a heartbeat.

As I start back up the stairs, I stew on this, pick it apart like a dog picks meat from a bone, bit by bit. It hits me. Why Mukta will agree. Why Mack isn't worried about anyone getting at Grace. Mack is going to take Grace to a black site. Once there, there will be no way for Mukta to get Grace out.

Mack could keep Grace in that limbo between being arrested and being set free for weeks. Grace would be a prisoner, tortured—no matter what they call it, not letting someone sleep, sit down, piss, is fucking torture—until she confesses.

The thing is, Grace won't confess. No matter what they do to her. I've seen her stubborn and it runs straight down her spine and deep into the earth. She'll die first. My heart tears open with that thought.

I charge up the rest of the stairs. I swear I'll do anything to keep Grace safe.

Chapter 47
Gracie

Standing in my computer room, with John making fists at his sides and my heart starting a *For Whom the Bell Tolls* gong in my chest, I tell John the truth. "There's a chance that Cee *is* with Tyler."

"A chance? What's going on, Gracie Divine? What did Leland say?"

"Cee isn't there. She's missing too. My brother—"

"Tony?"

For a flash my brain falters as the competing thoughts *Tony's dead* and then *Tony's alive* rush me. "No—"

My cell rings again. *Victor. Why does he keep calling?* "It's a different brother who might know something about where Cee and Ty have gone. I'm headed over there now to talk to him. Do you want to come?"

"To the Mantua Home?" His face says he'd rather eat a bug dipped in dog poop. "Fine. Yes. I can meet you there."

My cell goes off again. *Victor again?* I answer. "Victor?"

"Roja, escape route. Go now."

The tone of his voice has me following his directions before I ask one question. I head out of the room and down the hall, cell to my ear. John follows a step behind, asking, "Where are you going? Is this about Ty?"

"Victor, what's this about?"

"No idea. Message is from Dusty."

I stop dead. *Dusty?* What's he up to?

John pulls up beside me. "What are we doing?"

We? Stay or go? Stay or go? Should I trust Dusty? "He didn't give you any hint what this is about?"

"No. Didn't say a word but what I told you, and I know you have some serious issues with him, but if I have a vote, I say go."

"Thanks, Victor." I hang up.

The creak of leather alerts me to someone coming up into the hall. A fed and two cops wearing leather gun belts appear at the other end of the hallway. I take off at a run.

Voices commanding me to stop echo down the hall. I run faster. A weight slams into me and drives me to the ground. We go down in a heap. John's voice comes tight in my ear. "What are you doing? Stop! It's the police."

No way. I can't help Tyler from a jail cell. And since this isn't the first time I've been pinned, I fall back on my training. I elbow John in the face and as he shifts, I roll out from under him, race back down the hall toward my apartment.

One of the cops grabs me. I slip out of his grasp, kick him in the stomach. Another set of hands reaches for me, then the first cop gets back to his feet. I'm surrounded quickly.

I throw a series of punches, then kick Cop One's balls so he drops to the floor. I throw a sharp elbow into Cop Two's neck. He falls to his knees, gasping. Then I'm face-to-face with the Fed and his gun, which is trained on me.

"You are under arrest," the Fed says, breathing heavily. Though he wasn't in the scuffle, it can't be easy to breathe through that nose. "We have a warrant to search the building and remove evidence, including your servers."

I put my hands up. "Evidence of what?"

"Evidence that you and your mother have been bribing numerous elected officials and businessmen and using the money to fund child sexual exploitation."

Is he out of his mind? It's crazy. I'm stunned by the implication for me and for my family. He intends to bring us all down, destroy the entire family. On any other day, I'd take him and this ludicrous charge on and fight the good fight legally, but not on this day. I can't help Ty from jail.

John gets to his feet. He has a red, just-getting-started bruise on his cheek. He looks around like his head is attached to a swivel, back and forth, back and forth. "I think she took my son. She lured him away, got him to give her money, too."

What the hell? *A-hole.*

I'm starting to panic. There's no way I can get out of here without seriously hurting these men. I'm debating taking my opportunity to grab the feds gun when I see Dusty sneaking up behind him.

The moment freezes in time as his gaze locks with mine.

My face grows so hot so quickly my cheeks sting, but, other than that, I don't react as I read the message he is sending me with his unflinching honey eyes. *Trust me.*

Toots. Not likely. I curse the day I first saw those eyes, the pull they have on me. Those eyes lie. Just like the rest of him.

Cop Two, not the guy still moaning on the floor with his hands covering his scrunched scrotum, takes out cuffs as the Fed intones, "Grace Parish, you are hereby under arrest for bribery, extortion, human-trafficking, and arson."

Chapter 48
Dusty

Sneaking down the upstairs hall of Club When?, I keep my eyes on Mack and the gun he has trained on Grace. For a moment, her eyes lift to mine, and I thank God. I send her a *get-ready* nod.

She looks away. *Fuck.* Why is she so mad at me?

The sound of handcuffs being taken out works like a pistol at the starting gate. I thrust my arms under Mack's upraised ones and lift. Mack fires into the ceiling, but it's too late for him to get any kind of control. My arms are just plain old longer. I wrench the gun from his hand and toss him at the cop who, dropping his cuffs, is now reaching for his own weapon.

They crash into the wall and fall over each other, landing on the floor in a heap.

The final cop—I like to think of him as Crushed Balls—stays down. That leaves John. Wouldn't you know it, that fucker tries to grab Grace.

She chops his outstretched arm down, spins away, and runs. I'm a step behind her, but a take a sec to slam John into a wall and hiss, "You fucking fuck" in his face.

A bit childish, sure, but, knowing the guy doesn't like cursing, it feels great.

Grace and I race into her apartment with Mack shouting behind for us to stop. *No can do.*

Gracie slams the steel reinforced door closed, running her fingers over a trackpad.

I hear the steel pins sliding into place a blink before Mack

247

tries to turn the handle. Steal blinds fall in place over all the windows, making things dimmer inside the room.

Mack beats on the door. "There's no way out, Dusty. Open up and I'll forget your part in this."

Pushing away from the door, Gracie turns to me. Her expression, one of distrust and confusion, punches me straight in the chest. Feels like someone took the business end of a pickax and slammed it into my breastbone. Hurts like a son of a bitch.

She whispers, "But you rescued me."

"Not yet, but I intend to. Does that elevator still work?"

She looks toward it then back at me. "Yes. It does, but…"

"Go to your momma's and call me when you're safe. 'Til then, I'll sit here and negotiate with Mack. I'll keep him busy and focused here while you lawyer up. You need to know, Mack means to take you to a black site, Gracie."

"What?"

"Listen now. It's much better if we negotiate you turning yourself in to the police from a position of power. The charges are trumped up. We can get you out of jail easily as long as you're not under Mack's control, hidden at a black site, or someplace where Rush can get at you."

She looks at the elevator again, then at me. "My son… someone, my sister Cee, I think, has taken him."

Her sister took her son? What the hell? I pull a hand across my face, because now I understand what John wanted. "We'll find him, darlin'."

Her spine stiffens with the endearment. She shakes her head. "You're a liar."

Mack begins pounding on the door. "You're throwing away your life here, Dusty."

I keep my focus on Gracie, waiting for her to absorb this moment, what I've done, what I will do, because it's the only testimony I can give since I've no idea why she's so pissed off at me.

Her face folds into confusion. She turns toward the elevator and begins walking away.

That pickaxe draws blood, but I turn toward the door. Why call me a liar? "Mack, we're going to want a couple of concessions before we open this door."

Behind me, I hear the elevator rise and open. I glanced over my shoulder to see if she's gone. She climbs inside and pauses the door from closing with a hand against it. She says, "Unless there's a fire or some other emergency, you can't open that door or the windows without me."

"Well, that sucks for me. Looks like I'll be spending some time here, judging by your security system, it'll take a couple hours for the Feds to break in here."

She bites her lip, releases it, and says, "First half of the elevator code is on page seventeen *Of Mice and Men*. It's the first seven letters going down. The other half is on page three hundred of *Anna Karenina*. The last letter of the first six lines of dialogue." She lets out a breath, a tear on her cheek. "Thanks for holding them off. I'll see you at Momma's."

She lets the elevator door close, and I have the most inappropriate sensation I've ever had in any situation in my entire life—joy.

I feel joy despite being trapped inside her apartment with my SAC on the other side of a steel door, knowing I've lost my job, and am probably going to go to jail.

Joy. Huh. Maybe I can plead crazy. Wouldn't be the first agent to blur the lines during an undercover operation. Yes, sir, I might only end up in a mental institution. And that shouldn't make my heart even lighter and put this smile on my face, but here it is.

Because Ms. Grace Parish, despite whatever her head told her, just decided to follow her heart with me and that is pure joy.

I intend on making sure she never regrets that decision.

Chapter 49
Gracie

Slamming my hands on the armrests on either side of Rome's chair, I growl into his face, "Stop ignoring my questions."

The mood inside Momma and Leland's sun-streaked office drums with tension. They watch uneasily from behind her desk.

The only person who seems immune to this palpable stress is Rome himself. He's as cool as he is unmoved, handsome, and young. This close, I can smell his deodorant and see the acne on his chin.

He shifts.

It's the first sign that I'm getting to him. Uncomfortable with someone invading his personal space? Good. I lean in closer. "Look, Rome, I get it. Cee convinced you to help root out this group, this fraternity, acted like everything you did was related to that, but, clearly, something else is happening here."

Silence.

"Did you know she'd reached out to Ty for money?"

Silence.

"Do you know where she's taken Ty?"

Silence.

Come on, kid. "Why involve Tyler? Did she need his money? Or was it just some way for her to get back at me?"

Rome's eyes snap from staring at the wall to boring into me. "Why would she want to get back at you?" Is that disgust in his voice? "Just because you said you didn't want her to become part of this family and live here?"

"So, she's talked to you about that?"

Rome's eyes narrow. "Do you know what she's been through?"

I do. I interviewed her extensively. Cee told me her story, each and every horrible, gut-churning detail, with an anger that had been chilling. Not sadness. Anger. That's why I hadn't wanted her to come here. I knew Cee was the kind of angry person the power of The Guild could warp.

Pushing off the chair, I lean back against Momma's desk. "I know."

He stares at me as if *I'm* the monster. "Then you know she's not soft. The fact that you didn't like her or didn't want her here doesn't matter to her."

It obviously matters enough that she mentioned it to Rome. "So why reach out to Ty? Why lure my son to... wherever? Why have him deposit money into an account? Did she use that money to set the fire? Did she hire a hitman to kill me? What is she doing with Ty?"

Rome slams his hands against his thighs, lurches forward. "She didn't do any of that. This isn't her. They were supposed to meet, yes, but not what you're saying."

His trust of Cee is just sad. It brings a lump to my throat, but I have to press, for Ty's sake. "I know it's hard when people lie and abuse your trust, but I'm telling you she did this. We have text messages and proof."

Rome flops back against the seat, casts his eyes down with a sigh that says it's all so futile. He starts to pick at the seam on the side of his jeans, making a flicking noise that rides down my spine like a nail. "She wouldn't do that. She loves us."

Kneeling at the side of his chair, I soften my voice. "Look, my son is in danger. The Feds are after me. They have a warrant for my arrest. Somebody set me up, and I'm running out of time. I need to know everything you can tell me about what Cee was working on and how she involved Ty."

He flinches. "I'm sorry about all that, I am, but why aren't you worried about Cee? She's out there. She rates as much as your son. Doesn't she?"

What? My stomach turns. Good thing I haven't eaten anything today. "Are you saying Cee went to meet Ty, but somehow she's in danger, too?"

"Yes." He straightens. "That's what I've been saying. She went to meet Ty—that part's true—but she was supposed to pick up a burner phone and contact me. Except she never called and never got in touch with me. She wouldn't disappear like that. She wouldn't do that. Not to me. Not to Jules. Not to the rest of our unit. And not to you. She wants you to like her."

He's tone is so sure, so completely confidant, that it takes me a moment to recapture thought. "You think Cee wants me to like her?"

Anger dive-bombs his face like a kamikaze. "What, just because you're afraid to trust and love someone, you think Cee doesn't want to be loved?"

Jolted by his anger, I jump back to my feet. "No. I—"

He shakes a fist at me. "You're never going to convince me of that. Never. There's something else going on here. You're not listening."

His words slap me like an open hand. Warmth spreads from my cheeks and down to my chest, a steadfast certainty that I can't deny. He's right. This doesn't add up. Something else is going on here, and my fear of trusting too much—both Cee and Dusty—has prevented me from seeing that truth.

Trying to relax my tense shoulders, I say, "You're right. I asked a lot of questions, but I wasn't listening. I'm listening now. Please tell me."

Rome wipes his palms across his jeans. "Cee wasn't the one to reach out to Ty. Ty reached out to us about the fraternity."

My brain stumbles for a moment; a thousand questions push forward then land on, "Cee told me it was a student at the Mantua Academy who told you about this fraternity. That's not true?"

"*Plus minusve.*"

Latin for more or less. "Explain that."

"Jules got an email right after the drone attack from a school email address, from a student who goes to the Mantua Academy. She told her about a girl who'd been victimized and that no one was helping her. We began to do research on the dark web on the girl and on the group."

At this, Leland comes around Momma's desk and stands beside me, looking down on Rome. "You went undercover on the dark web?"

Rome, looking a little less cocky, nods. "Yeah. We managed to get into the group, and then get into their online… uh"—his eyes lower—"red room."

Leland slams his hand on Momma's desk, causing the cell Cee had left behind to jump. "You bypassed school security to visit the dark web." Leland's voice drops to an ominous rumble like an earthquake. I'm pretty sure I feel the ground shift. "You then used school computers to go to a site that live-streamed coeds being drugged, tortured, and raped?"

Rome shakes his head emphatically. "No, no. The security here is too complex. We went to Starbucks, used their Wi-Fi, an anonymizer, and a laptop I purchased and stored off campus."

These kids. I rub my face. "Anonymous isn't the same thing as secure. A laptop could serve as some damning evidence. They don't differentiate between accessing those sites to help people versus going to those sites to hurt people."

Momma, who'd been unusually quiet, takes that moment to say, "Which is why we don't allow teenagers to conduct unsupervised operations."

Rome doesn't glance at Momma, but he'd have to be a robot not to hear the disapproval in her voice. He whispers, "We were smart about it."

I wave that off. They obviously hadn't been smart *enough* about it, but I have bigger fish to fry. Like finding out where Ty fits into all of this. "Okay, you used the laptop, infiltrated the group, and Cee went after them in North Philly?"

"North Philly?" Leland and Momma say at the same time.

Whoops. I hadn't told them about that little incident. Honestly, I wanted Cee to like me, too. I give Momma and Leland a quick rundown of the incident, then ask Rome, "What happened after that?"

"A few days after the Philly sitch, someone reached out to us and asked if we were the vigilantes who took down the North Philly house."

What? No.

With this information Momma moves to stand with me and Leland. Her hands go on her hips, a sure sign of agitation.

I don't blame her. This is unbelievable, as in, something is not right.

Rome's shoulders tense under the tri-person scrutiny.

"The dark web is anonymous," I say, talking quietly and gently because I can see he's spooked and beginning to understand his many mistakes. "What we do at The Guild is secret, so didn't you wonder how some random person online figured out what and who you were?"

"Of course. We asked."

"And?" Leland asks.

Fidgeting, Rome keeps his eyes on me, on the person who seems least angry right now. He says, "We asked and he told us he was your son, and that his father had told him all about us. He said he'd taken over a school email address, but that he was actually the one who'd given us the lead on the group. He also said that he had others."

This makes absolutely no sense. "You'd have no way of knowing, Rome, but I know that John would never, ever tell Tyler about me and our family... lifestyle." He'd see it as putting him in danger.

My stomach flip flops and I put a hand against it. Someone had set Cee, Ty, and me up in a very smart, very detailed way. "It wasn't Ty sending those emails. You were catfished."

Rome's skin heats with red and he starts to stammer a

protest that dies on his lips and is replaced with desperate truth. He says, "Cee wouldn't tell me where she was supposed to meet Ty because she said it was better if I didn't know, but I got the impression it was in the Poconos."

I swing my head between Momma and Leland on either side of me. They aren't looking at me. They're looking at each other. I say, "It isn't Ty. It isn't Cee. It's someone drawing them together while pretending to be both of them. Someone with enough computer experience to set all of this up and someone with motivation."

Momma and Leland are nodding to this speech, but it's me who names her. "It's Layla."

My cell beeps. My heart picks up its pace as I look at the text from Cee. Coordinates along with the words: *He's here. Come alone or Cee, who's not here, will die.*

I hand Momma the phone and she shows it to Leland. Layla has them both and apparently at separate locations. My eyes travel across Momma's desk to Cee's cell, the number Layla sent her text from. She's good. She hacked Cee's phone, which had layers of security. There's no doubt she even used that phone to spy on her, to listen in on conversations, to gain information, to manipulate.

That's how she'd known about the elevator. She'd been listening in on our conversation in my apartment because, unlike the Mantua Home, my apartment doesn't have a countersurveillance system.

Come alone. Fudge.

The desk phone rings, and Leland reaches across his desk and picks it up. He frowns. "Wave them inside." He hangs up. "Dusty and Victor are here."

Dusty *and* Victor?

It's a lot for one day, but I can't keep what I know about Tony a secret. I grab Momma's hand, look her in the eyes, and whisper directly into her ear, "Tony's alive. He tricked us."

She smiles slowly. "How did you finally figure it out?"

Chapter 50
Dusty

I'm done arguing with Victor, who I'd texted after I finally escaped through Grace's elevator and tunnel to pick me up. The man has a look of pure rage on his face. Though that could be from the pain of driving an Expedition with his arm in a sling.

"I offered to drive your SUV," I say.

"I'm not trusting you with my ride. I saw him—Tony is alive, which means you knew about it, which means you're full of shit."

Images snapshot into my head, Tony dead, Tony standing over me, a needle, and the words... *Leave it...* A sharp pain lances through my skull. I rub my aching head.

I fight down nausea. The setting sun right in my face doesn't help this throbbing headache. Neither does the pounding words, *Leave it be, man. Leave it be.*

"I can't leave it be!" I shout. I bend to get away from the words and the sun, and I nearly vomit. "I don't give a fuck what you saw. As far as I know, the man is dead."

Victor looks over at me. "You okay? You look awfully pale."

"I need to worry about saving Grace's son. I can't think about Tony, about..." I sit back up, tilt my head to the ceiling. "I have to leave it fucking be."

"Calm down. Fuck. Your nose is bleeding."

I can barely hear him over the roar of noise in my head, which pounds each word into my skull over and over. LEAVE. IT. BE.

He slams to a stop at the manned gates of the Mantua Home and pushes back against the seat as a guard comes out. Victor texts something on his phone, and I lean back as my head settles and my stomach tries to right itself. I wipe my nose, and, sure enough, there's blood.

After a surprisingly quick check of the car, the guard waves us through. We drive inside and over a speed bump large enough to jar my teeth. Still recovering from his injuries, Victor cries out, "Mother. Fucker."

Looks like the Mantua Home has themselves a new scanner. *Swanky.* "Pretty sure that motherfucker speedbump has a scanner in it that just weighed our balls."

Victor's eyebrows rise. "Could've bought me dinner first."

I laugh, more at relief that he didn't bring up Tony again. It hurts my head so badly to think of him.

After passing through campus and going up the hill, Victor pulls into a spot, then turns off his car. He texts again on his phone, but I can't care about that.

I'm here.

I climb out of the SUV with my stomach in knots. I have no idea how I'm going to convince Grace that I didn't know about Tony. Hell, *I* wouldn't believe me. I can't even bring forth details from that last hour in Mexico without a blinding headache.

I take the front steps two at a time and, at the top, the door opens for me. I walk inside, and she's there. Grace.

My heart gives a whoop of joy and a rallying cry of *Steady, man.*

Victor sidesteps me, then nods at Gracie. "Where's Mukta?"

She points down the hall. "She's waiting for you."

Beginning to walk in that direction, Victor throws back, "Go easy on him, Roja. He's fucked in the head."

I'm not sure that's the kind of support I want right now. I brace myself to look into her eyes, knowing I'd rather she hit me than see the same look she gave me earlier, the one that screams her pain.

There *is* pain in her eyes, but it's not the same. It's not directed at me, but... *for* me?

She says, "What happened with Tony after we left?"

Searing pain lances my head again, but I fight it, knowing she needs the truth. I try to think, try to remember what happened at the end. Tony. Dead. Tony. Standing over me. A needle.

My head aches like someone is trying to cleave it open. I can feel the blood running down over my lips. I put a hand to my aching head. "I... fuck."

I bend forward and she's there.

Her hand runs along my cheek. "It's okay, Dusty. It's okay."

I blink at her. "I swear to you, I can't fucking remember."

Her eyes look strained and hurt. Hurt not *by* me but *for* me. She puts her arms around me.

A thread of sharp alarm wings up my spine. Why can't I remember? I wrap my arms instinctually around her. "Me not remembering is bad, isn't it?"

She holds me tighter. "Yes. I'm sorry."

Again, that sharp slice of alarm. Something is fucked here. Something is fucked in my head.

Her tears soak into my shirt.

She steps back then wipes her eyes.

"Tony did something to me?"

She nods. "It won't hurt you, not..." She bites her lip, takes out a tissue, and wipes my nose. "Oh, Dusty, I'm so sorry. It can be fixed, but we have a dire situation here, and I need your help, so I don't have time to explain M-erasure to you, the levels of mind-wiping, or what a complete and total Moby Dick Tony has been to you."

Tears spill down her cheeks and that thread of alarm turns to seething anger. What *did* he do to me?

Grace says, "I promise to help you fix this after Tyler is safe. Can you trust me to do that? Can you trust me enough to wait for that?"

My throat swells with emotion. She's asking me to trust her? I nod, then bend to kiss her.

She lifts up onto her toes, and I taste her, rejoice in her, and let this moment fill my chest with joy. So sweet, I can hardly breathe.

She puts a hand on my face and plops back onto her heels. "You are brave and sincere, strong and loyal, kind and fair, and I love you."

I suck in a breath, swallow, and manage. "Love you more, Grace."

Chapter 51
Gracie

Victor's headlights slice a resolute triangle up the winding dirt road. As the car accelerates, I look out the window at this rural-as-Pennsylvania-gets remote part of the Pocono Mountains. The deeper in we get, the rougher the thread of road becomes and the thinner. Moonlight brightens the night sky, but the dense trees block much of it.

Victor curses as we rock over the pothole-strewn road. I know it's not easy with his injuries, but he insisted on coming with us.

Beside me, Dusty asks, "You sure about your intel on Layla?"

"Trust me," he says, "I did a deep dive into her, deep enough to know this chick is a control freak, and I'm telling you that her text might've said different, but she's going to want Cee close by. Plus, it makes the most sense to get you all together and clean up this mess in one swoop. Why else have this meetup on John's property? She obviously wants this as far from her family and their stuff as possible."

Letting out a breath long and low enough to empty my lungs, I try to calm my nerves. What if Cee isn't here? What if…

The big warrior next to me scoots across the back seat and puts his strong, protecting arm across my shoulders. "Focus on the plan. On what you can do."

I lean my head against his shoulder, getting a face full of scratchy Velcro from his bulletproof vest and a rib full of weapons.

Dressed all in black, including his hat and long sleeves, Dusty has a two-way communicator and small armory on his person. Come alone? No thank you.

"You're right." I check my cell, but it stills says No Service. Layla insisted I bring my phone, so I know she's got something up her sleeve.

I fidget in my seat.

Dusty grabs my hand. "Let's go over the plan again."

"Yes. Perfect," I say because I need to feel like this drive has a real and definite end. "I approach the front of John's cabin, as Layla insisted, which will distract her for you to come in the back."

Dusty squeezes me close and says, "I'll be quick as can be. Have the layout of the house memorized and a good sense of the land."

I say, "it's forty acres square in the middle of wild, brush-filled forest."

Victor says, "The perfect family getaway for an angry psychopath to take her victims. "

I groan.

Dusty snorts. "Not that I'd brag, darlin', but the woods and I are fine friends."

"Not that you'd brag."

"Never." He kisses my head. "But if I *were* to brag, I'd say you'd picked the right man for this job. You keep that psycho busy and, when I get close enough, I'll switch on my jammer, which has a good range but shit battery. Once I flick the switch, it'll slow down the signals to her security and her communications. Enough that I can ghost into the house, get Ty, find Cee, if she's there. And—"

"Get out," I say because to me that's the most important part. "I'll handle Layla."

"Don't underestimate her," Victor says. "Whatever she has planned, she has her fiancée and her bodyguard as backup. Those are likely the two men who attacked you in your apartment, Gracie."

"You don't think she'll have anyone else?" I ask.

Dusty says, "She might have Porter, but I think Victor has the right of it. It's doubtful she'd involve anyone who wasn't completely devoted to her, not in something this personal."

Which means, we still have no idea if Porter and Layla are working together.

"She doesn't need more than a few people," Victor adds. "The major thrust of Layla's execution will be electronic. That's her comfort zone. When Dusty signals me via the two-way that he's close, I'll break from my hidey-hole and head straight down the driveway. And *my* jammer"—he inclines his head toward the huge black box that Momma gave him—"has lots of juice. With it, we'll roll over whatever Layla has up her sleeve."

"Easy peasy," I say, over my pounding heart. Layla could do anything. She's terrifying and brilliant, with access to powerful technology and the darkest places on the web through which she can reach the darkest of human minds.

We round another corner and start up the steepest incline yet. Trees crowd the road like a threat. This is the final road, the one that leads to John's driveway and the cabin he'd purchased years ago.

"Victor, this is close enough," I say. "Stop and hide under the cold pack in the back so she won't be able to read your heat signature." Assuming she's that prepared, and I do assume. "Dusty can get out here, and I'll drive us to the spot Layla indicated for me to park."

He pulls over, turns off the lights. "You sure we shouldn't try to get closer?"

"No. I'm nervous enough about bringing you guys." Momma and Leland had tried repeatedly to get me to let them organize a bigger team. That would've been a disaster. The time it would've taken, for one. The risk for the family—this is getting beyond complicated with the FBI without adding people. Plus, I have enough dealing with Layla; I can't add siblings hopped up on revenge to the mix. "Get in the back now and stay quiet."

"Sounds like I'm going to be all kinds of comfortable," Victor complains.

"I'll try to make it in fast," Dusty says. "It's a few miles from here through these woods on foot."

My shoulder muscles tighten so hard they feel like they're barely operational. Is all of this a mistake? Should I have come alone? What if something happens to the kids, to Victor, or to Dusty?

Reading my mood, probably from the tension in my body, Dusty whispers, "We're going to be just fine. You concentrate on your part."

I angle my head to meet his lowering mouth and kiss him, long and hot. The ache that shoots through my body is as much emotional as physical. "Just be careful."

"Yes, ma'am."

From the front, Victor clears his throat. "Do I get one of those? Either one of you can answer."

Dusty smirks and gives me a *you-take-this-one* wave as he climbs out of the car.

I say, "You're staying in the car two miles from the cabin and only coming in at the last minute to a jam party, so what could possibly happen to you?"

I open the door and climb in the front as Victor gingerly climbs between the seats on his way to the cold pack in the back.

He says, "Knowing my luck with your family, a bear attack."

#

The dirt road leading up to the cabin is an uneven, ankle-turning mess, and it's not easy to sprint up it in the dark. Though I'm comfortable looking at the world through night-vision goggles, they don't help with the altitude.

I arrive at the driveway that marks the property and slow to a stop, sweating and panting. Layla must be enjoying this, and though I haven't seen any cameras, she sees me. So says the instructions that started to appear on my phone a half mile after I left Victor. Normally, I wouldn't get service up here, but my phone was recruited into a network Layla must've set up. I catch my breath at the top of the driveway, then a text alert beeps. I lift off my NVGs and read it.

Leave the goggles on the road.

I'd love to know where the cameras are. It irks me that I can't spot them, and I've been trying. I peer down the long driveway, scan as far as I can into the woods, before reaching up and pulling off my night vision. I put them on the ground before starting down the driveway—which is, thank God, downhill. I reduce my speed, mostly because I can't see very well.

When the cabin lights come into view, I slow even more and do some recon. There's one person on the porch. Probably Layla. She's a shadow in the dark at this distance. I spot no one else, but I can't see very far into the woods without my NVG. I'm sure, as Victor said, Layla has at least one person covering her—and maybe more than one.

Not a pleasant thought, but I hope anyone helping Layla is focused on me and not the back way to the cabin.

I might not be in the best shape of my life, but my above-average conditioning means my breathing quickly evens out. My sweating, on the other hand? My black cargo pants and shirt cling to my sweat-soaked body. I wipe my face, then swing at the swarm of gnats circling my head like a rain cloud.

"Stop right there."

Startled by the disembodied voice, I do stop. This time, I spot the small device attached to a tree.

"Strip."

"Is that necessary? You must have sensors."

"Strip."

She also must have a camera, binoculars, or a scope on me to see this far. I pull off my boots, struggle out of my sweat-drenched pants, lift off my shirt, and stand there in my undies. I twirl to show I have no weapons and am not wired.

"You have a tattoo?"

"Can I put my clothes back on?"

"What does it mean?"

The calmness of Layla's voice turns my blood to ice. What was it Victor said about her? She was a control freak. Add she's a game player to that list. "Why do you care?"

"If you tell me, I'll tell you where Cee is."

I fist my hands at my sides, even as my heart starts to pound. I want to know where Cee is and if she's close, but I also feel like this is part of Layla's plan, to feel me out on my affection for Cee. The yellow lights of the cabin fall across Layla, but I'm not close enough to read the expression hidden by her baseball cap. I say, "Tyler, too. I want to know where they both are."

"Okay."

She sounds so calm and confident, I feel played. My tattoo isn't only a symbol, it's the story behind the symbol. Still, a deal is a deal. "I got the tattoo when I was fifteen. My sister Justice and I snuck out."

"You ran away?"

"Sort of. For two weeks, at least, and during those two weeks, we got up to a lot and got in a lot of trouble. That's when I met a cool, hip young tattoo artist. She started the tattoo for me. It was supposed to symbolize my take on the world, grab the sin, the apple, the bad decision, and don't let go."

"Bold. You said *started it*."

I don't want to answer this lunatic's questions, but as long as she's paying attention to me, she isn't paying attention to Dusty coming in the back way. "Yes, well, my adventure was cut short when we were caught after an incident involving a stolen vehicle. Anyway, I had the tattoo finished a few years later, after the birth of my son."

There's a moment of silence, a moment that stretches as wide as the years between us, a moment in which I sense her trying to pin me down in her own mind.

She says, "Ty is sleeping in the house. Cee is in the woods. Does that make you feel better?"

Not at all. "Is Cee alive? Injured? Why is she in the woods?"

"Oh, she's healthy and uninjured. In fact, she's been doing a good job of following the instructions being given to her through an earpiece, and judging by where your friend Dusty is, he should come across her soon."

Fear sends my adrenaline spiking. Blood whooshes in my ears.

Layla continues. "She's wearing an explosive vest. She's a booby trap. I really wish you had arrived alone, as instructed, because two bodies that far out are going to be one hell of a mess for me to clean up, but, as always, I will figure it out."

I nearly choke on the boulder of anger that avalanches into my throat with a thousand pounds of pressure. I can't react, can't let myself think anything other than Dusty will handle it, to do so is to ruin whatever chance we still have here.

Still, I also understand that Dusty has his hands full and is out of the plan and likely Victor is, too, as I doubt Dusty notified him. I have no weapon and no idea how many people are working with Layla—though I'd wager a guess the two big guys that broke into my apartment through the elevator are probably here.

Crud. I need a new plan and fast. "Can I get dressed?"

"Yes. Please do. I'm starting to feel self-conscious, and you can proceed the rest of the way down the driveway to the house. Keep your hands raised, though—I only wish to talk to you, but if you try something, I will shoot."

She only wishes to talk. Funny. Hysterically funny. "Good. That's what I want, too, to talk."

And to kick your crazy ass.

Chapter 52
Dusty

Walking through the woods at any time of the day, but especially on an overcast night, is a skill that I perfected. I know well the minuscule adjustments and awareness needed to avoid tripping or getting caught up in brush. I learned this from Uncle Harvey, who had a negligent parenting style and a big woodsy property filled with old junk.

Once you've tripped over a car bumper in the dark, you learn to look after yourself in those woods. After life with my overbearing father, life with Uncle Harvey had been a blessing. Being alone and able to make choices for myself had seemed a miracle to me. Uncle Harvey understood that, and though I got lost many times in those woods, he never came for me. It never scared me, not even on the darkest night in the deepest part of the forest, but I'm scared now. Downright terrified.

Adjusting my night-vision goggles, I glance again at the small device in the tree. It's some kind of drone that looks like a bird, and it's definitely spotted me. Layla, the computer genius and AI creator, would've made one hell of a Parish. If I didn't need the battery on this jammer for when I get closer to the house, I'd use it to keep that creepy thing from following me.

I do need it, and it does follow. It's an impressive bit of technology, and I can't help but marvel at Layla's skill and at how much money she's going to pull in with these things. That means that Mukta and Leland were right. This is personal to Layla, which has me incredibly freaked out.

This is a different kind of war she's set up for us. One built not on knowledge of guns and warfare, but on ones and zeros and tech.

Not having the benefit of surprise means that as I stalk forward, I'm already adjusting the plan. I pull up short when I see the teen. She's wearing some kind of helmet, but I recognize her anyway. We first met at Gracie's club, after that time in Philly. We met again at the Mantua Home during that fancy dinner. Her name is Cee.

Cautiously, I move toward her, scanning the area as I go. I don't spot anyone in the woods other than the kid. As I get closer to her, I see the helmet has a camera attached to it and some kind of wires that appear to be sensors. Not just that. The kid is rigged with explosives. No wonder she's carrying herself a little herky jerky.

Trying to keep it calm, I ask, "You okay, Cee?"

She stops and her lips tighten into a line of determination. "I'm"—she looks down at herself—"strapped with something."

"Yep. Looks like." I take a deep, steadying breath. I don't know a lot about explosives, but a quick look tells me that the wires and explosives are hidden inside a vest, so it's not easy to get at without setting it off. No wonder Cee shakes like a leaf despite the fact that it's as hot as hell. A hell Layla is doomed to spend eternity in, if there's any justice.

Through my NVGs, I try to get a better read on how it might go off. Not a timer. Not a wire trigger. Nope. A cell phone on the front says it's set to be remotely detonated. By who?

Cee jolts and says, "Okay. I'm going." To me she says, "We have to leave the woods right now. There's a man talking to me through a device in my ear. He tells me if we get far enough away the explosives can't be triggered, but if we stay here or get closer to the house, he will have no choice but to blow it."

Layla is one step ahead of us, employing some guy with an itchy trigger finger. Looks like the jammer in my pocket is going to be needed a bit earlier than I'd intended. First things first.

Figure out what kind of a visual itchy trigger finger has on us. "Okay. You good to run, Cee?"

"No." She almost shouts this. "We can't run. We have to walk or he'll set off the device right away, and he says you have to walk in front of me with your hands up."

Okay. Layla's not only smart; she's devious. I start walking, hands raised, knowing that if we get far enough away to avoid being blown up, I can get back in time to help Gracie.

As I walk, I scan the dark for more of those drone cameras. I need to know how well Itchy can see me. "No problem, Cee. So do you know who's talking to you?"

"I—I'm not allowed to answer that."

That clears up nothing. Fine. If there's one thing I'm good at, it's a distracting conversation. "Ain't it just a nice night for a walk in the woods?"

Cee makes a small, pained sound. "I don't want to die, but if you can save yourself…"

She trails off. Chills race down my body and my heart fills with a heavy weight. This is one brave kid. I shake my head. "That's a nice offer and all, but wouldn't really be much of a life knowing I abandoned such a fine young person as yourself."

She sniffs an obviously runny nose. She's crying. "I should've known better. I thought I was helping Gracie and her son reunite. I thought her son reaching out would make her happy. I wanted to do that for her, you know. I was stupid. I don't deserve…"

Aw, damn. "Sometimes you can't outsmart Loki."

She sniffs again. "Loki?"

"Trickster god. And he's got all sorts of minions. So, sometimes, you get tricked. Live and learn, my uncle Harvey always said. And then he'd tell me, 'People always emphasize the *learn* part of that, son, but it's really the live part that's most important.' I tend to agree. Live. Don't really matter if you learn shit. As long as you can greet God and tell him you lived a full and happy life."

"I think I want to do both, live and learn."

"Fine by me. Uncle Harvey died from too much chewing tobacco, so you might have a good point there."

She doesn't laugh, as I'd hoped. Instead, she says with that soft Spanish accent, "I'm sorry for your loss."

This kid. Sweet as honey. "No worries. Harvey lived a big life, but here's the thing—I'm pretty fast, long legs and all. So, you tell me if you have trouble keeping up."

I pray she gets what I'm telling her. We might not be able to run, but we also shouldn't be moseying either.

"Okay."

I pick up my pace. She doesn't say anything, but when I glance over my shoulder, I see her keeping up.

Smart and brave. Yeah, she'll live and learn and, thanks to The Guild, use her knowledge to change the world.

Assuming whoever's manning the controls on that bomb isn't herding us to a better location to blow us up.

Chapter 53
Gracie

I near the house, a Victorian cottage, almost gingerbread in its cuteness, wide wraparound porch, wicker rocking chairs, and, though it's too dark to see now, the online photos had shown a cheery lavender-and-royal-purple color scheme.

A more appropriate setting would've been an old cabin with a stained rocker on the porch and the carcass of a bear on the floor.

Large moths flutter around the lights by the front door and try to get inside through the screen door. Layla sits on a wooden footstool on the porch, a rifle with a scope pointed at me. She isn't looking through the scope, but she looks very comfortable with the weapon.

I'm not surprised. Research showed Layla to be a computer genius working on groundbreaking tech and AI who's hunted with her father and brothers since she was a teen.

She's wearing camouflage from head to toe. Her eyes are wide, almost horror-movie wide, as if someone else has control of her body and she fights them internally. Her smile is coy and self-assured, her posture eager.

I wasn't sure I could kill her if it came to it, but I realize now I probably won't have a choice. This is a person way off the deep end, someone who thinks they're still totally in control, but anyone with even a toe in reality can see she's not.

All of this tells me exactly how obsessed she's become with me and this game she's been playing with me, Tyler, and Cee. It also tells me how much it means to her right now to be in this position. It means everything to her. She wants this. She's enjoying this.

Layla's head bobs in consideration and her blonde ponytail bounces behind her camo baseball hat. "That's close enough."

I stop. Right now, my only plan is to get close enough to disarm her, which means making her comfortable with me or rushing her. I say, "It looks like you won. Congratulations."

"You made it easy. I can't believe you never figured out it was me. I thought you were a feminist."

I shrug. "You didn't seem the hitman type."

Her wide eyes go squinty mean. "That wasn't me. That was Porter. I was annoyed when I figured it out, faster than you, but that's what romance gets you—distracted."

So, she hadn't been working with Porter. Knowing that, sending James to follow me makes more sense. Porter freaked out after trying to kill me, and he wanted information to use against me. He had no idea what Layla was up to. And I thought my family had issues.

Turns out I had two killers after me, and one of them had better helpers. I can see him now, hanging at the edge of the woods. He's a large man, a shadow.

Layla continues, "Even after you were shot at, when you should've been on high-alert, it was unbelievable how much I was able to mess with you. It kind of got boring. Do you want to know how I pulled it all off? I can dumb it down for you."

A genius, AI tech wizard, good with guns, and also a mean girl. Too bad, I've never been susceptible to mean girls. I have way too many siblings to be insecure over a rude comment or two.

Of course, this actually might be my one advantage. Layla's all about the brag right now. She believes she's won and that I'm under her control because it's all going her way. Hard to argue with that right now, but I know enough about the psychology of psychopaths—socially cunning, glib, high self-esteem—to know that this moment, this very second, is why Layla did all of this. Not to kill me, but to humiliate me, prove she's better than me, then kill me and anyone who she sees as a threat to her, which obviously includes Ty. The first grandson born of Rush's first daughter, me. That gives me an advantage.

I swallow all the anger and fear bubbling away inside like a cauldron with a too tight lid. "Where's Ty?"

Layla squints through her sight at me "You're not much of a sharer, are you?"

My hands are slick with sweat, and I can practically feel the heat from the red dot of a laser pointed at my head. "On the contrary, I'm glad to sit down with you and have a long talk as long as you give a little to get. How is Ty?"

"Did you know you're who I should have been? You're her."

Layla didn't just lose it tonight; she'd lost it a long time ago. Helping her father and his career is nowhere near as important to her as the slight to her ego.

"Where's Ty?"

"Inside." She stops peering through her scope and smiles at me. It's a wide, elegant grin, the kind of smile a politician would covet. "He's a good kid, so polite. It's too bad you don't really know him and that knowing you doesn't matter to him. He's happy without you, and, as a mother, that should mean something to you."

Layla's trying to manipulate me into the humiliation she had planned. She wants me to grovel, to be injured, to show all the emotions that she must've felt on learning about me. Only then can she repair the damage to her ego.

I know that I matter to Tyler because that's how Layla was able to abuse and manipulate his trust.

Taking a page from Dusty's book, I casually say, "You're really enjoying this."

She bites. "Of course. This is why I did it. This moment right here. I could've hired a hitman like my stupid brother, but where's the fun in that? This moment, this electric, delicious moment where you are helpless and I'm one step away from ending this nightmare has been worth all of my trouble."

"Ah, I see. You saw the movie, the ending where the villain reveals the master plan, and decided that was it, that was your big life goal."

"Don't fuck with me," she says, raising her weapon.

This, too, is the typical grandiose mindset of a psychopath. "I have to admit, I'm impressed. Brava. But if you don't mind, *sister*, I want to see Tyler."

"Don't fucking call me that! You will do what I want. *When* I want it. You need to hear me." The change in Layla's demeanor is instant and blinding, like a light switch being thrown in the dark. She's angry and determined and bent on revenge.

I begin to inch closer. "Look, I'm your prisoner. I will do whatever you want. Hands up. Lips shut tight. As long as you let me see—"

"I used analytics to track your son through the internet, to watch where he went, to gauge who he was. I tailored content to him, lured him into asking the question: 'Can I find my mom?' I even wrote articles about how to track down a birth parent, and he paid me for the privilege. Of course, he thought he was paying a private detective ten thousand dollars to find his mother."

Layla's laugh is a light tinkling sound that chills my blood. It's a laugh coated in the delusions of a brilliant but unhinged mind.

"Once he knew who you were, I hired someone to follow him. To mimic you, what you were doing when you'd stalk him in Manayunk, but to be a little more obvious. You're very good at not being spotted. I'm better, though. At everything."

Oh God. No wonder Ty had waved at me. He'd paid for information on me, had tried to find out about me, and had been looking for me.

My usually tell-a-tale skin stays cold and under control at Layla's outburst, but, inside, I'm panicking. This devious nutter went out of her way to manipulate Ty. "Why would you do that? Why involve him in this?"

I know the real answer—because he threatens her ego—but I also know she'll have a more detailed, more logical reason, so she won't have to admit that to herself.

"Me involve him? Oh, no. *You've* been stalking him. *You* contacted him. *You* got him to give you sixty thousand dollars to help fund your teen vigilantes, including Cee. *You* set him up on an expensive laptop in order to get him to help you—the location of said laptop will be anonymously sent to the FBI. You lured him out here, and then, when he realized what a nut you were, he had to defend himself, so he shot you dead."

Cold sweeps down my body. "You're going to kill me and make it look like my son did it?"

Layla tsks. "Simple minds conceive simple plans. He *is* going to kill you."

"Ty would never do that."

"Of course he would. After all, you killed his whole family, his mom and his dad and his little brother. It's pretty awful of you."

I saw John a few hours ago. There's no way Layla could've set this up and gotten to him, not when I left him with a Fed. "They aren't dead."

"Or course not. Why would I go to the trouble when it's easier to make it look like they are? The deep fake convincingly showed Ty his family's dead bodies. Poor kid, he was very upset afterword, and I had to slip him a little sedative to calm him down."

"I sure hope it also doesn't confuse him when he wakes up, which should be any moment now."

A bullet to my heart would hurt less than knowing the pain Ty has been put through. I can barely breathe. *Oh, Ty.*

"Seems to be a family trait," I say through clenched teeth, not giving Layla the drama she craves, "drugging people to get what you want. I get why your father did it, but I don't understand why you did this, risked this. You already broke into my club and set me up with the FBI to clear your father's name. If you'd done nothing else, there's a good chance I would've gone down for a crime I didn't commit. Or, at least, been charged with it and been embroiled in years of legal difficulties. Your father would probably be president before it was all said and done."

"Your ego is incredible. Not everything is about you. You're not the only player here. The materials at your club were placed to take down your mother." Layla intones the word *mother* so strongly saliva shoots from her mouth. "But you? You don't get to fucking live. My dad has one daughter. One."

Rage and murder glistens in her too-wide eyes. She wants to shoot me and there's no doubt in my mind she will. She's out of control.

"It's fine, Layla. It's all good. You *are* his one daughter. I honestly don't care. I have a family."

"Fuck you," she says, standing as she raises her gun.

I dive to the side a moment too late and feel the sting of a dart pierce my leg as I hit the ground.

A dart?

I reach down try to pull it out, but my hand isn't cooperating. Missing the blurry end twice, I struggle against my drooping body but fall flat on the ground. My vision begins to dim as I gaze up at the night sky.

Layla comes into my view, leans close to my face, and whispers, "Yeah. You see, that's the problem. I'm *not* his daughter. You are."

Chapter 54
Gracie

I blink awake confused and inundated with the sound of lapping water. A toilet? I try to locate the sound, but everything is so blurry even blinking doesn't help. I try to lift my head, but all I manage is to realize I'm on my belly on the floor. What floor?

An alarm sounds in my head, sending adrenaline racing into my body, and my blood rushing enough to wake me. My heart pounds as I lift my head and gaze around the room. I'm in the cabin.

Fully awake, my nerve endings deliver a staggered situational report—dry throat, pounding headache, and incapacitated arms and legs. My arms are tied behind my back to my legs. I've been trussed up like a pig.

I rock back and forth in order to get a better feel for my orientation. I'm on the floor halfway across the room from the front door. I'm partially situated on an oriental rug with my upper half pressed against the scarred wooden floor of the cabin and my lower on the rug.

Layla and whoever I saw in the woods likely dragged me inside. The water sound is a fountain on the floor, a meditating Buddha with water flowing from the center of a lotus flower nestled in his lap. *Disturbing.*

The room, dimly lit by one fringed lamp on an end table, is old-lady-having-an-English-tea-party style with Victorian seating, paintings, and decorations.

Rocking, I manage to turn to get a better look at the room

and I spot Tyler. He's pacing the floor and, now that I've stopped moving around, I can hear him muttering to himself.

"Tyler?" My voice comes out like a whisper, but he still pivots as if I yelled at him.

He has a gun in his hand and tears line his face.

The hand with the gun shakes against his leg. "Why? Why kill them?"

"Ty—"

"Why!" He raises and points the gun at me.

My mind comes online with a jolt that has me thinking and speaking fast. "Tyler, what you saw was deep fake. I promise you that your family is okay. Listen to me."

He wipes tears from his eyes with the back of his hand, the very hand holding the gun, and I cringe at how close he is to his own head. "Done listening to you."

My heart tramples through my throat like a bull through anyone careless enough to get in its way during the run of Pamplona. "Be careful with that gun, Tyler. Please. You're going to hurt yourself."

He snorts a desperate sound, an agonized laugh. "You want me alive, but you don't get it. I'm not alive anymore. You took them. You took me. You—"

His voice breaks and he begins to sob. The weapon goes down, points toward his own feet again.

"Tyler. No. Listen—"

"Shut up!" He points the gun at me again.

The cold calculation of my training washes the panic from my body, and I realize I'm not going to convince him of the truth. Ty isn't able to distance himself from the beliefs Layla so carefully installed in his head, so I have to try something else. "I'm sorry. I'm so sorry. Please. You're not a killer. You don't want to hurt me."

He laughs, the gun shaking in his hand. He says, "You're right." He points the gun at his own head.

"No!" A spasm runs through my body.

Tears stream down his face now. "This is what you wanted: me. You killed them for me. Now, you get nothing. Spend your whole life in jail. Empty."

No, no, no. I have to stop him. I have to do something. Fuck! I rock on the floor, try to get closer to him, but I can barely fucking move.

Something. Something. Make him angry. Make him point that weapon anywhere but at himself, make him point it at me. "They deserved it," I spit. "Those fucking idiots. Especially that little one. Stupid fuck. Kept asking for you. I enjoyed killing him."

Fury takes over the pain in Tyler's eyes. He jerks the weapon away from his head, aims at me, and shoots, shoots, shoots.

Chapter 55
Dusty

These woods have a lot of dips and roots, a lot of places a foot could be put wrong, but nothing that has me as off-center as the fact that I'm getting farther and farther away from Gracie.

I need to get that vest off Cee and head back to the cabin. I have a pretty good idea of the vest setup right now. It's held on by Velcro. But I still don't know how quickly I can get it off her, how well my jammer will work, or what kind of workaround Layla might've setup. Cee isn't giving me any information I can use.

I've asked her a dozen questions, including if it's heavy and if she can see wires, but she only answers with, "I'm not allowed to answer that."

Doesn't matter. The questioning itself gave me information—like how closely we're being monitored. Verbally? Like a hawk. Visually? Not so much.

Because while I asked my questions, I also slowly altered direction, shifted course to the left and then to the right, subtly. Whoever was monitoring didn't flag it or tell Cee to stay a certain course or walk a certain way.

In addition, the guy has never asked me to remove my night-vision goggles. Which I take to mean he can't see me all that well. And if I'm not mistaken, there's a lag in his communication that's gotten a bit longer the deeper we go into the woods. Sometimes when I ask my questions, Cee is able to get a whole word out before saying, "I'm not allowed to answer that."

So, whoever is operating this rig isn't too close by. Good to know.

I keep walking, talking up a storm, because I also noticed whoever monitors us gets distracted by my stories. Always knew what my uncle had dubbed my "chipmunk chatter" would come in handy one day. *Voice had been a lot higher in my younger days.*

Twigs break under Cee's feet and leaves crunch as we walk. After making hundred percent sure there aren't any more drones, I ready myself to put my plan into action.

I scan up ahead and pick the perfect spot. Slowing my pace, I wait for Cee to catch up.

Her eyes are wide and intense as she sees me gaze back at her. She's picked up on the shift. Good. I make sure she's close enough when I put a foot wrong and trip over a root. "Dang it. Twisted my ankle."

She gasps, bends over my prostrate body. "Let me help."

I reach and flick up her camera, so it'll show only trees and darkness. Her eyes widen, but I put a finger to my lips.

Proving quick and smart runs in her family, she says, "Take my hand."

I speak loudly, have to hide the pulling off the Velcro. "Fucking root. Did you hear that snap? I think that was my ankle."

"Oh, it's twisted," she says. "It looks bad."

"Yeah. Give me that hand?"

"I need to step back. I'm being told…"

Too late. I flick on my jammer, get her out of the vest, tossed it into the woods, followed by the helmet. I pick her up and run like the devil himself is after us.

Boom! The blast sends me sprawling, but I shift so that I don't crush the kid. We lay in the dirt, gasping, sore, and alive.

She's up a half second before me, looking around the woods as if expecting an enemy. Once I'm standing, she turns back to me. "You did it."

She hugs me and I hug her back, then hold her away from me, so I can see if she's injured. "You okay?"

"I'm fine," she says, though I can see she has a minor cut on her cheek. "What do we do now?"

"We gotta work fast here." I take off my bulletproof vest and put it on her, tightening it. "You take this, my two-way, and my night-vision goggles."

She lets me give her the vest, but pushes back on the NVGs. "But how will you see?"

"Take them and walk north. This two-way is set to the right channel, but don't use it until you get farther away. Whoever strapped that bomb to you might think you're dead, but not if they pick up your signal. If you keep heading north, you'll find a car on the road, an Expedition. The guy inside, the guy on the other end of this two-way, is named Victor. He'll take care of you."

"I know Victor," she says, then shakes her head. "But you take the goggles. There's tripwire set up near the house. I don't know where."

"How many people are working with Layla?"

"Two men and one of them is huge." She pulls back a little. "Even bigger than you."

Bigger than me? Not sure she can see so well in the dark, but I'll take her word on it. "Okay. I'll take the glasses. You take the two-way and call Victor."

Distant gunshots end our conversation.

"Go!" Cee shouts.

I run like hell, arms pumping, legs fighting for speed. Every obstacle comes into sharp focus and I jump fallen logs and large roots with ease.

My heart pounds in my chest and a prayer forms on my lips. *Grace. Please Lord, give me Grace. Don't let me be too late. Please.*

Chapter 56
Gracie

My body convulses with the *thuck, thuck, thuck* impact of each bullet being fired into the floor around me. The shooting stops, the echoes fades, and the smell of gunpowder fills the room.

I'm so tense, I have to fight to unclench my locked jaw and pry open my eyes.

Across from me, Tyler has lowered the gun. He's staring at me. His face is a mask of fear, confusion, and childish hope. He sucks in snot. "You promise they're alive?"

His voice sounds so young, so hurt, that my throat grows tight with tears. "Yeah. I promise, Ty. They're alive."

A brutal curse, a sobbed "Fuck," breaks from his mouth. "That bitch lied. She really lied to me?"

He begins to tremble, and I recognize the adrenaline backlash. I need to get him focused on moving out of here before Layla comes back. I have no doubt she's watching this all from someplace close. "It's all lies. That woman you met pretended to be my sister Cee and pretended to contact you for me, but, at the same time, she contacted my sister, pretending to be you."

Ty wipes snot from his face, blinks. "They're for sure alive?"

Oh, kid. Goose bumps race down my body. We need to get out of here. "Yes. I promise. I promise you, Tyler. The scene was faked. You know how they fake stuff like—"

"Aliens or ghosts caught on video?"

"Yes. Like that. We have to get out of here." *Now.* "Can you untie me?"

283

The skin on his cheeks heats red, a flush I know well. He rushes over to me, dropping to his knees and placing his gun on the floor.

His fingers shake as he unties me, so does his voice. "I saw what you were doing. When I put the gun to my head. I saw it. You'd let me shoot you. You'd let me do that if it meant that I got to live."

I can't stop the small, pained sound that escapes my throat or the tears that fall from my eyes. He sees me, understands me, believes in me. "Yeah. I would've."

He loosens the knot and the slack is instant, releasing my arms enough that I can roll and swing my hands under my legs, so they're in front of me. I untie my feet.

Tyler pulls the rope away from my wrists. "Do you think she's around here somewhere?"

"Yes. Layla, that's the woman you met, is likely close by and not alone. Did you see anyone else in the house?"

"A limo driver brought me here." He blushes. "I thought he was from your family, the Parishes, but when we got here, he drugged me. After that I only saw… uh, Layla."

Freed, I grab the gun, put a hand on Ty's shoulder, and he helps me to stand on wobbly legs.

Ty puts an arm around me to help steady me.

"Don't worry about me. Move quickly," I say. I put one hand on Ty's upper arm, making sure he moves as I direct so that I'm able to protect him. I use every bit of caution I can while moving quickly on partially numb legs and scanning for any sign of danger.

Adrenaline heightens my senses, and I became sharply conscious of every pop and creak of the floorboards, the slide of Ty's canvas sneakers, the way my boy holds then releases terrified breaths, the gurgling sound of water. *Water?*

The fountain, the fountain that is running despite the fact that the rest of this place is covered in a layer of dust. I examine it from across the room and see that the water inside is shiny, slick with rainbows. And the smell of it... I hadn't noticed in the ensuing drama. It's not water.

Pulling Tyler's arm, I shove him in front of me. "Go!"

He slams against the front door and stumbles onto the porch. A step behind, I scan the trees, knowing she's here somewhere.

And then I see Layla, no more than a shadow, a dark figure moving through the woods, raising her gun, intent on making sure me and my son will be dead in a moment, our bodies burnt in the explosion.

Everything unfolds in one terrible instant of brutality that sears itself upon my horrified, witnessing mind.

As calm as a woman who has never lost a thing in her life, Layla steps from the woods with her weapon raised. No darts this time—she's holding an AK semiautomatic rifle.

Launching forward, I shove Tyler hard, propelling him off the porch and into the air. I follow behind, my body covering his as we fly forward.

My one hand pushes him down while the other brings up my gun and a panicked voice screams in my head—*not fast enough, not fast enough.*

That moment plays out in blinding clarity. The feel of Tyler's warm back against my palm, the smell of the summer woods, the startled silence of time standing still as the electric prayer fires through my brain as quick as the shot I fire, quicker: *Please, God, keep Ty safe, let the bullets only strike me.*

A *rat-a-tat* of gunfire erupts a split second before my finger depress the trigger of my own gun. And then Layla's skull explodes and her body spasms against a spray of bullets that mangles her muscle, tissue, and brains on impact.

A whoosh of air is knocked from Tyler's lungs as we slam to the ground. I land partially on top of him, spin off, and scramble to my feet with my gun raised and ready.

I spot movement on the driveway and pivot with my pulse pounding in my throat and my ears muffled from my not-fast-enough shot.

"Hold your fire, Roja. It's me," Victor says as he limps forward, face pinched with pain, semiautomatic sticking out from his sling. His injured arm rests by his side. "Anyone else?" he asks, and a nearly simultaneous cry of pain rises from the woods. "Layla!" The shout tears through the woods along with a large figure I recognize from earlier. Rage and disbelief contort his face. An eye patch on one eye, he charges forward, levels his gun at me.

I swing my weapon around.

Victor turns, too.

A figure, bigger than the first, bursts out from the woods. He slams into the enraged eyepatch man like a fullback, knocking him to the ground.

Dusty holds the man's gun arm down while bringing his own gun down on the man's skull again and again.

There's a *crack, crack* and a splatter of wet darkness shoots up into the space between the man and Dusty, then there's stillness. Dusty lurches to his feet and scans the darkness. He says, "Cee said there were two of them. Where's the fiancée?"

A second of definitive silence as if, for an entire heartbeat or the skipping of one, the world goes quiet. then I remember… "Explosives! Run!"

Tyler gets to his feet and runs. A split-second later, I'm running beside him, with Dusty veering to the side to meet us on the driveway. Bringing his two-way to his mouth, Victor yells into it while running.

A moment later, car lights appear at the top of the driveway. There's only one person who could be driving that car. I make a looping gesture with my hands, and Cee follows my directions, swinging the vehicle around with a slide and shriek of tires.

I end up in the back between Ty and Dusty. Victor climbs into the front, his door still open as Cee accelerates back down the driveway.

The house explodes.

The SUV lurches forward, like a giant hand gave it one firm shove from behind. Victor's door slams against his arm and he screams. We fly forward in our seats then backward with the fiery momentum.

No sooner have we been thrown back then a series of concussive blasts explode with a *bam, bam, bam* down the driveway.

Cee swings the car left and right in rapid, jerky movements as trees catch fire, sending pockets of fiery debris raining down around us.

My body rocks between Tyler and Dusty, and I loop an arm through each of theirs to keep us all steady. I'm unable to articulate a single word.

A fiery branch falls into the driveway, but Cee goes around it now as if she's been doing this her whole life. She reaches the end of the driveway and swings hard left. The glow from the fire lights the night sky behind us.

Without being told, Cee jerks to a stop. She looks at Dusty. "You drive."

I smile, because the kid has mad skills and great teamwork.

Dusty kisses me gently on the forehead before climbing out.

And beside me, Tyler squeezes my hand and whispers, "Thanks for rescuing me… Mom."

Chapter 57
Dusty

Standing behind Grace outside the new and improved *Staff Only* doors leading into Club When? I tie the blindfold—a long strip of black silk—over her eyes.

Pretty as a picture in spiked red heels and a short red dress that laces up the back, she doesn't object. The curve of her fine ass under that dress reminds me of an apple. Ripe. Juicy. Begging to be bitten.

One thing at a time.

I put my lips by her ear. "You ready?"

She tilts her head back, brushing a soft kiss against my chin. "I've been ready for weeks."

I have been too, but the things needed to be perfect.

Taking a small nibble of her earlobe, the silk from the blindfold soft against my cheek, I whisper, "Is that excitement or wariness in your voice?"

She laughs. "Excitement. If I hadn't promised, I would've peeked in there to see what you've been up to long ago."

"Have to say, I was impressed with your self-control." Especially since we're both living at Club When? now. It'd taken all my powers of persuasion after the club had been repaired to her specifications to get her to allow me to take over designing the theme for the grand reopening.

I hope she likes it. Hope what waits beyond these doors is our future.

"Good thing you hadn't peeked," I say, giving her a light pat on the round swell of her ass. "You would've been in big trouble."

Fingers itching to pull that bow, I grab her by the hips and steer her through the doors, using my foot to kick them open for her.

Lord, I'm starting to sweat.

Inside, the ceiling of the club is draped in black fabric. Projected on that silk is an endless night sky, brilliant stars, the Milky Way's glimmering sweep of silver dust, and the ethereal pinks and golds of distant galaxies. Sculpted white trees draped in lights perch along the perimeter of the dance floor. And on each of the white-linen tables twinkles smaller handcrafted versions of those trees.

A light show of white shimmers slowly over the floors and walls. All along the bar are a series of glowing tall and short silver candles—the fake kind, because we are super conscious of fire hazards here.

Mouth dry, heart pounding, I fish the remote out of the pocket of my jeans and hit the button. The sounds of the piano play quietly through the speakers at first, and then Garth Brooks begins singing, "Make You Feel My Love."

"Dusty?"

"One sec."

I try to still my pounding heart as I fumble the ring from my pocket. Dropping to one knee in front of her, I hold up the gem that reflects the purity of my intentions and my undying love. "You can take off the blindfold, Grace."

She reaches up and pulls it down. Her hands fly to her mouth. Her eyes bounce around the room, glittering with the reflection of all those lights. By the time her gaze settles back on me, tears streak her softly blushing cheeks.

I find my own eyes growing wet. *Aw, hell.* I adore her. "Grace Divine Parish, will you do me the honor of marrying me, making me the luckiest man in all of the universe?"

She drops to her own knees, takes the ring, and whispers against my lips, "Yes to that."

#

Feels good to be back behind the bar of Grace's Club When? Especially when I'm putting together what's come to be one of my favorite drinks, Blood and Guts.

Going to be a busy night, judging by the crowd. Let's hope it goes smoothly. First week back, and Club When? is experiencing a bit of a hiccup. There hasn't been a night this week that there wasn't at least one fight in the club.

Starting to feel more like a club bouncer than a bartender, and I can't help but wonder if it has anything to do with the "costume change" as Grace calls it.

She'd loved the wedding theme—so said her enthusiastic yes to my proposal—but she later pointed out that we needed to tie the theme to a specific date in history.

What's not to like about Kate and William's wedding? Pomp. Ceremony. Crazy hats. Maybe it's the hats.

I pass the drink to the customer, telling her, "It's called Blood and Guts because you need some to drink it."

She smiles as she clinks her blue swirly drink with her boyfriend's beer.

Squaring my shoulders, I move to the other end of the bar and the guy I saw come in earlier. Apparently, the man doesn't understand the *get lost* signal I've been sending him. Can't really help the curl of my lip as I reach the end of the bar. Guy deserves a sneer.

"What do you want, Mack?"

Mack scratches at his scruffy new beard. He looks a little older. Nose a little less straight. His face a little rounder, like he's put on a few.

"Guess you're wondering why…" He trails off.

I'm not wondering. I know exactly why he's here. Turns out, the FBI doesn't take kindly to agents using manufactured evidence against innocent people. Mack's case and career fell apart, but not before he took the low road.

"Naw, I think I get it. You need a job."

Mack's eyebrows jump, but he laughs. Just a little. He waves around the club. "Pretty romantic."

Yeah, it is. Every time I walk in here, I'm struck by the overwhelming truth that she'd said yes. I'd had nerves the night I asked her to marry me like I hadn't had in... well, ever.

The word *yes* had never sounded as sweet in the history of mankind. Made even sweeter by the sharp *yes*es I'd coaxed out of her fifteen minutes later upstairs in that big bed of hers.

"I came to apologize to Gracie Parish. It got messy there."

Messy? Fucker arrested Grace after we'd come back from dealing with Layla and her crazy vendetta. I'd gone insane trying to find Grace. Fucking Mack had had her transferred to a black site.

He'd tried to get her to confess, hoping to salvage his career—and Rush's.

Honestly, I've never been more grateful for the Parish family pull than when they'd joined with me to help locate Grace. Now, I'm a fan for life of writing wrongs. I've been an employee of The Guild ever since me, Justice, and Sandesh went in there and busted Grace out.

Still makes my blood boil what Mack did, so, no, I'm not going to give him the absolution he's looking for. It's all I can do to stop myself from punching the guy in the nose again before forcibly hauling his sorry ass out of the club.

It's the eyes of that beautiful redhead watching me that is stopping me from following that exact course of action. Beautiful doesn't cover it.

"If you want to apologize to Grace, turn around. She's standing behind you."

Mack blanches and spins around on his stool. Grace stands there, wearing her Club When? Finest, and looking hotter than any woman has a right to.

"Apology accepted," Grace says. "Now, if you don't mind, Dusty and I were just going to rewatch the shockumentary on disgraced Senator Andrew Lincoln Rush. Did you hear that, when the authorities finally came to believe my version of events and searched Layla's home, they found she had numerous videos showing the disgraced senator had drugged and raped girls? Including several recordings of him, drunk and slurring, admitting his despicable behavior to his son, Porter, who went to criminal lengths to hide the truth?"

Mack nods. "I did, yes. I guess you just can never tell what people are like behind closed doors. Sometimes people confuse you."

"Yeah," I say, "it's so difficult to figure out that someone drugs and rapes people when you've seen the video of one of his rape victims telling you that she'd been drugged and raped. Maybe next time you join forces with a political candidate and his son, you'll do a better job investigating them."

Mack has the good sense to stay quiet as he slips from his stool and begins to walk away. He glances back at me one last time and says, "Your dad died. Did you know?"

I know. I also know his congregation tried to stay together, but, in the end, couldn't. I hope they all end up better for it.

Seeing I'm not going to answer, Mack keeps walking. *Good riddance.*

Grace climbs up onto the stool Mack left, leans across the bar, then runs her thumb along the shadow of stubble on my chin. "You're still mad at him, huh?"

She looks worried for me, like she thinks I'll hold this grudge forever. Might at that. But how to explain to her? Those panicked, brutal moments of not being able to find her, then realizing she was locked up, taken somewhere where people could and did hurt her. How to explain the anger and the lengths I'd gone to rescue her? I can't and won't.

She has her own stuff to deal with regarding that mess. But she's here now. Safe. And—as much as she'd object and tell me the word means ownership, though that's not how it feels to me—she is mine.

Mine.

Maybe seeing the thoughts playing across my face, Gracie scoots over the bar and drops down next to me. She wraps her arms around my waist.

Aw, hell. This woman.

I kiss her for all I'm worth. Kiss her like a man who almost lost the best thing that's ever happened to him.

And she kisses me back, just as sweet and hot as every minute I'm lucky enough to spend with her.

When we pull apart from that scorching kiss, it's to the approach of three twenty-somethings, who take seats at the bar and begin singing with the music pouring through the club's speakers—"Going to the Chapel"—out of tune and without the correct words.

Gracie grabs me by the belt hooks and moves her sweet ass to that god-awful song.

Actually, now that I think about it, proper like, I kind of like that song. Of course, it might just be the company. Or the friction. "Love you, Grace."

The singing trio whistles and hoots as I bend and kiss my bride-to-be.

Mine.

Chapter 58
Gracie

Making my way into the Parish Palace, as Dusty now calls the Mantua Home, I try not to let my tell-a-tale face show how freaked out I am about what's going to happen today. It's unprecedented, unusual, and scary.

Now that the lower levels of The Guild are back in operation, Momma and my super cool scientist sister Zuri are going to try to reverse the M-erasure that Tony performed on Dusty. Unfortunately, it's much easier to hide a memory than to retrieve it, so they aren't sure it'll work.

I close the front door and bring Dusty's hand to my mouth, kissing his knuckles. He smiles at me, a little goofy and a lot afraid.

I squeeze his hand. Momma promised to try to make Dusty whole, to give him back his memory, and I'm going to be there for the entire procedure, holding his hand.

We walk past the gym as a soccer game echoes from inside. We don't stop. We go all the way down the hall to the elevators in silence. We turn into the side hall, and I press the *Up* button, even though we aren't going up.

The elevator doors slide open and we walk inside. The doors slide shut. I think this is the longest I've ever heard Dusty not talking. He even talks in his sleep.

Dusty reaches for the B—basement button—but doesn't press it. "Not really four floors, right?" he says.

"Not really." I put my wrist up to the control panel. The elevator beeps. I say, "Subfloor 4B."

Another beep. The new system has added security. A small door on the panel slides open and I let it scan my eyes. The elevator says, "Grace Divine Parish. Welcome. Rider two, identify yourself."

Dusty turns his wrist over, eyeballs the elevator like it's a demon. "So I just…"

I grab his chipped wrist and hold it up to the sensor. The elevator beeps. He bends toward the scanner. It reads his eyes and says, "Leif Eric McAllister. Also known as Dusty. Also known as USA. Also known as Southern Accent. Welcome."

He laughs in a way that's both amused and disturbed. "Rome?"

I nod and he shakes his head. "Kid's gonna pay for that."

When he reaches for indented handrails on the sides of the elevator, I stop him. "Justice would never let you live it down."

He smirks.

The elevator intones, "Proceeding to Subfloor 4B."

"Well, I'm all about impressing your…"

The elevator drops. Fast.

Dusty jerks sideways, hits the wall, and grabs the handrail with a, "Shiiiit."

Feet braced wide—I've had practice—I stand my ground and grin at him.

He uses the handrail to regain his footing and mutters, "You got a lower center of gravity."

And that only makes me smile wider.

The elevator slams to a stop, but Dusty stays standing by, white-knuckling the handrail.

Looping my arm around his, I ask, "What do you think of Elevator-X?"

His easygoing grin is nowhere to be found. He says, "That's just not natural. That's what that is un… natural."

I tiptoe and kiss him. The stubble on his chin scratches pleasantly against me. Heat rolls through my body, and I grab his shirt to press myself closer.

The doors open and the elevator announces, "Sub-floor 4B.

Welcome, you are being monitored. Entering unauthorized areas will result in immediate expulsion."

I pull back from the kiss, and he rubs a thumb across my lips. "Sweet as you are hot."

"I really love you," I say, heart hammering with lust and fear. I grab his hand and squeeze. "It's going to be okay."

He winks at me. "Hadn't been nervous at all until you said that."

I lead him down the hall to a door that meshes with the walls so seamlessly it takes me a moment to remember exactly where it is.

I hold my wrist up. After the beep, Dusty does the same. Two eye checks later and there's a mechanical, "You are cleared for access to Neuro Room 3D."

"Sounds like we're going to a holodeck," Dusty says.

I snort. "You have geek in you?"

His eyebrows furrow. "Gotta ask? Used to work for the FBI, remember?"

There's a rush of air and the smell of chemicals as the door slides open. We're the last ones to enter the clinical-looking room.

Momma and Zuri are busying themselves with computer equipment. Zuri said recreating those last moments in Mexico will make retrieving the hidden memory easier.

Justice, Sandesh, and Victor chat as they wait by microphones on the side of the room, ready to recreate that last day.

Dusty eyes the chair in the middle of the room with obvious unease. It's a cross between a mad scientist's and a dentist's chair, with a large arm connected to a helmet with wires and submerged sensors.

I have to remind myself that he chose this. I have to remind myself that he said he wants every memory that belongs to him. Every one.

If this works, Dusty will be able to remember what happened with Tony. If it works, he'll be whole.

If it works, we'll be able to use that information to track down Tony and bring that stupid ass home.

Epilogue
Dusty

Standing guard against a horde of trespassers as the summer sun scorches the earth, I'm beginning to think, once again, that I have John McClane's *Die Hard* brand of luck.

I wipe sweat from my face. We're outnumbered. The field, some call it a quad, is awash in red. The enemy hides everywhere behind the huge boulders that line the field, stationed atop the guard tower—a raised deck with telescopes the school uses for stargazing—and crouched behind trees and bushes.

We've lost many today. My crew now consists of me, Gracie, and Ty. We're hunkered down behind a dumpster, hidden by a fancy wooden fence at the field's edge. Our teammates need to be freed, but that means getting across a field guarded at every conceivable ambush point. I've seen episodes of *Game of Thrones* that are less messy.

"I've been in tighter places," Grace says.

I raise an eyebrow then grin, because so have I, but that'd been a lot more fun.

Maybe reading my mind, she elbows me in the ribs and says, "Here's the plan."

She outlines a decent game plan, using some stones and Popsicle sticks to mark it out. It could get at least one of us through alive. Only need one to free the other players.

Tyler takes note from the edge of the dumpster, but his eyes keep straying to the field.

"Ty," Gracie says, "Did you get it?"

"Yep. Got it," he says. Raising his paintball gun, he turns and runs out onto the field, screaming, "Leroy Jenkins!"

Can't help but grin at the big kid. I shake my head. "That's your son."

Gracie laughs, then takes off to follow him, firing randomly.

I have a good mind to let them go it alone. *Nah. What fun is that?*

I run out, balls to the wind, or what I like to think of as Butch-Cassidy-and-the-Sundance- Kid style, AKA, Leroy Jenkins.

The paintballs pelt the ground and our jumpsuits in no time. Tyler and Gracie are tripped up and go sprawling onto the grass. I fall over them, covering their bodies with my own. Paintballs slam into me. *Hurts. No fucking kidding. That hurts.*

Grace pushes against me. "The paintballs are less dangerous than being smothered by you."

"Stop shooting," Justice calls from her spot on the guard tower. "It's a fucking massacre."

I roll off them, stand up, then help Gracie and Tyler to their feet. The two of them burst into laughter. They even high-five each other. Makes my heart do something funny, a bit of gymnastics in my chest.

I reach out and draw them in for a bear hug, lifting them in my arms. They complained mightily, but what's a man to do? We just survived a massacre together.

Yes, sir, John McClane's brand of luck. I'm that damn lucky.

#
Gracie

Autumn trees of yellow, red, and orange fill the Mantua Academy campus lining streets, and along brick buildings and beside park benches. The sun is starting to set, spotlighting the tops of those glorious trees with an orange glow.

My heart is light as I leave the quad with Tyler by my side, sharing this day with him, this place where I grew up, is a dream come true. The wind smells of earth and a summer well spent, and I could not be happier.

There are several pockets of people walking, spread-out, along the campus grounds. The teams split up after our war games. Dusty, Justice, and Sandesh stroll together, discussing the "fucking massacre," a conversation I have no doubt will, once again, turn to tracking Tony.

Now that Zuri has successfully returned his memory, Dusty's determined to find my wayward brother. Tony is smart, but Dusty is pissed and former FBI. Thanks to Dusty's help, the video of Tony outside my club, and some cyber-sleuthing, we have a beat on him. Justice and Sandesh will leave tomorrow to track down the first lead. If it pans out, we'll join them in a few days. It's already been agreed that we bring Tony home together.

"You don't mind that I didn't do your plan, do you?" Ty asks.

I smile up at him. "Honestly, I like your way of ending things. Now, the memory won't be the same as one of a thousand times we played here. Now, it'll go down in family history."

"I like to make history wherever I go," he says with a cheeky grin.

I laugh. He's so funny, and he's smart and interested in the world and details of my life. I love his curiosity. I love everything about him.

"Is it weird having the campus so empty?" he asks.

"It kind of is. This late in September, the campus is usually full, but it won't be much longer before classes resume."

Cee, Rome, and Jules jog past us, heading toward the house. One of Leland's rules for training I remember well from childhood: *Don't walk, run.*

Rome bumps Tyler's shoulder as he passes us and says, "Ask again."

I yell after him as he jogs off, "Don't encourage him! Remember who you're training with tomorrow morning."

Jogging backward now, Rome spreads his arms wide. "Dusty said he'd train with me."

I turn to look at Dusty, who gives me a sassy Southern grin, or, at least, that's how I take it, when he winks at me.

"You're lucky you're so cute," I tell him.

"So can I?" Tyler asks, taking Rome's podding to heart.

Letting out a breath, I grab his hand and hold it as we walk. Yes, he's too old to hold his mother's hand, but, strangely, he never objects. "We've been through this, Ty."

"But Rome goes here. Why can't I?"

Oh boy. This is the third time he's asked, and as happy as the idea of him making his home here—even if it's only during the school year and at the school—I know it will be a fight with John and Ellen. I don't want to bring that kind of drama into their lives.

I try to dissuade him, again. "You know school won't start for a few more weeks and there's only a short holiday break this year and a shorter summer break next year. Going here wouldn't be the same as in your current school. It would be harder. Plus, I don't think your parents—"

"That's not true." Ty brushes slightly sweaty bangs from his green eyes. "My parents know. I talked to them."

They know? Surprising. Well, maybe not. John and Ellen have become a lot kinder to me since I saved Tyler's life. Not just saved his life, but almost lost mine because, after we escaped Layla, Mack arrested me, in part using John's accusation that I'd kidnapped Tyler. Because of John, I was taken to a dark site.

I shudder thinking of those days in solitary. Best not to think of it, but if it made John rethink the way he acts toward me, rethink how far he'd almost gone to keep me away from Ty, then it was worth it.

Truth is, I'd love for Tyler to go to school here, and maybe I'm starting to believe I even deserve to have my son in my life. "I'll talk to Momma."

Tyler perks up and swings our clasped hands back and forth. "She'll let me in. Momma loves me."

I can only whisper, "Yeah. She does."

As we near the main gate, I can see John and Ellen sitting in their car with Henry in his booster seat. I wish they'd come onto the grounds. "Ty, are you sure your parents are okay with you coming here? They won't even come onto the grounds."

He cringes. "They're okay with it, promise. Mom, um, I mean—

"No *um*, she's your mom, Ty, and I respect that and her."

His face reddens. "Yeah, Mom was the one to suggest I go here to the school part, you know. They don't come on campus because they're worried it's intrusive or something for them to do that."

That's good to know—that they won't come on campus out of some misguided belief that it would bother me. I'll let them know that's not true. "So, it's okay with both of them if you go here?"

"It's okay with Mom, but Dad said it's too expensive."

That Ellen suggested Ty go here flushes warmth through my body. We've made great strides in learning to parent Ty together. She's actually been a great teacher, which, to me, is proof of how much she loves our son.

And John might've only been saying it was too expensive as an excuse, but I'm going to take him at his word. I'm done feeling guilty or wrong about being present in my son's life.

I grin up at Tyler. "Did you know that family goes here for free?"

ACKNOWLEDGEMENTS

Before I'd gone through the extensive and exhilarating work of readying my novel for publication, I was unaware of how many talented and dedicated people would add to the shape and texture of my novel. I am so very grateful to all of them.

As always, a huge thank-you goes to my agent, Michelle Grajkowski, for cheerleading my work and being there every step of the way on this wonderful journey.

I'd like to thank my editor, Mackenzie Walton, for her incredible talent and insights. You transformed this manuscript, making it so much more than it would have been without you.

A huge thank-you to my copy editor and production editor, Judi Fennell. I sincerely appreciate all of your hard work and advice as I've navigated this self-publishing process.

To my incredible cover designer, Elizabeth Mackey, I can't thank you enough for your incredible artistic talent. You've managed to create a gorgeous cover and series of covers that capture my story and my heart.

Another big and beautiful thank you goes to my Advanced Reader Team. You all provide me with valuable insight and support, and I truly appreciate each and every one of you.

A big, sloppy virtual hug to Patricia Gussin, who not only read my work but championed me and my novel!

A sincere thank-you to everyone who has read this book and series. I consider it a privilege and an honor to be able to make this connection with each and every one of you.

ABOUT THE AUTHOR

Diana Muñoz Stewart is a bestselling author who writes romantic suspense with a focus on diverse characters, action, adventure, family, and love. Her work has been praised as high-octane, edgy, sexy, and fast-paced.

Diana's work has been a BookPage Top 15 Romance, a Night Owl Top Pick, an Amazon Book of the Month, an Amazon Editor's pick, a Pages From The Heart Winner, a Book Page Top Pick, Golden Heart® Finalist, Daphne du Maurier Finalist, A Gateway to the Best Winner, and has reached #1 category bestseller on Amazon multiple times.

Diana lives in an often chaotic and always welcoming home that—depending on the day—can hold a husband, kids, extended family, friends, and a canine or two. A believer in the power of words to heal and connect, Diana has written multiple spotlight pieces on the strong, diverse women changing the world.

Sign up for her newsletter to receive the latest information on her new releases including the novella, "Rescuing Grace," which tells the story of how Dusty rescued his Gracie from a black site with the help of her sister Justice: https://dianamunoz stewart.com/newsletter/

If you'd like to read the first two chapters of Tony's story, Daring Honor, you can do so here:
https://bookhip.com/KVMATCQ